BACK
OF THE
YARD

MEG LELVIS

Black Rose Writing | Texas

ISBN: 978-1-68433-737-8
PUBLISHED BY BLACK ROSE WRITING
www.blackrosewriting.com

Printed in the United States of America
Suggested Retail Price (SRP) $18.95

Back of the Yard is printed in Garamond

*As a planet-friendly publisher, Black Rose Writing does its best to eliminate unnecessary waste to reduce paper usage and energy costs, while never compromising the reading experience. As a result, the final word count vs. page count may not meet common expectations.

For Gary

SPECIAL THANKS TO:

Reagan Rothe and his staff at Black Rose Writing
David King, Design Director at Black Rose Writing
Danielle Hartman Acee, Tech assistant
Mark Pople, Editor

Houston Writers critique friends and beta readers: Landy Reed, Carolyn Thorman, Connie Gillen

For help, advice, and anecdotes about growing up Catholic: Maggie Dunne, Monica Winters, Connie Gillen, Carolyn Thorman

As always, Carole and Myrna

My family: Kristy, Rebecca, Cate, Nolan, Teddy, and Gary, who provided historical and railroad advice

Finally, in fondest memory of Rita Zralek, who told me colorful stories of her childhood in Back of the Yards, and toured the area with us.

BACK
OF THE
YARD

"It is the music which makes it what it is; it is the music which changes the place from the rear room of a saloon in Back of the Yards to a fairy place, a wonderland, a little corner of the high mansions of the sky."
–Upton Sinclair, *The Jungle*

"Canst thou not minister to a mind diseased,
Pluck from the memory a rooted sorrow,
Raze out the written troubles of the brain
And with some sweet oblivious antidote
Cleanse the stuffed bosom of that perilous stuff
Which weighs upon the heart?
–William Shakespeare, *Macbeth*, Act V, Scene III

CHAPTER 1

South Chicago, 1930s

Some neighborhoods are just neighborhoods. They harbor the rich, the poor, and everyone in between, like me, Betty O'Leary. Other places have a unique history, reflecting not only their city, but a growing America. My neighborhood was one of these. Established in 1865, it evolved and grew alongside the Chicago Union Stockyards. Yes, the stockyards of Sinclair's *Jungle* fame, and Sandburg's *Hog butcher to the world* fame. The brutal, relentless workplace of my father, grandfather, uncles. An area vibrant, dirty, tough, foul-smelling, colorful, and compassionate. This was my neighborhood. I loved it. I despised it. But it was mine. My own Back of the Yards.

I didn't dislike the neighborhood as much as Mama and Maureen, my older sister. They'd tell strangers, 'we live around south Chicago, you know, Bridgeport,' once mostly Irish. If pressed, they'd reluctantly admit, 'yes, we live in Back of the Yards,' but Mama would hasten to add, 'We live six blocks down from the gate.' In other words, not the closest street to the stockyards, almost to Garfield Boulevard. Aunt Agnes said Mama put on airs.

By the time I was born on June 22, 1930, the Great Depression had gripped the country with its iron fist and wouldn't let go. I was the fourth O'Leary child, unplanned, a grim reflection of our Irish Catholic circumstance. Of course, Mama never admitted in so many words that I was unexpected, but I'd hear bits of conversations with Aunt Agnes and the cousins. *Yes, Betty came as a surprise, but a happy surprise of course.*

Dennis was the oldest, then Maureen, followed by Joey. Our home blended in with the other drab bungalows and two-flats in the neighborhood. Like many others, our house was a plain one-story brick bungalow with a tent-shaped wood attic, shingles dangling from the roof. The Zraleks lived next store in an identical house, and on the other side, Billy's family resided on the top floor of a basic two-flat. The homes were close enough to shake hands out the window.

Mama tried to make the inside of our house nice and insisted we not mess up the living room. She cut lilacs from the bush out front and put them in a green glass vase on the coffee table. *Remember girls, we're not shanty Irish, we're lace curtain Irish.* When I said our curtains weren't lace, she'd shush me and tell me it was just a saying, and I was too young to understand.

Our furniture was worn, but not shabby like Billy's, where someone had burned a hole in the couch with a cigarette. I didn't mind sharing one of our two bedrooms with Maureen, but she hated it. *Why do I have to share with Betty? She's always getting into my private things.* Mama ignored her, since the only other bedroom was hers and Daddy's. The boys slept in the basement in a makeshift bedroom next to the coal bin. Sometimes Joey would let me come down if I promised not to touch his Buck Rogers gun. In the heat of summer, we'd lug mattresses onto the back porch to sleep.

Like everyone else, I grew up with notions of truth. We knew we were poor compared to some Bridgeport kids who went to Nativity of our Lord Catholic School. *Roses are red, violets are blue, the stockyards stink, and so do you,* kids would chant on the playground. I think that rhyme had been around since our grandparents' time.

But we were better off than others, like the Prestons and Andersons several blocks away, closer to the yards. At least my Sunday dresses didn't come way above my knees like Alice Preston's. Mama said the poor girl wore the same dress year after year because she stayed just as skinny.

I recall one day right before Christmas two ladies from Trinity Lutheran waddled to our front door with a large basket. I hid behind Mama's apron and saw them hold out a turkey and some other food, smiling and yapping about ladies' aid and helping out in these hard times. Mama got upset and refused to take their offerings and said we were not about to take charity and why on earth were they on our doorstep? Her face grew redder and redder. *Who told you we needed free handouts? How dare you?* In later years, when I asked about the ladies who brought us a Christmas turkey, Mama would hush me and pretend it never happened. To this day, Maureen won't admit it either. And she was right there beside me.

Some would label my childhood as troubled, dysfunctional, painful, but you only realize that later. At the time, I knew nothing else. It didn't help that people compared me to a pretty older sister, well liked, even adored. Maureen was born with red, wavy hair and green eyes. I'd been stuck with dishwater brown hair with a cowlick on my forehead. After she discovered the movie star, Maureen O'Hara, she'd raise her chin and say they looked alike, which they didn't, truth be told.

She was sought after by girls at school to be their friend, and she held court in any group. Sassy and confident, she began to develop in sixth grade. The boys really ogled her after that and would hang around her, flexing what they thought were biceps.

The family poured all their attention on Maureen. Our two brothers, Dennis and Joey, just did boy stuff and got in trouble with our father, whose dreaded razor strap hung on a peg by the bathroom sink. They dodged Mama's wrath because she didn't find out about taboo activities like Dennis sneaking out to steal coal at the railroad tracks. Dennis was smart that way.

We walked the few blocks down Peoria Street to St. Basil's Church School. Our teachers were Dominican Sisters who wore pure white habits, sometimes with black capes. I can still see their thin leather belts, black rosary beads attached, swinging to and fro as they breezed by, gliding like ice skaters.

Sister Agatha scared the heck out of me. She viewed God as an angry judge. And life itself? Evil to the core. She once knocked Jimmy Flynn onto the floor where he hit his head on the steel bottom of the desk. In spite of all the blood, he didn't need stitches. However, he got the strap when his father found out. I'd like to see the old Sister try that in this day and age. One day she called on me, asking me to name the largest continent. I hesitated and stammered, even though I knew the answer. *Speak up, mouse, I can't hear you. Well, are you going to be a scared little mouse all your life?* My cheeks burned. *N-no, Ma'am. It's Asia.* I heard snickers behind me.

Thankfully, most of the Sisters were kind, and one or two took pity on me, perhaps because I didn't compare to Maureen in personality and looks. Luckily, I did excel in one area: school work. Classes and assignments came easy for me. Sister Cecile patiently taught us to read from the same primer used by most American children. *Fun with Dick and Jane* instilled in us middle-class values, and once I learned to read, I never quit. My imagination soared beyond my own drab walls. I saw myself as a new sister living with Violet and the orphans in *The Boxcar Children*, and Nan's best friend was me in *The Bobbsey Twins at Windmill Cottage*.

When I was six, a new library was built next to Sherman Park, a half mile from my house. The one-story gray stone building perched at the edge of the park on Racine close to Garfield. The first time Mama guided us through the glass doors, I gazed around the enormous room, awestruck. A wonderland of books. Where did they come from? I loved the timeworn, woody smell in the air. A large picture of a gruff-looking man with a walrus mustache named John B. Sherman hung on the wall near the entry. Mama said he founded the stockyards in the eighteen-hundreds.

I wanted to explore the whole library and clung to her hand so I wouldn't get lost. Women and kids of all ages milled about. Everyone whispered. A lady in a white ruffled blouse and gray hair piled atop her head sat behind a shiny wood desk with books piled here and there. Several children and their mother waited as the librarian stamped books and handed them to the woman.

Mama found the children's section in the endless stacks of books. She followed us around as we extracted from the shelves pages of fictional lives waiting to be discovered by curious young minds like ours. I located books that would become favorites: *The Bobbsey Twins* and *The Boxcar Children*. One day the librarian, Miss Brune, taught several of us how to use the wooden stand with lots of little drawers in it called the Dewey something.

The library became my refuge every Saturday morning for years to come. Mama went with us at first, but then Maureen was stuck taking me. The boys weren't invited, since we knew they would chase each other around the stacks, eliciting a harsh *Hush* from Miss Brune. Still, I remember Mama wanted them to read more. *If you boys read like Betty does, you'd do much better in school and amount to something in life.*

In upper grades, my favorite class was Latin, which helped me understand the meaning of Father John's words as he celebrated the Mass. The idea of different languages fascinated me. Perhaps someday I'd understand Billy's grandpa next door yelling at him in Polish.

We also learned Roman history, and I dreamed of visiting Rome and seeing the Vatican and Colosseum and Pantheon. Awfully big dreams for a girl like me. Only presidents and movie stars went to Europe.

· · ·

Looking back, I was invisible. Only a few nuns truly saw me, like Sister Cecile. *You keep on reading, Betty, and you can go to college someday.* My only friend was a girl named Joan, who carried more than a few extra pounds. Kids called her 'fatso' and chanted, *fatty fatty two-by-four, can't get through the bathroom door, so she does it on the floor.* Back then, no one thought much about how cruel children could be. We were just resigned to it. Kids teased me about Mrs. O'Leary's cow starting the huge Chicago fire. *How's your grandma, Betty? Started any fires lately?* So clever. They didn't get far when Dennis, my big brother was around. With a single glance, he'd send the bullies scattering.

With my mousy brown hair, drab hazel eyes, and stick figure, I wandered through the world unnoticed unless Sister Agatha picked on me. *Are you really Maureen's sister, little mouse? She was never shy like you.* But I escaped into my world of books, including Laura Ingalls and all her houses.

When I reflect on it today, the structure and rituals of Catholic school gave me comfort and stability. Comfort and stability I lacked at home. Comfort absent in Mama's and Daddy's fighting, Daddy's yelling and strapping the boys, Daddy's drinking at the corner bar, Mama's moods—warm and affectionate one minute, banging kitchen pots and pans in a frenzy the next.

The origin of my own descent into darkness was yet to come.

CHAPTER 2

At times I wonder if my childhood in the yards affected the mental illness that would plague me in later years. Would I be the same if I'd grown up in Bridgeport or a small town like Evanston? Would the Accident have happened in another neighborhood? Aware that my classmates' fathers also worked in the stockyards, I was curious about Daddy's job. For some reason, he never spoke of it. *You're better off not knowing what goes on inside the yards. Way back when, your grandpa had the shit jobs, got the pickled hands. Didn't have protection then.* I wondered how hands could look like pickles, but he explained workers got skin infections from pickling meat and sausage. Daddy would hold out his hands pretending to grab us and describe in gory detail how ugly the skin got. Maureen and I would squeal and run away.

At school, I heard tales about splitters and other grisly jobs on the floors of the slaughterhouses, but I willed myself not to believe those things. After all, animals were like people, especially when Sister Cecile read chapters from *Doctor Doolittle*. Just to be mean, some nasty boys like Jimmy and Butch would hang around us at recess and sing, *Mary had a little lamb, and it began to sicken, they took it down to packing town, and now they call it chicken.* When I'd tell Mama, she just pooh-poohed it and said they were dumb boys and don't pay them any mind.

• • •

One blistering summer day, Dennis asked Maureen if she wanted to see some cows up close. I was no older than six, but I begged Dennis to let me tag along. "I guess you can, but don't tell Ma. We're gonna meet Billy and a couple more kids, so you gotta keep up with us."

Bursting at the seams, I followed Maureen, Dennis, and Joey out of our small, sweltering house. My first adventure inside the yards. I couldn't wait to pet the cows and maybe even a calf.

I was so excited, I almost tripped on the concrete steps of our front stoop as we scurried out to meet the other kids.

I'd seen the outside of the stockyards, but never the inside. This was a special day. We picked up Billy and met two other boys at the next corner and finally met up with Alice. We followed Dennis and the boys for nearly six blocks up Morgan Street. I tagged along in back of the group, trying to keep up with Maureen and Alice. The sun blazed upon us as we kicked up sand and grit along the sidewalk for the long journey. The top of my rompers stuck to my skin, and beads of sweat shone on all our foreheads. We saw other scruffy-looking kids on the way and waited for a couple old cars rambling down the street. We passed forlorn houses, bars, and grocery stores along the way. Everything was hot and sandy.

The air grew foul as we reached Forty-ninth Street. "Pee-ew. The stockyards stink, and so do you." The boys continued teasing us girls. "Ready to pickle some pigs?" Laughter. "Hey, Betty, maybe we can see a pig get spl—"

"Shut up, Dennis," Maureen cried. "She'll have bad dreams and tell Mama."

That hushed them up. I didn't like keeping secrets from Mama. She worked three days a week at Casey's, the corner grocery store on Garfield and Union, other side of Halsted. Daddy's uncle owned it, and Mama helped out for a lower wage, she said. On Saturdays she'd bring us a treat if we'd been good. I loved Tootsie Rolls, swirly lollipops, and Black Jack or Clove gum. Sometimes the boys didn't get anything if they'd been bad, and they'd beg me and Maureen for some of ours when Mama wasn't around. I was more likely to give in than my sister.

• • •

To this day, I can still smell the yards. They say you become immune to the pervading pungent manure stench, which perhaps is true. I remember when we approached the fences and dirt lots on Forty-seventh, I "Ewe-ed" with the other kids and pinched my nose. After I let go, the stench hit me. I smelled the huge piles of cow poop outside the pens, along with a rancid stink of rot and smoke.

"Come on," Dennis said. "Let's crawl under here and sneak in the stalls." The whole square-mile area looked like endless fencing around several blocks of open land, buildings, and animal pens. I don't know how anyone could find their way around the entire place.

On hands and knees, we crawled under a rickety portion of the weather-beaten wooden fence. It was common for "children of bad influence" to play in certain parts of the yards, so my brothers weren't supposed to, but they did with Dennis in the lead. It would be easy to get lost amongst all the buildings, pens, pathways, lots.

As we drew closer, the sound of constant lowing from thousands of cattle and grunting from pigs grew louder. I heard men yelling in funny languages as they ran cattle from trucks into to the pens. I looked around, confused by all the activity. Fear gripped me as the noise grew louder, the stink of sewage stronger. I grabbed Maureen's flowered dress. "I wanna go home." I fought back tears that threatened to expose me. I couldn't let the others know I was scared to death.

"Betty, don't be such—" Her voice trailed off as she looked at me. "Just a minute," she yelled at the boys. Her hands held onto my shoulders. "I know it's scary to be the littlest one. Here, hold my hand."

"Come on, Betty," Alice chimed in. "We won't stay long. You can find a cow you like and give it a name."

The next thing I knew, we pressed up against a pen surrounded with wooden fencing, brown cows moaning and swishing their tails back and forth to shoo the flies. The stink hit me with a vengeance, stinging my nostrils. I wanted to leave. The cows were too large, and the flies pestered me, swarming and buzzing around our heads and arms.

"Hey, let's give them names. We'll each pick one." Dennis yelled out his orders. Then Joey chimed in. "Yeah, then they'll have a name before they go to the slau—" Dennis shut him up. I always sensed something bad happened to the animals in the yards, but no one would say. My instinct told me not to beg for details.

After everyone named their chosen ones, I pointed to a sad-looking cow who turned and looked right at me with half-closed brown eyes. Her huge black nostrils with protruding hairs twitched. "I wanna name her. She'll be Flossie after the Bobbsey Twins." My happiness was short lived when I heard the boys' raucous laughter.

"That's a steer, dummy, not a girl. Pick a boy's name." Smarty pants Dennis. I hated to look stupid. "All right, his name is Freddie then." Satisfied, I whispered to Maureen, "I want to go home and go potty."

Since all of us were hot and sticky, Dennis and Billy agreed to go home. Dirt and sweat streaked Billy's face. Dennis kept tugging at the shoulders of his workwear denim overalls, trying to fan himself. Joey's freckles turned red, his cowlick plastered to his forehead. Maureen and Alice wore everyday dresses sewn from flour sacks. Mama found colorful ones at the store, since the company started putting the flour in decorated bags to make clothes look better. But today, they wilted with sogginess.

The walk home seemed longer, harder to trudge along, and I tried not to wet my pants. We were taking a shortcut through a vacant lot to Fifty-third Street, when something caught my shoe, and I fell flat on my face, cracking my chin on the ground. My teeth clamped down on the tip of my tongue. "Wahhhhhh," I wailed. My hand flew to my mouth. I heard Maureen yell to the boys, "Wait up. She's bleeding."

The metallic taste of blood filled my mouth.

"Did her tooth get knocked out?" Alice sounded panicky. She flipped her brown pigtails away from her face.

She and Maureen helped me stand up, not easy because I was still bawling and knew I'd wet my pants.

"Mama will kill us," Maureen moaned.

"Aw, shaddup. She's okay." Dennis never worried about anything.

Still sniffling, I whispered to Maureen, "Don't tell them I piddled in my pants."

"God, Betty. Let me clean you off." Maureen's red curls stuck to her forehead and cheeks.

She and Alice brushed sand and grass from my arms and legs. Both knees were skinned red, and my tongue bled down my chin and onto my yellow pinafore top. No one had a hanky or anything to clean me off. Maureen looked around and found a brown leaf which she used to wipe my face. Then she rubbed the hem of her dress on my bloody romper, but the stains wouldn't come out. My tongue throbbed and bled as I limped the last two blocks toward our house.

"Don't tell Mama where we were," Maureen said. "We'll say we were playing with the Doyle kids."

I quit crying, feeling ashamed of myself, and when we stumbled through the front door, Mama stood straight as a soldier waiting for us, hands crossed over her faded apron.

CHAPTER 3

She took one look at my dirty, bloody face. "Betty! What happened to you?"

I felt my chin quiver, my tongue formed a ball, and I started bawling again, running into her arms.

After several seconds, she held me straight out and inspected me top to bottom. She glared at my brothers and sister. Her voice soft, chilling. "And where have you been?"

"We were playing at the Doyle's house," Maureen and Joey tried to say at once.

"Where else?" Mama had a dangerous look on her face. "Betty?"

I wiped my nose on the back of my hand. "Ah—I—"

She dragged me into the kitchen and proceeded to run hot water onto a cloth, examining my skinned knees. The other kids started a getaway to their rooms. Mama said, "Don't go anywhere. You must think I broke my nose. I smelled you a block away. Of course, I know where you were, so don't lie to me." I waited while she wiped my cheeks, neck, arms, legs. She rinsed the cloth and rubbed it with gritty Lava soap, then scrubbed the stains on my romper. In all the fuss, she didn't notice my damp pants.

"Damn. The one outfit you have that isn't a hand-me-down from your sister. I'll have to soak it in cold water."

"I'm sorry, Mama," I whimpered. I opened my mouth and pointed to my tongue. "Look." I hoped she'd feel sorry for me.

"Oh Lord, it's all swollen. At least the bleeding quit." She ran cold water in a small Mason jar, and then she chipped ice pieces from the icebox to add to the water. "Here, stick your tongue in there. It'll help the swelling and won't hurt as much." She sat me at the kitchen table bent over the glass of icy water. My tongue was instantly cool, and the stinging faded away.

Mama faced the others. "Good thing your father isn't here. You'd get the strap for going to the yards, especially for taking Betty." She shoved at the boys. "Go to your room and don't come back till you have your bath after the girls do, get that stink off. Then maybe you'll get supper." Joey looked at her like a lost puppy, but Mama didn't cave in. With his endearing smile, green eyes, light red hair and freckles, Joey was Mama's unspoken favorite.

Maureen started to leave. "Hold on, young lady. What got into you? Betty could've been trampled to death. You're ten years old. You should know better." Mama's hair escaped from its bun, long brown strands sticking to her neck. "People like us don't go to the yards. I have half a mind to take the ruler to you."

"I'm too old for the ruler, Mama. I said I'm sorry. I'll never take Betty anywhere again."

"Hush now. Go run a bath for you and her. You're gettin' too big for your britches." Maureen could stand up to Mama and Daddy like none of the rest of us could.

"And then run clean water for the boys so your father won't smell it on them." We knew Daddy's nose was so ingrained with the stink of the yards, he wouldn't know the difference, but I knew better than to argue with Mama.

•　　•　　•

After our bath, Mama dabbed her special Lily of the Valley toilet water on me and Maureen so we'd smell like ladies. But Mama still stomped around the kitchen. "Now I need to make supper. You're getting One-eyed Sams tonight."

I didn't dare complain, but I couldn't stand the soggy toast with an over-easy egg in the middle.

I don't recall if the boys got the strap that day, but I never asked to visit the stockyards again.

CHAPTER 4

Mama always tried to protect me from unseen horrors. *Look what happened to the Lindbergh baby, Betty. He was exactly your age. You have the same birthday.* I heard those words time and again through the years. *Don't ever go out alone. At least they got that awful German brute. He'll get the chair for sure for killing that poor baby.*

No one could have predicted Mama's greatest sorrow was yet to come.

•   •   •

I was nearly four years old when the big fire destroyed almost the entire stockyards. I briefly recall Mama holding me inside the front door when I wanted to rush out with the other kids and see the commotion. I remember the smoke, burning air, and neighbors hustling about worried and chattering. It's hard to tell my memories from stories I heard from other people— flashbacks, splintered scenes of me at the front door, but they'd only last a second, then vanish. A fleeting picture of me talking about the odor. *Is the house burning, Mama?* I'm looking up at her. The image disappears.

In years to come, I heard the fire could be seen in Indiana, over a hundred miles away. It was a miracle that more livestock and people weren't killed. One worker died, a watchman like Daddy. Thankfully, Daddy didn't work on Saturdays and went to work that Monday. The yards were up and running after a day, which was unbelievable, as I heard more than once.

•   •   •

Finally, the day came when Mama allowed me to play outside with the neighbor kids without Maureen or my brothers around. I loved roller skating on the sidewalk with metal skates clamped to my shoes and the key swaying on a string around my neck. I played hopscotch with Billy's cousin Dee and sometimes Maureen and Alice. My favorite game was kick the can when the boys would let me join in.

Yes, there were good and bad times in our family when Mama laughed and Daddy hadn't been to the corner which meant drinking at Kerry's on Fifty-third and Morgan. He usually met his mates from work there on Fridays and then Saturdays, he'd stop in for a pint after neighborhood meetings. Lots of people joined the council, which was officially Back of the Yards Neighborhood Council. I later heard it was started by Saul Alinsky, who, according to rumors, was in cahoots with Al Capone, but he helped the neighborhood in many ways.

The council met once a month, and Daddy took great interest in its doings; I heard snippets of conversation between him and Mama or the neighbors. I realized later that the group not only helped the packinghouse workers but also started programs of food for the poor, along with building a park and baseball field.

Sometimes Daddy drank too much at the corner. We'd hear him singing outside the house at all hours. *..tis my brother in the army, if I could find his station in Cork or in Killarney ….wack fol the daddy-o, there's whiskey in the jar.*

Mama would scurry out the door. *Hush, Mac, they'll hear ya all the way to Tipperary an' back.*

Then they'd stumble into the house. *"Too-Ra-Loo-Ra-Loo-Ral, Too-Ra...*
Shut up, you'll wake the kids. Now lay down on the couch. Sleep it off.
Aye, come on, Nora. Come join me here. I need yer lovin'…
Not on yer life, ye drunken maggot. Go on with ya.

Then all would be quiet, and if the boys snuck in later, Daddy was never the wiser.

•　　•　　•

I reckon Mama did the best she could. You hear people say that about their parents, but I don't know what it means, truth be told. Mama thought everyone was poor and life was hard. *At least we're not the tattered poor*, she'd say. But sometimes she saw the bright side. *Remember, we're not as bad off as those poor folks in Oklahoma, with no rain and all that sand getting in their houses, clothes, hair.*

I remember the fireside chats Mama and Daddy listened to on our Philco tabletop radio. Daddy would say FDR was pulling our country back together again and giving us hope that people wouldn't be hungry anymore.

When I was almost four, Mama talked about a mother having five baby girls at the same time in Canada. I couldn't understand how that possibly happened. Later, Maureen told me that before we're born, we start out like a shelled peanut, and this lady had five in her belly instead of one. People called it a miracle.

On Saturdays, a peddler came around with a suitcase full of knickknacks and stuff for women, like doilies, colorful babushkas, shampoo, and fragrant soaps. He called on all the women in our neighborhood, and Mama always welcomed him, even though we didn't know his name. We just called him Ivan because Billy's grandma said he looked Russian with his dark flashing eyes and black beard. Mama admired a pearl-like comb and brush set, ornate with sparkles on the back of the brush. He put it aside for her until she had enough money to pay for it.

No one I knew had it easy during the Depression. We scrimped, wore hand-me-downs, ate Hoover stew and fried baloney, didn't see a dentist unless we had the toothache. One time I'll never forget is when I had my tonsils out, the only one in the family. I was barely six, and must've been in a bad way because we didn't see doctors unless were at death's door. Daddy's uncle drove me and Mama to Dr. Gerlock's office upstairs from the haberdashery on Ashland. Dark and full of shadows, the stairway stank of medicine and hints of ether.

Shards of memory flash in my mind. I lay on a table and pushed the nurse's hand away that held the ether. Then I screamed like a banshee as strong arms held me down and the horrible ether mask was forced onto my face. Later we left the office and Uncle put me in the back seat of his battered car, and we were home. *I'll carry her in, Nora. She'll be sick for a few days. Here, take this grape soda. Good for her stomach after the ether.* Uncle was right. The soda helped. I still see my purple throw-up in the sink. To this day, I reach for grape soda when I'm queasy.

While I recovered, Mama wouldn't let me play outside for weeks it seemed. No one played indoors with me except Joey. We played gin rummy with an old deck of cards the grownups used for Whist.

When I was six or seven, we swam every day at the lagoon that circled Sherman Park. On hot summer days, kids trying to keep cool overran the place even though the water was warm and soupy. In winter, we'd ice skate in the park.

I wore Maureen's old skates and took to it right away. Before long, I was good enough to play crack the whip with the older kids.

Even though we were poor, we had fun times. I will always remember my eighth birthday because it was the last carefree time for years to come.

.   .   .

I turned eight that summer. For the first time, Mama said I could invite two friends for a birthday party, so Alice and Joan came over for ice cream and cake Mama baked special. Even Maureen was excited because she was in on the surprise gift. Before we ate our chocolate cake (called Depression or Crazy cake) and strawberry ice cream from Uncle's store, they sang the birthday song. I blew out eight candles in one enormous puff. Joey grabbed the center candle to lick the frosting, but Mama grasped his hand in midair. "No you don't, Mister. Wait your turn." This time, his impish grin didn't sway her.

Joan's gift was a pink beaded necklace, and from Alice, a cup and saucer picturing Minnie Mouse. "Wow, brand new toys! All mine!" I sniffed at Maureen.

"I'm too old for those anyway," she huffed. "But close your eyes, and get ready for a big surprise."

I did as instructed, but when I heard her footsteps scurrying back from the kitchen, my eyes defiantly burst open. She stood with both hands behind her back. I ran toward her.

"Hold your horses, Betty." Mama put her hands over my eyes.

I heard Alice and Joan gasp. Mama said, "All right, now you can look."

Maureen dramatically held out a small box. When I tried to look, she laughed and held it over her head. "Maureen, behave. Don't tease her," Mama said.

She slowly lowered the box. I peeked inside and squealed like a pig. "Oh, is it Marie?"

"Yes, it's Marie, Betty." Mama and Maureen looked at one another as if their big secret had hit the mark.

"What's the big deal about a dumb old doll?" Dennis put his two-cents worth in.

"It's one of the Dionne quints, dumbbell." Joey seemed proud he knew something his brother didn't.

"Let's see her pin," said Alice as the girls crowded around the box.

I carefully lifted the prized treasure from its resting place and held it out for all to see.

Alice squinted at the gold bar pinned on the front of the doll's lavender romper trimmed in white lace. A gold circle hanging from the pin read 'Marie.' "Betty, she's so beautiful. I want Emilie. I'll ask Mama." Alice turned to Joan. "And you can get Annette, and—and Maureen, you get um—"

"Cecile?" Maureen scoffed. "I'm too old for dolls. I want ruby red lipstick like Jean Harlow."

Mama harrumphed and said for the hundredth time, "Oh hush. You're too big for your britches."

The rest of the party was a blur of fussing over my new doll, taking her matching bonnet off and on, stroking her molded dark hair, admiring the rosy cheeks.

Joan took the chubby plastic leg in her hand. "Look at her socks." The girls admired the white anklets rimmed with lace.

I felt different that day. Everyone paid attention to me, and even Daddy came home with a package of Clove gum just for me. "How's my birthday girl?" He swooped me up and was about to turn me upside down.

"Put her down, Mac," Mama said. "She's full of cake and ice cream."

Afterwards, Maureen and I skipped with Alice and Joan to their houses. I was lucky to have two friends, even though Alice was closer to Maureen's age.

I will always remember my eighth birthday, my new doll, my family's attention. Those were days of blissful, gauzy memories.

But several months later, everything changed

CHAPTER 5

Time scatters details to the wind. I only recall bits of everyday life, joy, tears, my house, the people in my little corner of the world. That summer I basked in the warmth of my birthday, splashing in the lagoon, nights sleeping on the back porch, promise of a new school year.

·   ·   ·

I liked my third-grade class, mainly because Sister Gertrude was nice to shy girls like me. She never compared me to Maureen, but she'd ask about my brothers at times. People said winter came early that year, and a thin layer of new snow dusted the ground and streets on Halloween. Going to school, I wore my hand-me-down green wool coat over sweaters, knit scarf, hat, mittens. Frigid days passed with the usual worry in the air. *Christmas will be sparse this year. Do we have enough coal to last the month? Will there be another war in Europe?* Grownup talk. Flickers of pictures in my mind, like flying down the hill after school at the park on flattened cardboard boxes. Mostly carefree days for kids. Everything the same, normal. Until one day it wasn't.

·   ·   ·

Was I dreaming, or were the voices real?

I must've been sleeping. Darkness wrapped itself around the room, Maureen gone from her bed. Voices. Men's voices. What were they saying?

Then daylight. Shivering, blanket around me. Frost crept inside the window making swirly designs. Maureen sitting on her bed, doing nothing. "Joe—Joey—gone—gone." Scenes like fragments of glass popping up, a rapid-fire slideshow of people, words. A kaleidoscope, reds, oranges, blues. Sometimes black and white.

How did I get in the living room that day, so full of people? My faded flannel pajamas hung from my shoulders, the legs sweeping the floor. Grownups come, go, stay. Father John standing with Daddy, voices low. Where is Mama? I don't like it here. Where is she? I feel like crying. I clutch Maureen's arm. "Where's Mama?"

"Oh Betty, you can't bother her now. She's feeling sick."

"But I want—"

"Now, Betty, don't fuss. This isn't the time." Auntie Agnes suddenly appeared, her eyes red-rimmed, her flowered housedress rumpled. "Maureen, honey, take her somewhere. She shouldn't be here right now."

Maureen's lips pressed together like a pencil line. "But where? More people are crowding the place."

"Go to your room and close the door. Play some card games." Auntie didn't know how unreasonable that suggestion was.

Maureen whispered something in Auntie's ear. "Oh dear." Auntie bent down, gazed at me. Then took in Daddy and Father John. People surrounding us.

To this day, I don't know precisely how I learned about Joey. Maureen said she told me about the Accident. Then Daddy and Father John, but all I knew was Joey wasn't coming back. Ever.

• • •

What I remember most was Mama's silence. She'd sit and gaze into her own thoughts and sorrows. As if she heard voices inside her head no one else could hear. Or she lay in bed for hours, dozing or whimpering. Her low, throaty moans scared me. She left her room only to use the bathroom and refused to go in the kitchen. Maureen and Daddy brought her food now and then, but it remained cold, uneaten, drenched with gloom.

During that time, I glided about in a netherworld of shock and emptiness. Vaguely aware of events in my peripheral vision, I eventually pieced together what happened to Joey from what Dennis told Maureen and me one night.

• • •

Of course, I knew Dennis, Billy, and their pals went to the train tracks to swipe coal. Other kids did it too, was their excuse. No one thought it was like robbing a store; it was just gathering coal that spilled onto the ground. But they still weren't supposed to do it. Railroad bulls, or cops, patrolled the area, but clever boys like Dennis knew how to avoid them. Mama cast a blind eye to Dennis and his pals but said Joey was too young to go along.

Odd how I remember a golden pinkish sunset that day. I ran into the house to tell Mama, but she wasn't in the kitchen. Maybe she was downstairs washing clothes. I opened the basement door and heard Dennis. *Joey, we have a gunny sack for you, but you gotta keep up. Can't be a slow poke like last time.* I was on the top step as Dennis and Joey clamored up. *What're you doing here, pipsqueak?* Dennis glared at me. *Ya better not tell Ma, or else. Don't be a tattletale.* My memory was stuck in that command. That order. That decree. *Don't tell Mama.* Did I promise not to?

Yes, I must have promised. The boys left to play with the neighbors, their typical excuse to sneak to the tracks. I'd heard Daddy say the coal bin was getting low, so they needed to stock up before it snowed.

Dusk crept over the neighborhood as the boys left to meet Billy next door, and then on to Fifty-fifth and Racine where two or three more boys joined them. Everyone carried a gunny sack, Joey for the first time. *You won't fill it though. A full load is too heavy for you.* Dennis, the know-it-all.

Heading east on Fifty-fifth, the boys crossed Damen and scrambled up the embankment to the tracks. Patches of snow and ice crunched under their feet, and the pungent scent of burning coal filled the air. Dennis recalled Joey's red cheeks and runny nose, his green wool scarf around his neck. At the top they paused for a good look around. Nobody there and no trains coming their way to illuminate them with their headlights.

. They made their way south toward the huge coal chute where the steam engines would have their tenders loaded with coal. Plenty of scattered lumps of it on the ground, there for the taking. That is, if the railroad bulls didn't catch them in the act. Even some switch men were tough enough to use their brake clubs on them. So far Dennis and his mates had been lucky.

Darkness nearly hid the coal chute looming over them. A quick look around, and Dennis led them over four sets of rails and underneath the trap door where, when opened, the coal would avalanche into the tender of the idling steam locomotive. The trapdoor would always be closed a trifle late, allowing a large amount of coal to pile atop the tender and spill off the sides onto the ground. The boys' personal little coal mine.

Dennis knew the routine, stopping the boys about 100 feet from the office. They lurked in the shadows until several crew men ambled indoors so they wouldn't spot the boys making a dash for the chute. Joey's legs flew as he tried to keep up with the rest.

The job went quickly. With gloved hands, they scooped the coal off the ground and into the sacks. Soon everyone had a full gunny sack, except Joey, who had perhaps half. Now came the hard part as those bags seemed to weigh 100 pounds, and no one, not even Dennis, could carry a full one easily. It would be slow going home. Billy took a glance and motioned the boys toward the embankment. Joey trailed behind.

•   •   •

No one saw nor heard the boxcar gliding through the darkness; steel wheels on steel tracks. Not the boys. Not the brakeman. Not anyone. There was a tiny thud when it hit. Not even an outcry. All in a flash, when Dennis realized what he must have seen in the corner of his eye.

Oh God no! A sense of irreversible loss froze in his stomach. Panic gripped him. Surely the brakeman had seen what happened. He'd help. Boys yelling. *Oh God, Oh, Jesus. No. No. Over here. Joe—Joey. Help! Help!* Dennis sailed above the ground, above his friends. A lump of clothing lay on the ground away from the tracks. How did it get there? *Dennis, come here. Come on.* The voice blasting his eardrum. He opened his mouth to yell. Nothing came out. Just choking, growling sounds like an animal. A final glance at the heap of torn wool lying on a patch of snow and cinders. A green scarf in tatters.

I was amazed at the details Dennis remembered from that night.

• • •

The next thing Dennis knew, he was in our living room. What happened between the railyard and the house remained a mystery; a wall of blackness. Ma's screams, moans. On the sofa, Daddy beside him, men talking, asking questions, cops milling about. Maureen slipped in. Uncle and Auntie. Later, Father John. A woman's voice. *Here, Dennis, drink this. You need to sleep now.*

CHAPTER 6

The days passed with a pervading numbness, a dull ache, dark, muddled. Time did not help me remember details of those days, but emotions, truths, filtered into my being and took up permanent residence. I've been told many times how Mama refused to come out of her room. Daddy and Maureen, and sometimes Auntie took food to her. Maureen said I was full of questions about Joey. Where was he? I was not well acquainted with death. My grandparents on Mama's side, and Uncle's old dog, Shep. I cried about him because I loved him, yearned for a dog of my own. *We can't afford a dog, Betty. Times are tough. It's hard enough to feed you kids.*

Maureen explained that Joey was in heaven with Jesus and Mother Mary. I'd asked about purgatory, but she said Joey was in a state of grace and went directly to heaven and became an angel. *He's looking down on us, Betty. He's an angel now. He wants you to be happy, so don't cry.*

People told me that in his small pine coffin, Joey looked like he was asleep, freckles sprinkled on his face. Not a mark on him. Some called it a miracle that he was thrown over to the side, not run over and mangled. To my eight-year-old mind, it seemed like a normal statement.

•　•　•

I was not allowed at my brother's funeral, but the puzzle pieces came together as the days and weeks inched by. Like everyone in need of funeral services in Back of the Yards, Uncle called on McInerney's Sons, who had served the good people of South Chicago for over sixty years. Located east of Halsted on Wallace near Forty-seventh, the funeral home boasted its own legendary jingle, known to everyone, including kids like me.

Bring out the lace curtains and call McInerney, I'm nearing the end of my life's pleasant journey, followed by more words too numerous to mention. For whatever reason, the poem's first lines remain in my mind to this day.

The morning of the funeral, I was sent to Alice's house. I cried, saying it wasn't fair I couldn't go, but once I parked myself on their comfy couch, I calmed down. I rather enjoyed playing with Alice and her new Emilie Dionne doll, since I'd brought my doll, Marie, along. I had begged to go to the funeral, but the family said I was too young. It was just for older people, but I wanted to see Joey. I needed to tell him I was sorry I had not told Mama he was going to the tracks that night. Maybe he would be here and not an angel if only I'd been a tattletale.

Maureen had warned me to hush about that. *Keep that a secret, Betty. I think Mama blames Daddy and Dennis. You don't want her to blame you too.* Even though Mama didn't know my secret, I still had a part in killing my brother.

Later I heard most of the funeral party ended up at Kerry's after the Mass and burial. Daddy and his pals drank well into the night, and you could hear them down the street singing off-key. *Who threw the overalls in Mrs. Murphy's chowder? Nobody spoke, so I said it all the louder.* "Hey, come on Mac. We'll end the night at your place." *It's an Irish trick it's true, and I'll get the mick that threw....* "Eye, your boy Joey got a proper send-off. He's up there now with the saints and yer kin who went a'for us."

When the funeral goings-on finally ended, heartache and gloom filled our world, spilling into the sidewalks and streets. I don't know if Joey's death truly sank into my mind and heart. Whenever I wandered into the house, it was filled with his absence. Dennis no longer slept downstairs; he'd take his pillow and blankets and sleep on the sofa. Looking back, Dennis would not be himself for many months, if ever. He told Maureen he wanted to rewind the memory in his mind and make it go away like the picture show in Bridgeport when the film strip broke and a few frames mangled, they would just restart the projector and forget about the lost frames. Why couldn't he do the same and go on with life, losing the ruined frames, as if that night never happened?

Daddy spent more and more time at Kerry's, coming home late, sometimes singing an Irish jig, other times, he'd drunkenly clomp down the basement stairs and sleep on Joey's bed. He suggested they donate Joey's clothes to the needy, but Mama would have none of it. *Leave his things be. I will not forget him. He is still here.*

Neighbors and relatives kept knocking on our door, arms laden with casseroles, pies, sausage, more than our icebox could hold. The women bustled around like hens, chattering, hugging, directing like symphony conductors. *Where's your mama, Betty? I'll just go peek in, won't be more than a minute, don't you worry.*

Those wintry December days lugged their weary hours, veiled with a seamless leaden sameness. Soon the holiday season descended on us, stores and bars, their colored lights glowing. Candles on small tree branches blinked through several frosty neighbor windows.

We had no Christmas tree that year. I'd been expecting to string ropes of cranberries and popcorn around the small tree Daddy and the boys always brought home. Except we no longer had 'the boys.' *There's nothing to celebrate this year. Mama can't get up. Sorry, maybe no presents either.* Daddy felt bad, but we never expected much. We couldn't even hang our stockings on the nails on the window frame because one would be missing. But Maureen and Auntie Agnes wrapped up oranges, apples, and nuts for us. I also got a new comb and a toothbrush. Dennis didn't open his presents, not even the box of Boston Baked Beans, his favorite candy. I think Mama would've been upset if she knew Billy's mama and other neighbor ladies brought us extra candy.

I would later learn how the neighborhood council delivered baskets of food and had given Daddy a generous donation to help pay for Joey's funeral, because *they took care of their own.*

After Christmas Mass, only Maureen and I went to Auntie Agnes's and Uncle's place for a dinner of chicken, potatoes, cabbage, and pumpkin pie. Mama, still secluded in her room, ate very little during that time, and Daddy and Dennis stayed home. I think Daddy went to Kerry's later on, since the pub opened at noon.

I missed singing carols around the tree like we used to. Billy's family would come over, along with other neighbors, and Auntie and Uncle would join us.

•　　•　　•

On that frigid winter morning in 1938 we heard no bells on Christmas Day.

CHAPTER 7

That winter sorrow wrapped itself around our house and wormed its way inside of everyone who lived there. It latched into the seams of our clothes, grasped the folds of our skin, invaded our hearts, our souls. It hit Mama the hardest. Immobilized, she remained a prisoner in her musty, moldering room plagued by her ghosts and demons. Friends, neighbors, relatives quit knocking on our door. However, Sister Cecile visited one chilly Saturday morning. *Nora, your Joey is with Jesus now. Pray to the Blessed Virgin to ease your pain. Trust in God to—*

But Mama wouldn't hear of that. *God turned His back on me, Sister. The God I knew doesn't kill little children. Come back when you've lost a child, and maybe I'll listen to you. Now leave.*

Grief toppled our world upside down. It climbed on our shoulders and refused to leave. Maureen took over cooking and Dennis and I reluctantly helped sweep and dust the house. Once I swept Joey's red model car from under the sofa. I teared up, saddened at the tiny black wheels, the running board, the chipped paint. I hid it under my shirt so Dennis wouldn't see and then hurried to my bed where I slid it under my pillow. It was the only thing of Joey's I could touch and feel. At night I'd whisper to him. *I found your car, Joey. I'll keep it safe for you.* It rests in a special box to this day.

•   •   •

The following week, I was sent away. Daddy held me on his lap. "We've been talking, little miss. Just for awhile, you're going to stay with Uncle and Auntie at their store. Don't worry, you'll go to school and see us, but Mama is sick and can't take care of things."

"Bu-but—" I felt tears urging to spill. My throat tightened.

"I know, I know. Maureen and Dennis are older. They take care of themselves, but since you're only—" Were Daddy's eyes wet?

"No. I can take care of myself too. I promise I won't be any—"

"Betty, look at me. You'll have a good time staying above the store. Think of the candy you can sneak, and Auntie makes oatmeal cookies you like." I didn't care about cookies. I wanted to stay with my family.

But it was not to be. Daddy opened their bedroom door and cautioned me to "say a quick goodbye to Mama." I don't recall what we said. Maureen tried to make me feel better. "You'll be swell, Betty. Just wait and see."

Dennis hung around in the shadows. Maureen told me later that Mama refused to see or talk to him for weeks on end. It took many months for him to play with Billy and his other friends.

•　　•　　•

So, I found myself at Auntie Agnes's house, a roomy apartment above their grocery store. When we used to visit, I'd happily scamper up the staircase at the back of the store and dance my way into a large green living room with an adjoining kitchen and dining area leading into a hallway with two bedrooms and a bathroom in between. Silver-framed black and white aging family photographs sat on end tables, and two pillows embroidered with pink roses rested on the couch. A framed square of tan fabric with *Be Still and Know that I am God* sewed on it hung above the couch. Bluebirds and green ivy circled the words. Auntie had made it herself when she first married.

A tobacco scent from Uncle's pipe always lingered in the air. The space was larger than it looked from the outside, and two windows in the living room provided ample light. Outside the building, stairs on the ground led up to the kitchen.

Uncle was really Daddy's uncle on his mother's side. *In other words, Betty, he's your great uncle, your grandma's brother.* I puzzled why his last name was Casey and not O'Leary like ours. *Because your grandma's maiden name was Casey, and the men keep their last names all their lives, and don't change 'em when they get married.* Why was it so confusing?

We'd never called Uncle by his real name, Maurice, which he hated. He didn't like 'Maury' either, but the grownups called him that. So, they were Auntie and Uncle for me. Both had gray hair, and wrinkles branched from the corners of their mouths. They were ancient in my eyes. In later years, I realized they were only in their early or mid sixties.

I recall Daddy lugging a flour sack as a make-do suitcase up the stairs and into the smaller bedroom where I would sleep. We unpacked my school jumpers and blouses, underwear, socks, and several small dolls and their odds and ends. I carried my Marie doll in my arms so she wouldn't suffocate in the bag. I also brought a copy of *On the Banks of Plum Creek* from the library. Tucked into a wool sock was the small red car. I slid it into its place under my pillow.

Because of the cold and snow, I left my boots, coat, hat, and mittens in the closet by the living room stairs. I remember walking to school most days unless an overnight storm had caked the streets with snow and ice. Then Uncle drove me. The store was east of Halsted, but school was about the same distance.

My memory is fuzzy, but during that time, it seemed the teachers and kids paid more attention to me, were nicer. Some asked about Joey, some didn't. Girls like Gloria Sperry wanted to be friends, along with others in her group. They liked to walk to Uncle's store with me after school and get free Dubble Bubble gum and Tootsie Rolls. I didn't see Joan as much anymore. She'd hang her head and slip away when I talked to other girls.

Truth be told, the apartment was a happier place than I expected. Auntie and I listened to stories on the Philco radio, wooden and larger than ours. I loved the adventures of Little Orphan Annie and her dog, Sandy. When I brought up their dog, Shep, Auntie said they weren't ready for another one. *Think of Joey and Shep running and playing with each other in heaven.* I found comfort in those words.

The question of why Mama and Daddy sent me away still lingered. They didn't want me, but no one gave me a good reason why.

Thankfully, Auntie took me to the library Saturday mornings, so I could shake off my thoughts about Joey. I checked out *The Wonderful World of Oz* and dreamed of becoming Dorothy and the good witch, Glinda.

We had fun times too. It seemed the radio was always on, and Auntie would play music when the fireside chats ended. I think Uncle sang along to every song they played, like "A Tisket, a Tasket," "Goofus," and "Cheek to Cheek." Sometimes on weekends Uncle would dance with Auntie and me after drinking something called Bee's Knees. *Come on, let's dance, Betty. You're the bee's knees and the cat's pajamas.* Auntie would pretend to scold him. *Maury, settle down. What would her mama think?* Uncle would scoff and keep dancing. *She's seen Mac knock back a few. Simmer down.*

One day Auntie and I finished singing "Little Playmate" when she hugged me, and I could hardly breathe. I wiggled away and must've looked confused. "I'm sorry honey bunch. It's just so wonderful to have a little girl with me again."

Her children were grownups and lived far away, New York perhaps. "You had a little girl?" I immediately had the feeling I shouldn't ask.

Auntie cleared her throat, gave a little cough. "We don't talk about—" She inhaled sharply. "I don't like to think—oh well. You probably know most of our children and grandchildren live back east near New York City." She stared out the window as if she saw something far away. "We had four boys and one girl, Nellie. She was your daddy's cousin. But she got sick and, um, she never got well."

"You mean, she—"

"Yes, honey, she passed away like Joey. And Shep." Auntie's eyes were circled in red.

"Oh." I wondered why Nellie didn't get well from being sick. "Why did she get sick?"

"I'm afraid there was an illness going around at the end of the Great War. It was called the Spanish flu. I don't know why, I guess Spain was hit hardest. Anyway, thousands of people all around the world caught it, and so many died. Very tragic."

I couldn't think of anything to say. I knew you could catch chicken pox from people, so I guess it was like that. Spreading germs.

Auntie looked so downcast, I wanted her to feel better. "Maybe Nellie is up in heaven watching over Joey and Shep."

Then Auntie cried a little and hugged me again. "Sweet Betty, I'm sure they're very happy."

I never mentioned Nellie again to Auntie. I didn't want her to cry or be sad.

CHAPTER 8

Life slogged on through that snowy, frigid time, days fading one into another. During those blurry weeks, I heard Mama went to a hospital to stay for a month or so.

One Saturday morning, Maureen came over while Uncle and I were building a snowman in the small back yard away from the street. I had just wedged the coal eyes into the lopsided snowball of a face, and Uncle had stepped inside to look for a carrot nose. I was shivering, my fingers felt like ice in my thick wool mittens.

"Hi, Betty. Handsome looking snowman." Maureen trampled through the snow to my side.

"What are you doing here? Did something happen?" It was a day early for our visit.

"Don't worry. Let's get out of this god-awful cold." She didn't have sense enough to wear a hat.

Uncle returned with a purplish rutabaga. "Here's your nose. No carrots to waste."

I stuck the root under the black eyes. "That's all right. I hate rutabagas anyway."

"Betty, that's no way to talk. After all, you're staying with—"

"Ah, let her be. She's honest." Uncle looked at Maureen. "You gonna tell her now?"

"Yeah, when I get unfrozen. Come on, let's go inside." Maureen, bossy as ever.

• • •

Uncle returned to the store to join Auntie, and I led Maureen up the outside stairs to the kitchen. We left our coats and boots by the living room entry and flopped on the couch.

Maureen wore a green wool sweater Mama knit last winter and dark gray snow pants, since she wasn't going to school or church. "Um, you know that Mama hasn't been herself or done much of anything since Joey—ah, since the Accident, so after you came here to stay, she got worse." Maureen studied her worn-out wool stockings. "So, they took her to a hospital in Elgin to get well."

"A hospital? What do you mean 'she got worse?'" I sensed something chilling coming.

"You know how she just sat in the bedroom all the time?" Maureen pursed her lips. "She took some shirts and Joey's sweater she knitted and his Buck Rogers gun and a few of those metal toy cars he liked."

I thought of his red model car I swept from the floor. It was still under my pillow.

"What did Mama do with those things?"

"Nothing much, other than stroking and smelling his clothes and holding the toys." Maureen raised her palms. "Besides not eating hardly anything, she started saying strange things, talking about Joey like he was alive. She'd say 'Joey will want to eat soon,' or 'save some candy for Joey.' I could tell Daddy was scared."

I wasn't sure I wanted to hear anymore. I looked at my feet and put my hands on my cheeks.

"I think I'll call Auntie to come up and explain it to you." Maureen nervously tapped the worn arm of the couch. She rose and faced the door. "I'll be right back."

•   •   •

Auntie's wrinkles seemed to weigh down the corners of her mouth as she sat next to me on the couch and put an arm around my shoulders. "I know this is hard to understand, Betty, but just like people get sick with sore throats and get their tonsils out like you did, some folks get sick in their heads and hearts and feelings."

"You mean Mama's crazy?"

Maureen gave a short gasp. "Betty, you—"

"It's all right, Maureen." Auntie hugged me. "That's a word lots of people use, but doctors don't say it. There are names like melancholy, where people are so sad, they can't do their jobs. I think your Mama just can't get over what happened to Joey, and so your Daddy called Dr. Gerlock. He said she needed to go to the hospital where they can help her get well."

I thought about that. "Is it a loony bin? How long will she be there? Can we visit her?"

Auntie glanced at Maureen. "It's called a mental hospital, and we can't visit for a while, honey. These things take time. We'll pray to the Blessed Virgin to give her comfort and strength to feel better."

•   •   •

I would learn that Elgin State Hospital, once called the Northern Illinois Hospital and Asylum for the Insane, went through many renovations from its origin in the 1870s. The main entrance of the center building was eventually demolished, a long-overdue process according to general opinion. Until then, the façade with its dark pointed arches and narrow windows imparted a foreboding, gothic atmosphere, an appropriate setting for a Boris Karloff movie.

The hospital was about an hour from our house, and a few days ago Mama's cousin from Bridgeport and her husband drove with Daddy to the hospital. Maureen said Mama didn't want to go, and Dr. Gerlock gave her drugs to calm her down. She fought Daddy about taking them, but finally relented.

"I heard Doctor tell Daddy that they have treatments they use to help people, like giving you baths for a long time in hot or cold water and other things I don't remember," Maureen told me. "But don't tell anybody where Mama is. Just say she's visiting her cousin if anyone asks. Daddy doesn't want people to know where she really is."

"I don't want anybody to know she's in the loony bin either, especially the girls at school and the teachers."

"Quit saying that. It's a hospital, and Mama's not crazy. Anyway, we're better off without her around now. Billy's ma brings food sometimes and checks on us. Dennis is home more. I think Mama will always blame him and Daddy for Joey, but Sister Cecile said it was God's plan."

I looked at the floor. "It was my fault. If I'd tattled on them that night, it wouldn't of happened." I couldn't help my lips quivering.

Maureen cleared her throat. "Betty, I've told you, don't blame yourself. You're only eight years old. Still a little kid."

"I am not." I hated being the baby all the time. "Sister Cecile says I'm very grown-up for my age."

"All right, silly. I gotta go now. See you tomorrow when you come to the house." Maureen reached out her arm to me, hesitated, and jerked away. I think she was too embarrassed to hug me.

Could I go home and stay since Mama was in the hospital? Would Daddy want me back?

CHAPTER 9

Ivan, the peddler came to the door one Saturday after Mama was sent away. He hadn't dropped in since Joey's Accident, and maybe he thought Mama was feeling better. Maureen said Daddy was mean to him and told him to go away and never come back to sell his junk. When Maureen told Daddy to mind his manners, she thought he was going to belt her, but he didn't.

I felt sorry for Ivan. I heard later he'd come here from Russia to escape poverty and violence against people like him who didn't believe in Jesus. We never heard from him again. I think he just disappeared.

. . .

When my third-grade year ended, I was still living at Auntie's. I felt unwanted, like used-up newspapers. I gave up asking Daddy and Maureen when I could come home. Maureen told me I got better food because Billy's ma didn't bring meals much anymore, and Daddy only cut up wieners to put in soup or noodles. Maureen knew how to boil cabbage, and Auntie showed her how to add oatmeal to hamburger meat to make it stretch. She learned how to fry cut-up potatoes, which they had plenty of since they weren't rationed like meat and eggs and other things.

Most Sundays I went to my own home after Mass with Auntie to see my family. The house stayed the same, with the familiar aroma of pipe smoke and musty books, even though we had no books in sight. But something had changed. Whenever I hopefully entered the house, a huge black emptiness greeted me. An emptiness that was Joey.

According to Maureen, we weren't allowed to talk about Joey because it would upset Daddy. I didn't see Dennis much. He'd slink around the kitchen and then spend most of his time down the basement or go out to meet some boys from school. He wasn't supposed to see Billy anymore or the other boys who came with him the night of the Accident. I don't know who made that rule, but since Billy lived next door, it was hard to avoid him.

Maureen said Auntie told her it was normal for Mama to find someone to blame, but the Accident was nobody's fault. *When our Nellie died, I blamed everyone around, the doctors, nurses, government, anyone connected with the flu epidemic. I blamed Uncle for not keeping her safe. Even God and the Blessed Virgin. But after a time, I knew in my heart no one was to blame. That it's all part of being human, birth, death, joy, grief. Your mama will get better with time.*

Maureen told me that one night Mama cried and yelled to Daddy she was going to the railroad depot and find out how they could've let the boxcar hit Joey and she was going to get back at them. Daddy got her to stay home by locking her in the bedroom until she calmed down.

·   ·   ·

Mama stayed in the hospital for several months, but it seemed like a year. One day at the house, Maureen grabbed my hand and led me into her room. "Guess what? I'm gonna visit Mama with Daddy next Saturday. The doctor said she might be ready for me to visit, and it could help her get better."

"Can I go too?" I already knew the answer.

"No, you're too little. I'm allowed because I'm a teenager." Maureen tucked her red curls behind her ear.

"Is Dennis going? He's a teenager." I thought how unfair it was to be the youngest.

"Of course not, dummy. You know Mama blames him. She doesn't want to see him at all."

At least I wasn't the only one left out.

·   ·   ·

The day after Maureen came back from the visit, I heard details. She peeked down the hallway, took me in our bedroom and softly clicked the door shut. "Oh Betty, we saw Mama's room. It's so small, and she just has a bed and dresser and a few other things. Daddy said not to tell you, but we went to a room with tables and chairs and all these people sitting around. Some of them played cards and checkers at the tables."

"Did Mama play with them?"

"No, of course not. She was with us. We sat and she talked to Daddy and me."

"Did you see crazy people jumping around? Were you scared?" I would've been afraid.

Maureen laughed. "Jeez, Betty, they weren't crazy like that. They sat around like Mama. Auntie told me they take medicine to keep them calm. Daddy asked Mama about her treatments, and she told us about getting treated by taking a bath."

"What does that mean? She'll get better taking a bath?" I was confused.

"Daddy told me later that she sits in a bathtub for hours, and the water comes in and out, and there are no faucets. The water is hot sometimes and then cold." Maureen twisted an end of her wavy hair.

"How can that make her—"

"I don't know, Betty. They do that to lots of people there. Maybe the water makes them feel cleaner, who knows."

A knock on the door interrupted our talk. We both jumped as though we'd been caught with hands in the cookie jar until Dennis stuck his pale face through the crack. "Who's in there?" His light reddish hair hung straight over his eyebrows.

"Just Betty. Whaddya want?" Maureen sounded irritated.

"Wanna hear about Ma. Did ya see the Satan lady?" Dennis came in and slouched against the wall.

"What Satan lady?" I blurted.

"Oh yeah." Maureen looked at me. "Daddy told Auntie there's a patient there who thought Daddy was Satan. Probably thought all men were."

"Well, did you see her?" Dennis said.

Maureen frowned at him. "I wasn't going to tell Betty, but now that you spilled the beans, yeah, she was there. We were leaving the room and she came along wearing a ratty-looking gown. She looked at Daddy and said something like, 'the serpent deceived Eve, your minds are led astray.'"

"Cuckoo." Dennis raised his eyebrows and made circles around his forehead with his finger.

Maureen chuckled. "Yeah, then she stares at me and says, 'be careful young lady, even Satan disguises himself as an angel of light,' and she tried to grab me."

"Oh no," I gasped.

"What did Pop do?" Dennis said.

"He took my arm and hurried us away." Maureen paused. "It wasn't that bad. A nurse held her hand and led her out."

"I wouldn't want to go there after all," I said, knowing I wouldn't be allowed.

"I don't think Daddy wants to go again either. He told me the doctor said Mama might come home in a few weeks." Maureen straightened her sweater sleeve. "He couldn't wait to get to the corner after we got home."

Dennis snorted. "Yeah, he's hittin' the sauce harder than ever." He hitched up his overalls. "I'm gonna go. Won't be home for supper."

I guess he was meeting some friends from school and not Billy.

· · ·

In later years I learned Mama had hydrotherapy in the hospital that Maureen referred to. Apparently, several bathtubs sat in a row in a separate room, and the water flowed in and out of the tubs from outside tubes. There were canvas covers to fit over the tubs with a space for the patients' heads so they wouldn't climb out and would stay for several hours.

The water was usually warm, but sometimes they poured ice cold water on their heads.

Mama also received insulin shock therapy where the drug was given to induce seizures, which helped some patients, but it wasn't clear what effect it had on Mama. All I knew was she was never the same. Did the treatments cause her inability to find peace, contentment, happiness? I'm certain she never got past Joey's death. The guilt, the grief just hollowed her out of herself. There was nothing behind those vacant greenish-hazel eyes Her loss had ripped out her soul.

I don't know why Joey had been Mama's favorite. His impish personality? His green eyes and freckles? I thought something more set him apart from us. He touched a part of her heart no one else could reach, for a reason known to God alone. But Mama had rejected God and church alike, and wasn't afraid to let Father John know her opinion. *I said it to Sister and I'll say it to you. The God I used to worship doesn't kill little children. Anyone who believes is a fool. Now go, and never darken my door again.* And with those words, Father John left our house for the last time.

Mama never again entered the portals of St. Basil's Church, ridding herself of every religious picture or artifact she owned, or so she said.

Years later, after her death, her amethyst rosary beads were found under her mattress.

CHAPTER 10

Dark, nameless months and days kept inching by, one into the other, carrying the oppressive burden of grief on their backs. We lived in a gray mist of anguish and silence. Years later I thought of that time as The Hour of Lead from Emily Dickinson's poem, "After great pain…" I always felt a strong connection with the poet, who surely experienced the grief and loss she wrote of in those words. Her perfect description of simply going through the motions of everyday life, "The Feet, mechanical, go round…" We were mechanical toys; wind us up and we go forward, feeling nothing, not even a pinprick. Although I knew Joey was gone, he was still there.

. . .

One joyful event changed my life for a while. At the end of August, Auntie said she had a surprise for Maureen, Dennis, and me. She would take us to a new movie called *The Wizard of Oz*. I squealed with delight. "Gee, Auntie, will it be like my book? Will I see Dorothy and Glinda?"

I could hardly sleep the night before. We planned to pick up Dennis and Maureen in Uncle's car after Mass, and he'd drop us off at the Ramova Theater in Bridgeport. I'd never been there, but I'd heard about it from Maureen.

"Gee, Betty, wait till you see it. It's swell, like the palace in Cinderella. Huge ceilings with stars, you think you're looking up at the real sky."

The morning finally came, hot and muggy. I squirmed through Mass and only picked at the roast chicken and warm canned tomatoes Auntie made for lunch. We kept our Sunday clothes on for our special day. I wore a new dress Auntie ordered from Sears catalog several months ago, pink and navy plaid with short, puffy sleeves, a square white collar with lace trim. Short white anklets matched my white strap shoes, but they pinched my feet. "You need new dress-up shoes, Betty. Maureen wore those, didn't she?"

I hung my head. I didn't need to feel ashamed with Auntie. Of course, Mama wouldn't want people to know I wore Maureen's hand-me-down shoes, but these days, she wouldn't know the difference being in the hospital and all.

I almost tripped scrambling down the stairs and into the back seat of Uncle's brown Packard he'd bought used last year. When we stopped in front of my house, Maureen and Dennis waited outside the door. They hurried to the curb and Auntie stepped out of the front seat so they could climb in back with me. Strands of Maureen's hair stuck to her forehead. Dennis leaned into the side of the car as we squeezed together. He clearly disliked being close to his sisters.

"I know it's hot, but the theater will be cool. They have a system, you know." Auntie twisted around. I didn't know how the indoors would be cool, but I reckoned I'd find out.

We reached the theater in a few minutes it seemed. Uncle stopped at the curb on Halsted in front of the building, where we all emerged into the stifling heat. I barely noticed the back of my dress sticking to my legs.

"See you out here after the movie," Uncle said. "And don't lose Betty in the picture house."

"Now there's an idea," Dennis said. Maybe he was slowly getting back to normal.

The outside of the building reminded me of the ancient castle from *The Sword in the Stone*. My mouth dropped as I gawked at the pointed stone windows and the marquee with its glittering letters: *The Wizard of Oz*. Chills tingled up my arms.

Auntie laughed and took my hand. "Come on, honey. We can't stand out here forever."

"Wait till she sees the inside," Maureen said, as we made our way through clusters of people dressed in pastel cotton dresses and white dress shirts.

My eyes almost popped from my head as we passed through the massive wooden doors. The luscious aroma of buttered popcorn swirled in the air. My mouth watered. I suddenly felt cooler. I didn't know where to look first. I was transported inside a magical kingdom of marble pillars, towering ceilings, and scenes of medieval country sides on the outside walls.

"Wait here," Auntie said. "I'll get our tickets." She watched me closely. "Don't move, Betty. I don't want you lost in the crowd."

Maureen took my arm, but I jerked it away. "I'm not a baby, you know."

"Hey, pipsqueak, look up there." Dennis pointed upward.

"Wow," was all I could think of to say. "Wow." Way above us on a navy-blue ceiling I saw hundreds, probably thousands, of tiny pinpricks of stars glimmering. I was in a dream for sure.

Next thing I knew, we were seated in the most enormous room I'd ever seen, with a gold-curtained stage, rows and rows of cushioned red chairs where the seats were up until you sat on them. I parked myself between Auntie and Maureen, and Dennis picked the aisle seat. I gaped around and around until Auntie said, "Settle down, Betty. People will think you're staring at them."

The lights dimmed, the curtains slowly opened, and on a huge screen we saw a newsreel, with soldiers marching and a man talking about Germany and Russia signing something. I heard a man behind me say, "There'll be war for sure."

I didn't pay any mind to that; I was about to sail into the land of Oz. After a silly Donald Duck cartoon, the curtain closed for a few seconds and opened to an orchestra playing "Over the Rainbow." When the movie finally began, Maureen whispered that later on it would be in color, which meant little to me.

From then on, I don't think I moved a muscle the entire hour and fifty minutes of my life in Kansas and Oz. I loved Dorothy, and wished I could be her, and Glinda, the wonderful witch of the north, was the most beautiful person in the world. But the part that changed my life was Dorothy singing "Over the Rainbow" because that's exactly where I wanted to go. I longed to fly with the bluebirds to a place where dreams come true and you have no troubles. I painted a picture in my mind of a lovely rainbow above a green meadow, and there I am smiling at a bluebird perched on my hand. I knew Maureen and Dennis would laugh at me if I told them, so the bluebird and rainbow became my secret.

My heart sank when the movie ended, not only because it was over, but Dorothy telling her Auntie Em how glad she was to be home, and she'd never go away again. My eyes formed pools, and I willed myself not to cry. I missed my home.

When the music faded and lights came on, I didn't feel glum anymore. The whole afternoon felt magical.

Auntie laughed as we got up and made our way among the crowd toward the exit. "I think Betty will be in a daze for a while."

Maureen straightened the waist of her pink striped dress. "More in a daze than usual probably." Her new dress had puffy sleeves and white ribbon around a boat neck and a band of ribbon above the hem. White slip-on shoes and

Mama's nylon hose made her look older than her fourteen years. Several boys glanced her way, and I saw her give them a half-smile.

The savor of popcorn still hung in the air in the lobby as I took a last look at the stone, marble, and fancy tiles. People chattered about the movie, but I was delighted to simply be there during this special time.

Stepping outside felt like walking into a furnace, as Dennis said. He spotted Uncle's car down the block, but I didn't want to leave the theater and all its magic even though the air was fat with mugginess.

"Whew," Auntie gasped. "This heat wave better end soon, or we'll have to live in the cellar." I knew she didn't mean that. Who'd want to live down there with all the jars of pickles, jam, and potatoes scattered all over.

Uncle switched on the fan in the car, but even with the windows down it was sizzling. We reached my home, and when Maureen and Dennis clamored out of the back seat, I wished I could follow them into the house. It struck me that today nobody seemed unhappy about Joey. We had disappeared to Oz and left his memory behind. I hoped Joey didn't mind that we were lighthearted for a little while even with him gone.

I still didn't understand why I couldn't go home. I wouldn't be any trouble. I wish Daddy or someone would tell me what was wrong with me so I could change it.

CHAPTER 11

Autumn, 1939

The following weekend Dorothy, Glinda and bluebirds still danced through my daydreams. It wasn't quite as stifling outside when I went home after the library to visit at my house. Labor Day weekend was here and school would start this week. Daddy and Billy's father were drinking beer in the kitchen and talking about the news of Germans fighting in Poland. I didn't understand much, but Mr. Linsky was upset because some of their relatives lived over there, and now it would be another war just like the Great War which wasn't supposed to happen. "Ya know Churchill's sure to pitch in against the Germans any day now."

"Aye," Daddy said, "FDR said no war for us at least. Not again. Gotta keep our boys safe this time." Daddy didn't seem concerned about it. He said America shouldn't have to take care of other countries. *Let 'em fight their own battles.* But if Billy's relatives were over there, shouldn't we help them? Daddy never mentioned our relatives in Ireland. Maybe they were safe.

I hung around the kitchen, hoping to hear that Mama would come home soon, but I knew better than to ask. I didn't want to get on Daddy's nerves.

• • •

Maureen and I sat on the bed looking at her *Photoplay* magazine with Alice Faye on the cover. I was anxious to start fourth grade on Tuesday. Knots always tightened in my stomach the first day, and this year I'd still live at Auntie's. Dennis would return to Lindblom High School, an all-boys technical school, close enough for him to walk. He'd be in tenth grade, but didn't say much about it. Or anything else.

Maureen had graduated from eighth grade and was thrilled about starting ninth at Mercy High School. "I can't wait to get away from grammar school and take the bus to high school. Even though there won't be any boys, I'll meet new girlfriends." She strutted over to the closet.

"Look, Betty, how do you like my brand-new school outfit?" She took out two hangars and held them up for me to see. The skirt and blouse looked more grownup than our St. Basil's attire, consisting mostly of navy jumpers and white blouses.

"Yeah, they're swell," I said. I liked the pleated tan skirt better than my old hand-me-downs. The white blouse had a regular-looking collar too.

"And guess what." Maureen placed her clothes on the bed and turned to the closet. "Look, we get to wear blazers with the school crest on it." Like a queen, she held up a maroon collarless jacket with a gold and black patch shaped like a shield on the front.

I reached out to touch the patch. "Careful." Maureen pulled it away. "Are your hands clean?"

I sniffed. "Yes they are, Mama," I said in a high-pitched voice.

"Pooh, you're just jealous." Maureen lifted her head and strutted around like she was Ginger Rogers.

"Ha, you always think you're the cat's pajamas, but you're not."

Maureen knew better than to take me seriously. She sneered and hung her clothes back in the closet. We hadn't fussed at each other like this since—since Joey.

I was quiet for a minute. I looked at my shoes.

My lack of response prompted Maureen to turn from the closet. "What's the matter?"

"I was thinking—thinking that I can't see Joey anymore."

She sat on the end of the bed. "Betty, none of us can because—"

"No, I mean I can't see his face. I can't stir it up in my mind." I wiped my eye. "Unless I take out his picture in the drawer at Auntie's. I want to see his freckles, his hair sticking up. I don't want to forget—" I tried to dislodge the lump from my throat.

Maureen put her hand on my knee. "I know. What brought this on?"

I sniffled. I didn't want to talk anymore. For some reason I felt a little better, though I couldn't bear losing a picture of Joey in my mind.

I guess Mama always sees him, he's always with her. He takes up all the room in her. There's nothing left for us or anything else in her life.

At least I could speak Joey's name with Maureen. And Auntie too.

CHAPTER 12

I continued to live with Auntie and Uncle as the weeks wore by. I quit asking when I could go home. I liked my fourth-grade classes and teachers. They'd talk of the war in Europe, and Sister Anne was worried about her people in Lithuania. She didn't explain why, something about Russia.

Sister Cecile taught our reading class again, and I loved learning new words and hearing her read new books. My favorite was about a little girl who lived in a Catholic boarding school in France. I checked out two of the *Madeline* books from the library and read them to Auntie. *In an old house in Paris, That was covered in vines, Lived twelve little girls, In two straight lines.*

I admired the bright blue coats and yellow hats the girls wore, and their teacher was dressed in a matching blue nun's habit. I liked Madeline best because she was the youngest and the only one with red hair. I thought if they had to live away from home, at least they had lots of friends around.

.   .   .

One crisp October afternoon gold and yellow splashed the leaves like an oil painting. Kids were jumping in a pile of leaves in their front yard down from Uncle's store. We never had enough trees around us to make a pile, and it sure looked fun. Maybe I was too old for that.

I reached the store, and when I opened the door, Uncle said, "Hi little bluebird. What did you learn today?"

"Lots of things. Way too many to talk about." Truthfully, I couldn't remember learning anything I didn't know yesterday. I eyeballed the candy counter by the cash register.

"Too bad you're not old enough to have those licorice cigarettes, so I'll save 'em for—"

"No, Uncle. I love licorice." I pointed to a black-shaped stick with a knob at the end. "What's that supposed to be?"

"Why those are pipes. Just came in, but you're too young to smoke." Uncle's cheeks wrinkled when he laughed. He thought he was so funny.

"Please, let me try the pipe, even though ladies don't smoke pipes." I put my satchel down and took off my heavy knit sweater.

Uncle handed me the licorice. "Here ya are, but don't let your auntie see it." He winked at me.

Just then the bell rang and someone came into the store. Thank goodness. I was happy to sneak upstairs and smoke my pipe in peace.

Auntie didn't mind that I'd get candy from the counter after school. She said I was a hard worker and got good reports from teachers, better than Dennis and Jo— I mean, better than Dennis and even Maureen. I opened the door and took my scuffed brown shoes off. I liked to go stocking feet at home. I caught a trace of warm milk in the air.

"In here, Betty," Auntie called from the kitchen. "Come have a cup of cocoa."

I rushed in with the licorice in my mouth. She spun around from the stove. "Good heavens, what is that thing?"

"A licorice pipe. Uncle just got them in." I giggled at her raised gray eyebrows and disapproving look.

"What will they think of next?" She put two steaming white cups in front of us on the flowered oilcloth. She took some graham crackers out of the cupboard and placed them on the table.

I took a sip of cocoa. "Mmm, good and hot." Sometimes we have marshmallows on top, but I didn't ask so I wouldn't be a pest. We ate and sipped silently until Auntie cleared her throat. "Your father said your mama might come home this weekend. He didn't want to get your hopes up, but it looks awfully certain."

Butterflies flipped in my stomach. I should feel joyful, excited, so why did I feel uneasy, worried? "Will I get to go home then? She'll take care of me and everyone?"

"That's what we're hoping, honey. But the doctor said to take things slow. Maybe after a couple days, then you can go back." Auntie's brown spotted hands caressed the shiny cloth.

That meant the rest of the family would be there without me for a couple days. For the hundredth time I wondered why I was left out. You'd think I was a baby. Nine years felt old to me.

Auntie straightened the collar on her yellow polka dot housedress. "I know you're unhappy about being away, and it's hard to understand your mama's sickness." Her light green eyes seemed as forlorn as I felt.

"It's all right." I took a bite of cracker. Maybe if I didn't complain, they'd think I was more grown up.

"Come downstairs. You can help put some cereal and bread on the shelves." Auntie pinned a strand of gray hair that had fallen from the bun on her head. It almost reached her waist when it was down. Every so often, she'd let me brush it and even braid it when I learned how.

After I used the bathroom and washed up, I joined Auntie, Uncle, and two neighbor ladies in the store. They rambled on about the war and worried about their people somewhere across the world. I was just worried about Mama coming home in a few days. Would she be normal again and let me stay?

CHAPTER 13

I woke up early Saturday morning, the day of Mama's homecoming. Uncle and Daddy drove to pick her up. Auntie and I minded the store until Uncle came home after lunch. He said Mama got home, and she seemed all right.

"How is she? Does she look the same?" As with Joey, my mind's picture of her had dimmed.

Uncle chuckled. "Yes, she's the same. She wondered how you were."

I perked up. "Did you tell her I wanted to—"

"Hold your horses, bluebird." Uncle cleared his throat. "I told her you were fine as frog's hair."

"Okay. When can I go see her? When can I go back?"

"Soon," Auntie said. "Let's get ready for the library. Get your books to return."

After browsing the shelves, I checked out *By the Shores of Silver Lake*. I was distracted, anxious to get home to see if Uncle had heard more about Mama. I barged into the store, and a friend of Uncle's was on his way out.

"Hello, young lady. You like to read those books, I hear." He was bald and bent over, like he was crooked.

"Y-yes." I smiled and shifted my feet. My cheeks burned.

He joked to Uncle, "See you next week, Maury. Don't take any wooden nickels." He guffawed and let the door swing closed behind him, the bell ringing in his wake.

"Can I visit Mama today?" I knew I shouldn't ask, but I couldn't help it.

Uncle and Auntie exchanged a glance. Auntie took my arm. "Come on, honey, let's go upstairs, and you can read me your book."

My hopes sank as I followed Auntie up the stairs.

•   •   •

The day wore on and by bedtime, still no word if I could see Mama. After my bath with a new bar of Ivory soap, I crawled into bed and read about Laura Ingalls moving to South Dakota. At eight o'clock Auntie came in for prayers. We both folded our hands. "Bless me, Lord, as this day ends, Bless my family and all my friends, Keep me safe throughout the night, and wake me with the morning's light. Amen."

Auntie kissed my cheek. "You have sweet dreams, sleep tight, don't let—"

"The bedbugs bite," I finished.

I settled my favorite doll, Marie Dionne, under the covers as Auntie left the room and closed the door. My doll helped me fall asleep as I whispered my secret thoughts to her. Tonight I had plenty to tell. "Do you think I can see Mama tomorrow? I don't want to wait till next week. It's not fair that Maureen and Dennis live with her and I—" I hugged Marie and squirmed over on my tummy. I felt under the pillow for a little red car. "Good night, Joey," I whispered. "Maybe tomorrow I'll see our mama."

•   •   •

A chill was in the air when we left for Mass the next morning. "Look at the leaves in the Stengel's yard. They're more colorful every year." Auntie walked beside me, and Uncle followed us on the sidewalk along Garfield. When it rained or snowed, we'd drive the few blocks to St. Basil's, but today sunshine fell upon us and a breeze hinted of colder air to come.

The Mass lasted a lifetime. All I could think about was seeing Mama. Auntie had to nudge me to stand for the Eucharist. I prayed to Mother Mary that I could see Mama today.

After the service, people congregated outside to chatter on and on. I tried to pull Auntie's arm away from Miss Petronis, but they kept yakking about the price of meat and the war. "Just a minute, Betty. Mind your manners. We're talking. What will Miss Petronis think?"

"I'm sorry." I looked down at my white Sunday shoes. Why did grownups talk so much?

We finally reached the store, and after waiting for hours, Auntie served sliced boiled pork liver on buttered toast for lunch with corn meal mush. I hated liver, but forced most of it down with milk. I fiddled with it using my fork, trying to hide the rest under cabbage leaves.

After two helpings, Uncle exhaled loudly. "Baked apples for dessert, Ma?"

Auntie opened the oven. "Umm. Done just right." She held a singed red potholder and pulled out a pan of three steaming apples, cored and stuffed with currants, cinnamon, and brown sugar. My mouth watered at the buttery, spicy fragrance.

"Ah, tasty. My favorite dessert." Uncle smacked his lips as we all dug in. "How 'bout you, bluebird?"

"Oh yes," I said. "These are much better than Maureen's."

Uncle guffawed.

"Never mind. Maureen's just learning to cook," Auntie said.

We finished eating, and I helped Auntie clean up and wash the dishes. It sure took a long time for her to scrub the pots and pans. I used two thin towels to dry them all.

"Ah, everything's spic and span," Auntie said. "Let's see what's on the radio. Maybe *Little Orphan Annie.*"

In the living room, Uncle was already listening to a program and puffing away on his pipe. I never tired of the smoky molasses fragrance of his Prince Albert tobacco. Light streamed in the windows creating a bluish cloud of haze. Years later, a random trace of Uncle's pipe tobacco would give me a sense of solace.

"Time for you to make a call," Auntie said as she started for the radio.

Uncle grunted reluctantly. "Yeah, yeah, I'm going." He extinguished the tobacco in the curved pipe and lay it in a tin ashtray, the stem sticking out.

He stomped out the door and down to the store where the telephone sat by the cash register.

"He'll call your house and see how Nora—your mama is today." Auntie didn't sound hopeful. "Now, let's find a story to listen to or some music."

I wanted to join Uncle and hear him call Mama, but I knew better than to ask.

Auntie rotated the dial on the square face of the Philco until we heard the familiar strains of "Flight of the Bumblebee." "*The Green Hornet.* Let's hear that." I'd forgotten I was blue. I loved the adventures of Britt and Kato fighting crime.

I curled up on the sofa and listened to the story while Auntie set up the board in the kitchen to iron my school jumpers and Uncle's shirts. After a while she called, "Betty, I'm going downstairs to see what Uncle's up to."

I suspected they'd talk about his telephone call, and after a few minutes, I opened the door and snuck down several stairs. I heard muffled talking and then crept closer.

"Never heard the likes of that." Auntie's voice sounded angry. "Nora should just pull herself up by the bootstraps like the rest of us."

"Now, Ma—"

"Don't 'now Ma' me, Maurice Casey. She's always put on airs and is lazy if you ask me. What kind of mother—I knew she'd be trouble. Mac should've found someone else. I told you that way back—"

"Shush, Betty'll hear you. I'm sure by next Sunday—"

I didn't wait to hear more. My eyes welled up, and I wiped my cheeks as I whirled around and hurried up the stairs, slammed the door, and dashed into my bedroom, *The Green Hornet* still playing. Marie was lying on my pillow; I grabbed her and squeezed her hard. I lay down and rolled to the wall, trying to stifle my sobs.

I heard the door open and caught a hint of gardenia. Auntie sat beside me and stroked my back. "I'm sorry, honey. You heard. I wish I could change things." She handed me a white hankie with lavender edging around it. I took it and sniffled into the cloth.

Burying my head in the pillow, I rubbed Marie's plastic hair. I was tired of talking. Tired of hoping. Just plain tired.

"You rest here with your dolly, and later we'll go downstairs for a delicious ice cream sundae. You can pick the flavor"

I didn't care about ice cream. I didn't care about anything.

I was a candle going out.

CHAPTER 14

How many times can your hopes rise to the treetops? I knew I should keep hoping I could see Mama, but I grew bone-weary of hope that disappeared into the mist. I kept on with school and friends who would come to the store with me. Auntie told me that they could only come two times a week because they just wanted free candy. I sensed that Joan was the only girl who wanted to be my friend because of me and not the store or because of Joey. I overheard Uncle say soon it would be one year since the Accident. Auntie thought the time had gone fast.

I wasn't sure how I felt. In ways it seemed like another time and place. Did I ever have a brother? What did he look like? Could I still hear his voice in my mind? I didn't think so, yet the other day at recess, I thought I heard Joey calling out. "Hey throw the ball over here." When I checked, it was a kid in upper school.

The week stole by and faded into November. Halloween came and went without fanfare. Uncle reminded us that last year there was the scare on the radio that Martians had invaded us. Who would believe that?

Kids at school prattled on about parties where you bobbed for apples floating in a large steel tub of water. Joan said you couldn't use your hands, just your teeth to grab the apple. I wasn't invited to any parties, and Auntie said it was too bad so few kids lived near the store.

I wore my gray wool winter coat to school with a new pink hat Auntie knitted. It had a matching puff ball on top. She was working on a white scarf and mittens too. I knew Mama would pooh-pooh the idea because white would get dirty at the drop of a hat.

•　　•　　•

When Saturday arrived, I returned my library book and checked out two more. This time I got another Laura Ingalls Wilder book, *Little Town on the Prairie*, and *Heidi's Children*, that Miss Brune said had just come out. I told Auntie I wanted to hurry home and start reading the Heidi book.

After lunch, Uncle said we could all go to my house and visit Mama. "We'll stay for a short time, and see how things are." Ella Swenson, Auntie's friend and neighbor, would mind the store for an hour or so while we were gone.

The day had finally come. I would see Mama for the first time in many months. I washed my face, and Auntie fixed my hair with a big white ribbon on the side to hold my bangs back. "Remember, Betty, your Mama has lost some weight. She may look different than you remember. Try and act natural when you see her."

"Okay." I didn't give it much thought. How different could she look?

It felt like the first day of school. I didn't know what to expect. Could I go home and stay? I wore my winter coat over a green plaid jumper from last year and a white blouse. I climbed in the back seat of the car, and we reached my house in just a wink.

We walked to the front door, and Daddy swung it open. "Come on in, we're all here."

A hint of coffee and cinnamon floated through the air as Maureen appeared at Daddy's side. "All bundled up, I see. It's freezing out. It'll snow soon."

We stepped into the parlor, and Daddy took our coats. A skeleton of a woman, my first instinct a stranger, sat on the couch. "There's my little one." Rising to her feet, she creaked as if her bones were sore. She extended stick-like arms towards me. I melted into her yellow and white cotton dress, whispering of Lily of the Valley. I circled my arms around her back and felt her ribs. Could she hear my heart thumping? Mama held me at arm's length. "Let me look at you. My goodness, Betty, you've grown so tall."

I didn't think so. "I guess," I muttered and grinned shyly. Heat flooded my cheeks. Her brown hair was poofed up on the sides and fell to her shoulders in the back, threads of gray now visible.

"I want to hear all about your school and what you've been up to." She sat back on the sofa and guided me to her side. Auntie and Uncle went in the kitchen with Daddy to drink coffee.

I couldn't stop staring at Mama. Ruby red lipstick emphasized her gaunt, pale face. She looked as if grief had scooped her hollow, her face lined with hardship. I babbled on about my classes, teachers, friends, and books I liked. Maybe if I talked long enough, she'd realize she missed me and want me back.

Daddy came in the room to retrieve his pipe from the end table. Maureen had been sitting in the brown upholstered chair across from us. "Betty, you didn't tell Mama the best part. The movie we saw."

I nearly jumped. "Mama, I plumb forgot. We saw *The Wizard of Oz* at the giant picture palace. Gee, it was so—"

"My, that's wonderful, Betty." Mama sighed. "I already heard you saw the movie with Auntie. I'm sorry, honey, but I'm so tired. I might need to lay down now."

She looked at Daddy like she wanted him to take her away. "Let's let Mama have a nap now." Daddy reached to pat my shoulder. "Maureen made molasses cookies. You go try 'em out."

I felt like a balloon suddenly deflated. I wanted to tell Mama about the bluebird song and the beautiful witch, Glinda. Besides, Maureen's cookies tasted like cardboard.

Mama stiffly rose, like the Tin Man. "I'll see you later, honey." Her voice sounded like something dying. Daddy followed her as she sauntered to her bedroom as though measuring each step on a tightrope.

"Come on, squirt." Maureen got up and headed for the kitchen. "You can have lemonade with your cookie."

We joined Auntie and Uncle at the table, and as expected, the cookie was like eating watercolor paper.

Daddy came and sat down with us. "How would you like to come back home, bluebird? You can pack your bags and come after Mass tomorrow."

"Really? Honest to goodness?" My heart fluttered, but I didn't feel quite as delighted as I thought I'd be. "Oh Daddy, I'll be good and not be a pest."

Everyone chuckled. "I know," said Daddy. "You can help Maureen in the kitchen and housework too. We all have to help Mama."

Auntie's lips pressed together. Maureen said, "Oh Daddy, it's not like we're Cinderella." She looked at me. "Don't worry, we're not slaves."

"Maybe we want to keep her." Uncle made a poker face.

"Okay with me," Maureen said. I knew she was joking. Maybe

We made plans for me to move back after lunch tomorrow. I felt elated and scared all at once.

That night my dreams filled with bluebirds, black witches on bicycles, Auntie in a dazzling castle. I woke up in darkness. I nuzzled Marie until clouds of sleep carried me off.

. . .

The next morning, I could barely eat my oatmeal and toast. Most of my things were packed and ready to go by bedtime last night. I could sense Auntie would be sorry to see me leave. I still might have reminded her of her girl, Nellie, she lost to the flu years ago.

A layer of snow dusted the treetops, lawns, and streets. We drove to Mass, and the hour tugged its feet through the service. I spotted Joan in the next pew, and we tried to mouth words to each other until Auntie nudged my arm.

At last the time arrived. Uncle hauled my flour sack full of clothes and a worn satchel from Auntie for my dolls and books downstairs and into the trunk as I climbed in the back seat. I felt like I had ants in my pants as we drove to my house. My own house once again. The sun peeked its head through the silvery clouds, melting most of the snow away.

I couldn't wait for Uncle and the bags. I scampered to the door and turned the knob.

It didn't open. "Let me try," Auntie said. She wiggled the knob around and frowned. "That's odd. Why would they lock the door?"

CHAPTER 15

Uncle came with the luggage and looked at Auntie. He put the sack and satchel down and tramped to the back of the house. I felt warm in my coat and gloves. Uncle returned a couple minutes later. "Betty, can you go sit in the car for a few minutes? I need grownup talk with Auntie."

My stomach tightened. I knew better than to ask questions, so I plodded my way to the car and sat in Auntie's seat. I saw her throw her hands up in anger before Uncle opened the door and they both went inside. I could feel my throat thickening and tears threatened to spill down my cheeks. Another letdown looming. My own family didn't want me. What happened after yesterday's visit?

Seconds, minutes, what seemed like hours crawled on until the door finally opened. Auntie and Maureen came out and approached the car. I braced myself for another disappointment. Auntie opened the door. Her face was flushed, her eyes lit up. "Come on out, honey. Just a little misunderstanding. Come on now."

Maureen shivered in her long sleeve shirt and corduroy slacks. "Yeah, you can move in, squirt. Just don't—"

"We need to tell you a couple things," Auntie said. "Your mama needs a lot of rest, so try not to talk to her too much. I'm sorry, that sounds terrible, but her sickness is the problem. It's not you. You're as good as gold."

"And Dennis stays out of her way almost all the time," Maureen said. "It's a secret, but he's kinda afraid of her because—because—" Maureen stopped, then went on.

"I've said that she blames him for—even though it's unfair because it was an accident, but it's the sickness again that causes her thinking to be—"

"Crazy," I blurted out.

"No, Betty, don't say that," Auntie said. "Her thinking isn't normal yet, but someday we hope it will be. So, let's go in. Maureen will help you if you need it, won't you honey?"

Auntie seemed to glare at Maureen. "Of course, I will." She sounded insulted.

Whatever butterflies had fluttered in my stomach before now danced their way into my throat. We headed once more for the door. Inside, the familiar flavor of coffee and pipe tobacco wafted in the air. Mama wasn't there, so I figured she was lying down. Dennis came from the kitchen. "The pipsqueak's home again." He sounded like he approved. A little. "See ya later. Gonna go play some ball." He hurried out the door in his dungarees and knit sweater.

Daddy and Uncle came from the kitchen. "Gotta get back to the store. Ella won't stay there forever. Come 'ere. Give your old uncle a hug"

I wrapped my arms around his middle, savoring the comfort of his molasses-like tobacco. "See you next week. Don't take any wooden nickels."

"I won't," I said. Why would I? You can't spend wooden nickels.

Auntie gathered me into herself and squeezed. "I'll miss you honey, but this is where you belong. See you next weekend, and sometime, we can have a slumber party. We'll sing "A Tisket, A Tasket, a green an—"

"Let's go, Ma. Don't wanna torture them with your screeching."

"Horse feathers. You're a fine one to talk."

Everyone laughed politely, and I watched Auntie and Uncle walk away. A twinge of gloom came over me. I'd miss our special times listening to the radio.

"Do you wanna unpack yourself or should I help?" Maureen was extra kind today.

I didn't know what I wanted. "Yeah, I guess you can help."

We took my stuff into the bedroom, tiptoeing past Mama's closed door. I visualized her asleep, the patchwork quilt pulled up to her chin. Perhaps she'd join us before long.

We unpacked the satchel of dolls and books, and I put them in order here and there. I slid Joey's red car under my pillow. Maureen helped hang up my dresses and folded the rest into drawers. "You got some new underwear. Quite fancy."

I blushed. "Auntie didn't like my old stuff, so she ordered those pink ones from Sears catalog."

"I suppose you wonder why the door was locked at first and what was going on." Maureen sat on her bed and twirled a strand of hair around her fingers. Before I could say anything, she went on. "Mama had a bad night and got all scared she couldn't take care of all of us and maybe you should stay put at Auntie's."

"But why? She saw how good I was yesterday."

"That didn't matter. Just one more person to cope with sent her in a dither. She got all crazy-like and said, 'I can't let anybody else in, even Agnes and Maury.'" Maureen paused. "Daddy told her to take some deep breaths like the doctor said. And he got her a couple pills to take. But she locked the front door when he went out of the room."

I wasn't sure I wanted to hear more. But my sister, acting like she was all important, went on. "Then came the best, I mean the exciting part. Uncle and Auntie came in, and Mama said some things. Daddy tried to calm her. Then Auntie told her, 'Nora, you need to pull yourself together. You can't keep dangling that poor child like a puppet back and forth. It's downright cruel. She's your daughter, for God's sake.' Uncle tried to shut her up, but she wouldn't. Auntie said 'you've had plenty of time to get well and be a decent mother. After all, Dennis and Maureen are old enough, and Betty's no trouble. She needs love from her mother. You should be ashamed.'"

Maureen wandered to the window and back. "Then Mama got real mad and said how dare Auntie throw stones at her after she lost her Joey, and that she had no idea the hell she went through in the hospital."

"Then Auntie said when her girl Nellie died, she fell apart with grief but after a few months, she had to get back to normal. 'You have to go on, Nora. You're broken-hearted, but you gotta put one foot in front and soldier on.'"

Maureen acted like she was out of breath. "Whew, it was quite the fight. I didn't know Auntie hated Mama so much."

"Do you think they'll like each other again?" I didn't know what else to say. Their fight had been about me. Why was everything my fault?

"I'm sure it'll all come out in the wash. They can't stay mad forever."

With that, Maureen started for the door. "I'm going to Alice's. Be back by dinner. You and me can make spam and noodles with mushroom soup."

"Bleh." I stuck out my tongue.

Maureen laughed. "Sorry, squirt. That's what you get for coming home."

"What should I do now?" I felt uneasy in my own house.

"Whatever you want, but don't wake Mama. Maybe Daddy will play gin rummy or turn on the radio." She dramatically threw a wool scarf around her neck and pranced toward the door. "Toodles." And she was gone.

I didn't want to bother Daddy, so I stayed and rearranged my books on a so-called bookshelf constructed from an orange crate. I looked through Maureen's *Photoplay* magazine with a picture of Hedy Lamarr on the cover. How can an ordinary woman be as gorgeous as her? Creamy skin, rosy cheeks, green eyes, perfect red mouth Maureen said was shaped like a cupid's bow.

I'd never be that beautiful, but Maureen might get close, and she knew it. She was the lucky one.

CHAPTER 16

The following week felt different walking to St. Basil's the old way on Fifty-fourth Street. Auntie must've told people at school that I'd returned to my house because Sister Cecile said, "I'm pleased you're back with your family, Betty. Pray for your mother's healing."

"Yes, Sister. I've been praying every day." I hoped my prayers would finally do some good.

At home, Mama stayed in her room much of the time, but she ate meals with us. Then one day she started cooking dinner. I must say, she did a better job than Maureen and me, and the food tasted normal again. "The fried potatoes are good, Mama," I said one night. I wanted her to know I appreciated her. When Dennis joined us at the table, Mama ignored him, and he didn't say much other than to answer Daddy's questions about school and whether the Bears would beat the Packers.

Maureen yakked on about her friends. She told me she was sweet on a boy she'd met after school. "He's so handsome, Betty. Just like Clark Gable. He's the bee's knees. All the girls swoon over him."

She didn't talk about him with Daddy around because he'd say she was too young to think about going out with boys. I pretended to be interested, but I wasn't. I didn't care for boys except the reserved, smart ones like Ronald Stone, who never looked at me.

Time jumped around in my mind, and soon I heard Daddy and Auntie say that the anniversary of Joey's Accident was coming up. I wasn't sure what to expect because to me, anniversaries had always been causes for celebration. Maybe we'd have a better Christmas this year.

But it was not to be. Mama gradually spent more time in her room. She ate less, and one day stopped cooking meals and eating with us at the table. A gloomy fog hung the air.

One day when Auntie and Uncle visited, they had a hushed conversation with Daddy in the kitchen. Mama was in her room, and Maureen and Dennis were out doing whatever they did.

I sat in the living room with Marie and a book, trying to hear the conversation from the other room. Finally, they came in the living room. Auntie sat beside me. "Honey, I'm afraid your mama is going back in the hospital." I gasped. "Just for a little while."

I felt a punch in my stomach. "Will I have—"

"No, you can still stay here with Daddy and the rest. You've been very grownup, but your mama had a setback. She needs more medicine in the hospital."

What was there to say? What would Joey say?

Auntie hugged me. "We'll carry on, honey. We'll visit, and you can have a slumber party whenever you want."

Uncle coughed. "Yeah, bluebird, our door is always open for you."

"When is Mama leaving?" I whispered.

"Tomorrow when you're in school," Daddy said. The lines around his mouth seemed to drag down his face.

The house grew hushed with unspoken words, hopes, heartaches. Auntie and Uncle left as if they carried a bag of potatoes on their backs. I told Daddy I was going to read in my room. He seemed relieved. "Okay, little bluebird. See you in a while." He hesitated. "Things will get better, you'll see."

I'd heard those words more than once.

CHAPTER 17

I kissed Mama goodbye the next morning. She'd joined us for oatmeal and toast Maureen made. Mama's light green chenille robe, worn at the sleeves, draped wearily from her shoulders, and Tuesday's brown gravy stain spotted the front. Her stringy hair hung to her shoulders, framing a sucked-in face with tiny cobwebs etching her forehead.

"Who's your favorite teacher?" she said for the third time. She sipped coffee, her toast uneaten.

"Sister Cecile and Sister Gertrude, even though she's German." I'd heard that from older kids, but I didn't know why that was a bad thing.

Dennis must've left for school already, probably to avoid Mama. Maureen gabbed on about a boy she swooned over. Mama sighed and held her face in her hands, elbows on the table.

"You're too young to think about going out on the town with any boy, Missy. Don't try to talk your father into anything."

It warmed my heart to hear Mama's old familiar scolding of Maureen. Perhaps she was getting better. Perhaps she should stay home after all.

Maureen flipped her hair back. "Mama, I'm fourteen. I'm sure you had a boyfriend when you—"

"Never mind. You're wearing me to a frazzle." Mama peered at me and Maureen. "Finish up now, and be off. I'll clean up." Plain to see, Mama wanted to get rid of us.

At the door, she tied my wool scarf around my neck. "It's cold out. Wear your mittens. It's supposed to snow later."

I gave her a long hug around her waist. I felt like crying. "Now, now, Betty, it's all right. I'll come home in a few days. Don't fret, honey." She paused. "I'm sorry. Sorry."

I kissed her papery cheek and, not knowing when I'd see her again, I slipped out the door into the frosty November air.

.   .   .

I knew it would be a year on December ninth since the Accident. Maureen said we'd all go to the cemetery and lay flowers on Joey's grave. I didn't even know where he was buried. Maureen and Auntie told me where the graveyard was, and I tried to imagine his headstone. How big was it? What words were on it? Would everyone cry? The house had just started feeling normal again, even with one brother missing. Joey's chair from the table, along with his memory it seemed, had been taken away and put somewhere else. In the basement, I think.

.   .   .

The dark, nameless days passed. Mama didn't come home, and Daddy drank more. He spent most evenings at the corner. Dinners were usually just Dennis, Maureen, and me sitting at the table eating whatever Maureen and I felt like fixing. Usually wieners with baked beans, fried potatoes, or noodles. Maureen and Dennis bought groceries from Uncle's store from a list Daddy made. He didn't shop much anymore.

Maureen said she wasn't sure if Mama would be home by 'Joey's day,' as I called it. Daddy had only visited her once since she left. As time passed, I felt a shift in the foundation of everyday life, as if things were unraveling like Auntie's yarn. Unraveling into something unknown, something scary.

.   .   .

A white blanket of snow covered the ground when 'Joey's day' arrived on a Saturday, icy and cold. Mama was still in Elgin, as we said these days. Uncle and Auntie planned to drive us to St. Mary's cemetery in Evergreen Park, about a twenty-minute drive south. They picked us up around mid-morning, and we all climbed in, Maureen between Uncle and Auntie in the front, Daddy, Dennis, and I squeezed in the back. Auntie held a large floral arrangement of red and yellow flowers with lots of green. I think the flowers were carnations.

We arrived at the cemetery and circled around a clearing where I saw a light brick building with a steeple in the middle, its cross reaching to the sky. We stopped alongside the road where a couple more cars were parked at a distance.

"Should be down this way," Daddy said as we climbed out. I gazed up at a huge stone statue of Jesus in a flowing gown, seeming to watch over the dead people resting beneath the tombstones. The grownups murmured among themselves, while we tagged behind. Awestruck, I willed my eyes to take in the hundreds of tombstones; some large and tall, some small and square, some flat on the ground. I wanted to read all the names. "Hurry up, Betty. You're gonna get lost." Maureen, bossy as ever.

The sky was powder blue and the bare trees and gravestones cast shadows over the white ground. Several pines here and there looked like Christmas trees waiting for someone to put colored ornaments on their branches. A trace of woodsmoke trailed in the air.

Daddy hesitated near a path and headed another way as if he couldn't remember Joey's location. "I think it's this way, Mac," said Auntie pointing toward a cluster of small trees.

We headed to the spot she indicated, and Daddy stopped. "Yeah, here it is."

I was a little fearful as I trudged beside Auntie and Maureen toward a small marble slab on the ground. Daddy kneeled and brushed away a thin layer of snow coating the marker. Auntie handed the flowers to Daddy, and he gently placed them on the ground. Auntie, Uncle, and Daddy, all sniffled. Auntie took off her glasses and wiped her eyes. Then Maureen sniffed and dabbed her eyes.

I stepped forward, leaning in to read the words on the marker.

Joseph Daniel O'Leary
Beloved son and brother
August 3, 1927 – December 9, 1938
"Lo, children are an heritage of the Lord.." Psalms 127:3

I was taken by surprise when Daddy sobbed loudly and bent down on one knee. "I'm sorry, son, it was my fault—"

"No, Mac, he's with God now. He took him," Uncle said, his voice raspy, his hand on Daddy's shoulder.

"But why? Why did—" I cried out.

"Shush, Betty. We don't question the ways of God." Auntie pulled me to her.

Dennis stayed apart from us. "I—it was my—" he choked on his words. He faced the other way.

Uncle went to him and mumbled something in his ear.

I didn't understand why God wanted to take Joey to heaven when he wasn't sick or anything. Why couldn't he stay with us? Staring at his gravestone, I tried to imagine what Joey looked like buried in a coffin. I'd heard dead people rot away into just a skeleton. I couldn't bear to think of Joey that way, so I forced my mind to see him as he always was. I hoped he wouldn't get cold from the winter air down there. But I guess he was really in heaven. I wish someone would explain it to me.

Daddy put his hand on the gravestone and muttered under-his-breath words. Then he rose and started to walk away. We followed him in unspoken agreement. I looked at Joey's name one more time. "Goodbye, Joey. I'll come back."

On the drive home, we were silent, each of us reflecting on our private thoughts and grief. Joey had been with us for eleven years. He left an anguish in his wake which would shatter our family for years to come.

CHAPTER 18

We continued our lives in muted sorrow. How long would it take Mama and Daddy not to be heartbroken anymore? Maybe forever.

Mama didn't come home for Christmas. "She's not well enough," Daddy said.

I don't remember much, but we had a bony little tree in the living room with ten candles clasped on spindly branches. I loved stringing ropes of popcorn and cranberries around like a necklace. Mama had several red glass baubles wrapped and packed away, which Maureen dug out of the attic.

When Auntie visited, she warned us for the hundredth time about not starting a fire.

"Your cousins in Dublin almost burned the house down from tree candles a couple years ago." She straightened two candles leaning precariously, so she said.

Rolling her eyes, Maureen glanced at me. "We're going to Goldblatt's to shop for presents, Auntie. I'll take the bus with Betty."

I was excited to ride the bus to Ashland and Forty-seventh, right at the edge of the stockyards. I hadn't been in the huge store for a coon's age. I couldn't wait to look at all the treasures, like lace dresses, toy cars, dolls, and even real canaries chirping in cages.

This year we had a little more money from Daddy's work at the stockyards. He said his job as watchman had changed. Maybe he bossed other people around. At least he didn't work inside the slaughterhouse like Patty Murphy's father. When I was with her and Gloria, she'd sometimes talk about the blood and guts that stained her daddy's clothes even though he wore a covering. I'd plug my ears and screech at her to stop.

Thankfully, our second Christmas without Joey brought more joy than last year's. We attended Midnight Mass, held earlier on Christmas Eve so children could go. Even Dennis came with us.

The next day we opened gifts. I jumped up and down when I unwrapped a Kewpie doll with painted yellow hair, a diaper under her pink dress and a tiny plastic bottle for her mouth. We received the usual apples and oranges, along with Snickers candy bars and peanuts. I gave Maureen a bottle of Rose toilet water, and Daddy a shellacked handprint with my name scratched on it that I made in art class. Joey's handprint had hung in the hallway, but Mama took it down. I couldn't think of a gift for Dennis, so Maureen helped me find brown and orange argyle socks for him. I wrapped a large package of Boston Baked Beans candy, his favorite.

When Dennis unwrapped the stockings, he took one look. "Where am I gonna wear these?"

"Everywhere, goofus," Maureen said. "All the college boys and movie stars like Frank Sinatra wear them."

He held up the socks. "Yeah, guess you want my autograph now."

Daddy laughed. "Always knew the boy was headed for Hollywood. So much for being a priest."

It was good to hear Daddy laugh again. We all sounded back to normal for a short time, the Christmas of 1939.

We uttered Mama's name less and less. Daddy'd visited her right before Christmas, and brought her little gifts from us, Lily of the Valley talcum powder, blue furry slip-on bedroom slippers, and a pair of patterned knit gloves Auntie made. Maureen had told me not to ask Daddy if I could visit her because Mama didn't want to see us kids. It would make her cry. Besides, I was too young to go to that lunatic asylum.

Maureen was excited about her invitation to a New Year's Eve party. "It'll be such a gas. A real gas. My new friends will all be there at Rita's house."

We sat in the living room listening to Tommy Dorsey on the radio after dinner. Daddy took a swig of beer. "I dunno, Missy. You're awful young to go galliavantin' around with who knows what kind of goons."

"Daddy, my friends are swell gals. Rita's folks'll be there." She brushed pinpricks of lint off the sofa arm.

"I don't like the sounds of it. Gonna be blokes at this shindig?"

"We're not in Ireland. It's guys, not blokes."

"I don't care. Will they be there?" He gulped his beer.

"Probably not, so don't worry," Maureen huffed.

"Probably ain't good enough, Missy. Where does this Rita girl live?" His frown lines, deep.

"Not very far. Down Halsted less than a mile. It's in Englewood."

Daddy staggered out of the easy chair. He grunted. "I dunno. I doubt your ma would let ya go there. I dunno yet." He tossed the empty beer can into the trash.

Maureen looked at me and raised her brows. She didn't seem worried. She'd most likely sneak out regardless.

"Going to the corner. Back soon." Daddy shrugged into his jacket, pulled his wool hat over his ears, and let the door swing closed behind him.

"I'm sure he'll forget about the party." Maureen adjusted the radio dial to another station. "Let's sing."

We danced around the room belting out "Jeepers Creepers" with Louis Armstrong. Dennis came up from the basement, and I thought he'd join in, but he just snorted, threw on his jacket, and left.

"I think he's sneaking drinks with his pals," Maureen said. "Daddy will go bananas if he finds out."

I guess you had to wait till you're a grownup to drink. Then it was okay.

•   •   •

New Year's Eve I was drifting off to sleep with Marie on one side and my Kewpie doll, Sugar, on the other. Dennis had left without saying anything to anyone, and Maureen got all gussied up for the party in a fancy emerald dress she borrowed from Rita. Although I'd never say it to her, I had to admit she looked like that movie star, Maureen O'Hara. Daddy didn't like the way she looked. "Take off that lipstick. You're not a gaslight floozie."

Maureen laughed. "Daddy, you're so old-fashioned. It's almost nineteen forty."

"I don't give a damn if it's nineteen sixty. You're gonna look respectable."

"All right. I'll take it off." I knew Maureen would put it back on after she left.

Auntie and Uncle popped in and stayed for a while. We played gin rummy and listened to the radio, music, some news about the war, how people in Europe had canceled celebrations because of blackouts.

I went to bed after saying Happy New Year and kissing Auntie and Uncle. Later in the fog of blackness, a loud clatter woke me. Maureen was spending the night at Rita's, so she wasn't in the room. It sounded like someone banging on the front door, then Daddy singing, *In Dublin's fair city, where the girls are so pretty, I first set my eyes on sweet Molly Mal*—what the hell!

Then more banging, and Dennis's voice. Both voices. Angry. "Not that late, look who's talkin' ya ol' drunkard." Then a crash, like something fell. My eyes opened wide. I didn't move. Just looked at darkness edged with a dim glow from the window. "Ya drunken ol' sod, your fault fer makin' us go to the tracks." Silence.

"Get out," Daddy yelled.

A door banged, then someone running down the basement. Daddy mumbling, grunting, slurring words.

Silence, then clomping up stairs, "Go ta blazes, ol' man."

Front door slammed. Pause. Feet stumbling to Daddy's room. Silence.

When I woke up, light was creeping through the window blinds. I climbed from my bed, tiptoed to the bathroom, then back to bed with my dolls.

I don't remember what happened after that, but at some point, Maureen came in the room, her hair messed, her coat slung over a sweater and wool pants. She yawned. "Gotta brush my teeth."

My memory is hazy like mist, but later I learned that Dennis had run off to stay with a friend. I didn't know who, but Maureen guessed it was a boy named Tim.

Dennis didn't come home for a long time, and Daddy never brought up the fight they'd had.

So that was how 1940 began. Now we were down to three in our family. Unless Daddy sent me back. But my world had plunged upside down. I felt lost, like the stray dogs and cats that slouched around the vacant lots and yards.

CHAPTER 19

Early 1940

Many months would pass until Dennis came home. He was living with his friend, and I hardly saw him. Every so often he'd stop by when Daddy wasn't home and talk to Maureen. He slowly faded away from my daily framework of life, kind of like Joey.

Mama came back a week or so after the new year. She looked the same, sunken, fragile, as if a gust of wind would blow her away. I hugged her gently, not wanting her to break. In time, I would realize she was already broken.

Maureen had warned me not to mention Dennis, because truth be told, his absence probably spared Mama the grim reminder of his part in Joey's death as she perceived it. So, I had to remember not to say his name, nor Joey's.

The days passed, and I wasn't sent back to Auntie's. After a while, I grew accustomed to Mama's good days and dark ones. I recall one night after dinner, she switched on the radio, and the poignant words and melody of "I'll Take You Home Again, Kathleen" played in the room. "Oh Mac, let's dance." Mama went to Daddy's chair and pulled him up. Beer in hand, he glided her around the living room and into the kitchen. The song ended; the kitchen went silent.

Maureen and I eyed each other. She raised her eyebrows. "Let's go in the bedroom."

Most days I never knew what to expect from Mama. Would she sit and stare into nothing, at a world known to her alone? Or stay in bed all day? Or laugh, sing? Hit herself in a rage?

"It won't last," Maureen would say when I'd tell her Mama was better. And my sister was right. The good times didn't last. Years later I would think of Frost's "Nothing Gold Can Stay" …*Then leaf subsides to leaf, So Eden sank to grief.*

"She still blames Dennis and Daddy," Maureen said one night as we sat in our pajamas. "I saw her in her bedroom holding Joey's orange striped shirt. You know, the one she said matched his hair. She brushed it against her face and rocked back and forth on the bed like she was cradling a baby."

I thought about his red car under my pillow. "I guess she doesn't want to forget him, but wouldn't that make her sadder?"

"I dunno. His clothes are still downstairs. Daddy wanted to take them away last weekend, and she about went bananas." Maureen yawned and arranged strips of white rags in her hair to make it curlier. "Auntie said Mama was never strong enough to go on living after losing Joey, even though no parent is ever supposed to bury their child."

·   ·   ·

As the year wore on, Mama was in and out of the hospital. I learned the telltale signs of her descent into the black hole, as Daddy called it. She'd stay up all night, traipsing around the house. One time she went outside in her grungy flannel nightgown. I heard the next day that Daddy went searching for her and found her meandering down the middle of the road. "Good thing I woke up," he said at breakfast the next morning. "She's sleeping now, but hell, she could've moseyed off to Tipperary an' back."

Another warning sign was a reddish rash on Mama's neck. We knew when it reached her face, she would go all crazy, like blabber about things that made no sense. Once she held my shoulders at arm's length. "Hi, whose little girl are you?" She looked right through me. "Oh, do you know the muffin man, the muffin man—oh I need to go out and pick flowers, flowers for—" and on she'd go, jabbering away.

·   ·   ·

Maureen heard from Auntie that Mama was going to have a treatment where the doctors hook up your head with wires, and you have seizures like Mama did from insulin. Except they would use electricity. I thought of the time Dennis talked about a movie that showed Frankenstein's monster all hooked up with wires, and it came to life.

And Daddy drank more. Maureen said, "He's gonna get fired one of these days." He didn't miss much work, though. Only one time I heard him on the telephone talking about someone taking his shift.

·   ·   ·

My fourth-grade year ended, and I welcomed summer vacation. I still hadn't been sent back to Auntie's, but she and Uncle visited almost every Sunday.

Grownups talked about the war across the world. Billy's folks worried because they hadn't heard from their relatives in Poland. An important convention was going to be held in Chicago in July, not at the huge center by the stockyards, but another stadium farther away.

Daddy said everyone at work and at the corner was rooting for FDR because he promised to keep us out of war, and no one wanted to repeat the Great War.

.   .   .

Sweltering summer months festered into autumn at long last. I started fifth grade with Sister Gertrude as my main teacher. The nuns discussed the war, and Sister said she had aunts and uncles living near a city called Dresden. Some kids didn't like her because she was German, but I didn't understand why. She had nothing to do with German soldiers starting the war.

In early November, the country voted for FDR as our President for the third time. People didn't think we'd go to war, so our fathers were safe here at home.

In early December we went on our yearly visit to Joey in the cemetery. Both Mama and Dennis were missing, so Maureen and I were the only kids, although Maureen was in tenth grade now. She didn't think of herself as a kid. "I'm very mature for my age," she said, flipping back her hair like Rita Hayworth.

Auntie brought flowers for Joey again, and this time the ground was bare of snow and grass. I examined his gravestone; again, I wondered what we'd see if he was dug up. I could hardly remember what he looked like unless Maureen showed me hidden pictures of him.

"I can't believe it's been two years," said Daddy.

Everyone murmured in agreement. To me, it was a lifetime ago since the Accident.

We mingled around for a few minutes, all of us guarding our thoughts. I said a prayer to the Blessed Virgin that Joey was safe in her arms. I felt a lump form in my throat.

Then I thought about Dennis and prayed to the Virgin to help him know he didn't kill Joey and didn't have to feel bad anymore. And to forgive me for not saving Joey's life by tattling to Mama.

.   .   .

Time passed, and soon Mama's craziness, Daddy's drinking, and Dennis's running away became normal. A gauzy veil of sorrow still draped itself over our house and refused to leave. Auntie no longer hinted that I might come back to stay with them. I think Daddy's mind was in the clouds, and he got used to Maureen and me making supper and lunch on weekends. People said things were getting better, and according to Sister Noreen, the Great Depression would end soon.

And with that, 1940 melted into the next year, with the O'Leary family forging onward without Mama and Dennis, and of course, forever without Joey.

CHAPTER 20

1941

It seemed the country was bouncing back from the Depression because Daddy brought home more meat to cook for supper, like beef roast and pork chops. And Maureen and I went to Goldblatt's more often to buy a skirt or blouse. We saw movies too. I'll always remember *How Green Was My Valley* and *Ziegfeld Girl.*

As I began sixth grade in the fall, I felt grown up like Maureen. She kept fussing with my hair, trying to curl it with an iron and tame the cowlick on my forehead. She only had one year left of high school and then she'd graduate. She told me so a hundred times, as if I'd forget. She already had her eye on a fellow named John, who knew her friend Rita. Maureen was keen to marry him. "Just don't tell anyone," she warned me.

Dennis had moved home during the summer. Uncle convinced him to make amends with Daddy, who finally agreed. The two still ignored one another most times, but managed to live in peace.

• • •

Joey's yearly cemetery visit would soon arrive. Mama had been home for a short time, but was back in the hospital. Auntie said she didn't think the shock treatments did much good.

The day was warm for December as we prepared for Mass. No boots or mittens when we headed out the door and approached Peoria Street, turning south toward St. Basil's. Dennis had stayed out all night at his friend's house, so only Maureen, Daddy, and I went to church that morning. The service dragged on as usual, and Maureen was antsy to get home and visit Rita hoping to run into John, who lived in the same block.

Afterwards we circulated in the vestibule listening to people chatter on, mainly about the war. Daddy looked forward to that afternoon's game at Comiskey Park, so he wanted to hurry home and hear it on the radio.

We had finished a lunch of left-over spaghetti, and Daddy leaned forward on the sofa, tuning in the radio. Maureen was changing clothes and primping in front of the mirror above the chest of drawers we shared.

"What the hell? What?" Daddy yelled. "Jesus, Mary, and Joseph!"

We raced out of our room; Daddy had his ear right next to the radio. A man's voice was talking, or stammering some words, but there was static, and I couldn't understand anything.

The radio man kept sputtering, static, Daddy groaning. Maureen cried, "What's the matter? What's going on?"

"Shush, gotta hear." Daddy tried to adjust the dial.

We heard a jangling ring, and I beat Maureen to the black telephone resting on the end table. "Hello," I said, and heard Uncle's voice. "Betty, your pa there?"

"Y-yes."

"Put him on. Now."

I feared the world was coming to an end. I held the receiver toward Daddy. "Uncle wants to talk—"

Daddy grabbed the phone. "What the hell? The Japs bombed the base? Pearl what? Where the hell is that?" He listened. "Shit, what'll Roosevelt do now?" Pause. "Yeah, we're in it now. Goddamn Japs. Might've known. Yeah." Daddy banged the receiver onto the phone and went back to the radio. "Lousy Japs, we'll kill every last one. Yellow bastards—" He kept muttering and cursing the Japs, whoever they were.

"Daddy, what's happening?" Maureen lips quivered.

"The Japs bombed somewhere in Hawaii called Pearl—Pearl Harbor. Go get the map, see where the hell it is."

Maureen went to the kitchen and opened a drawer where several maps were kept, one a world map. She brought it to Daddy, and he spread it on the floor. He shoved on his glasses, and finally located the spot.

"Why did they bomb it?" I kneeled on the floor close to the map.

"Because we have a naval base there and they want to destroy our ships so they can take over our country."

A banging noise came from the front door. It opened, and Billy's father and grandpa charged in. "Did ya hear, Mac? Looks like war." The men all jabbered at once, the grandpa in Polish.

They clamored around the radio, ears glued to the speaker. They'd comment and curse in their on-going commentary; it sounded like the end of the world.

A short time later, Auntie and Uncle joined the party. Uncle listened to the radio with the men, and Auntie came in the bedroom with me and Maureen and closed the door. Auntie's brows were furrowed. "Don't be too scared, girls. The men are upset because they thought we'd avoid another war. But your daddy's too old to get drafted, and Dennis is too young, except—"

"Except what?" I didn't want Dennis going to war.

Auntie coughed. "Ah, nothing." She reached in her black Sunday purse and handed us two Baby Ruth bars.

"Thanks, Auntie." We both gave her a quick kiss on her weathered cheek.

"I have Boston Baked beans for Dennis. Where is he?"

Maureen tsked. "Probably staying with Butch or Jimmy." She ogled the candy.

"I guess you girls will have to divide it."

· · ·

The rest of the day, Daddy listened to the news and blathered on with neighbors both indoors and outside in their yards. Maureen left to see Rita, and I stayed in our room reading and playing with my dolls. I think I dozed off, tired and bored from all the war talk. Did Mama know about the bombing? I didn't think it was a good time to ask Daddy.

· · ·

The next day it seemed like all of America listened to FDR's famous radio speech and the declaration of war. Our teachers discussed it, and everyone voiced an opinion, some more than others. My friends and I grew sick and tired of war talk, so we jabbered about other things like music, movies, books, boys. They gossiped about boys, but I wasn't interested in the least.

A couple men from the neighborhood council went from door to door bringing flags for people to fly in their yards. "Here you are, Mac. Fly Old Glory for the cause."

Daddy stuck the flag in the dirt beside the front stoop, bent it at an angle so it showed the stars and stripes. "See what the council does for the neighborhood, kids? All for one, and one for all."

I think Daddy had been to the corner.

At supper, he said that windows were smashed at some oriental company, and at an important Japanese building, workers were burning documents. I never saw any Japanese people in my school or anywhere else, but folks sure hated them.

When the telephone rang, Daddy answered. Several minutes later, he came back to the kitchen and sat down. "We're going to visit Joey's grave on Saturday. A few days late, but there's too much going on now with the news. We'll wait till then."

I doubted Joey would mind what day we visited.

•   •   •

Dennis finally showed up a week after the Pearl Harbor news. He was sitting on the sofa listening to the radio when I came home from school. A ratty-looking suitcase rested on the floor beside him.

"Pipsqueak, guess what. I enlisted. Yeah, enlisted." He grinned, showing his white teeth.

"Enlisted?" I struggled out of my wool coat.

"Yeah, enlisted. In the Navy. I'm gonna join the Navy and fight in the war. Kill all the Japs."

I didn't like the sound of that. "Wha—what do ya mean?" My eyes watered. "You can't go to war and get killed." I hurried to the sofa and sat beside him. He slid away as if my closeness embarrassed him.

He guffawed. "I'm not gonna get killed, noodlehead. I'm gonna help win the war for us. For you. For America."

"Daddy's gonna be mad." I felt like crying, but was determined not to.

"Ha. He can't do nothin' It's already done. He'll just hafta live with it."

Maureen sashayed through the door. "Dennis," she screamed. "You're back."

"He's going to war," I burst out.

They both yakked at once. "You can't do that," Maureen said, taking off her coat.

"Oh yeah? Already did, you twit. Me and Jimmy took the El downtown and signed up. We're in. I'm gonna stay with him till we get our orders."

This situation was moving too fast for me. I didn't understand any of it. I didn't want Dennis to go to war. What would happen to him?

•　　•　　•

When Daddy came home, Maureen and I were cooking chipped beef on toast for supper. Daddy and Dennis started talking in the living room. Their voices grew louder.

"You're too young to enlist, boy. Wait for a few months."

"Too late, Pa. I already did. Just waiting for orders."

"You numbskull. Should've waited. You're just a kid." He paused. "I can't lose another—"

"I won't get killed. I'll—"

"You don't know shit, boy," Daddy yelled. He stormed into the kitchen. "You girls go outside for awhile. Just go. It ain't cold out."

So Maureen shut off the stove, and we went outside and slogged down the block.

The slam of a door behind prompted us to turn.

We saw Dennis hurry down the walk gripping his suitcase. He headed the other way toward Morgan. I started running after him. "Dennis," I yelled.

Maureen grabbed my arms. "Let him go. He'll be back."

I watched him disappear into deepening twilight shadows.

He didn't come home for a very long time.

CHAPTER 21

People say time marches on, but to me, time sneaks away, silently fading into memories you keep, and memories you wish you could erase. If I could erase Joey from my mind and from Mama's mind, she would get well and I wouldn't feel so empty. Five years ago, Joey left us forever, and I can't evoke his image in my mind. I can't hear his voice.

Our mother will never be the same, according to Auntie. It's hard to keep track, but once or twice a year, Mama's back in the hospital. At age thirteen, I cook and bake as well as Mama and certainly Maureen. Even with Mama home, we're stuck with most of the cleaning, laundry, and grocery shopping.

I heard the attack on Pearl Harbor ended the Depression. It was common to hear of going away parties for newly inducted men, barely past boyhood. Parents and friends were happier to throw welcome home parties to returning soldiers. Of course, some fathers and sons never came back.

Family members of those serving in the war displayed flags with red borders and a blue star in their windows. When I saw a gold star, I said a prayer for the family inside the house. I also prayed to the Blessed Virgin that the flag in our window would always have the blue star for Dennis.

In school, everyone threw themselves into the war effort. We brought tin cans, wire coat hangers, and scrap metal we'd find in vacant lots. Father John and the Sisters kept saying how proud they were of us. Our teachers encouraged us to plant Victory Gardens and grow tomatoes and lettuce to help the food shortage. Mama's tomatoes grew well at first, but the next year she wasn't around. Everyone had a ration book with stamps to use for food, fuel, shoes, and other things.

When Dennis's name came up with neighbors or acquaintances, we said he was in the Navy, and we didn't know exactly where he was.

The seasons and years withered away, leaving changes in our lives with Dennis off to war, Maureen graduating from high school, and her upcoming marriage.

Maureen had courted her sweetheart, John Bailey, almost two years earlier when she was sixteen. They went to dances, parties with friends, and movies. Sometimes he came to our house to visit, and I thought he was friendly. Handsome, with black hair and sky-blue eyes, he treated me like a real person and not a little kid. Daddy wasn't sure about John as a future husband for Maureen. He was a couple years older than her, and she told me Daddy didn't trust them. *Don't come crying to me if you get in trouble.*

I don't remember when Maureen discussed the birds and the bees with me. She'd told me about sanitary pads when she first used them. I was lucky to have her was around when I got my monthly. Mama was gone, and I wouldn't have dreamed of asking Daddy. Maureen told me a girl from her school got in trouble with a boy, and she was sent away to a home.

We all attended Maureen's graduation ceremony at Mercy High School that June. Mama was home, and we dressed in our Sunday best. John came with his folks, and they met Mama and Daddy for the first time. By then, Maureen had told everyone they were getting married that summer. Mama liked John, and Daddy finally admitted he was all right, and at least he was Irish.

Mama agreed on a July wedding, so they busied themselves making arrangements with the church and selecting fabric for the dress Mama would sew. Maureen had landed a job at Goldblatt's in the linen department, and she spent every dime she made on the wedding. John worked at the Dodge Plant on Cicero Avenue and was proud to take part in the building of B-29 bomber aircraft engines used in the war. He threatened to enlist at times, but Maureen strongly objected. "He better not sneak off like Dennis did and sign up. I'm not about to have my new husband get killed." She was lucky he had a deferment because of his job.

As the wedding approached, I noticed signs that Mama's sickness was threatening to take over. She slept later in the mornings and napped much of the afternoons. The pink rash appeared on her neck and lower face. She'd rant and rave when something didn't go right.

She had set up Auntie's old Singer sewing machine in the living room corner by the window. "Damn, this lace won't fit around the collar," she groused one day as she worked on the wedding dress. "Christ, I can't do this, can't do it." She leaped up and threw a spool of thread across the living room. She plopped down at the machine and thumped her feet on the treadle, faster and faster the madder she got. She started to tear the seams on the side of the dress and make her growling animal sounds.

"No, Mama, put it down," Maureen cried. "You'll ruin it."

Mama whirled around, inches from Maureen's face. I thought she'd get slapped for sure. "I'll ruin it? I'll ruin it?" Mama shouted. "We'll see about that, you smart little witch."

With that, she grabbed the dress, ripped the lace off its bodice, and threw the whole thing on the floor. "Now let's see you fix that, Missy." Mama stomped into her bedroom and slammed the door.

I seldom saw Maureen cry, but she sobbed as she picked up the dress and held it out. The lovely white satin material and delicate strands of lace didn't resemble the bridal picture on the Simplicity pattern.

Maureen hugged the dress to her heart and hid her face in the cloth. She looked up, her eyes brimming. "My God, what'll I do?"

Then it came to me. "I know. We'll wrap it up and take it to Auntie's. She can fix it on her new machine."

Maureen hesitated, glaring at Mama's closed bedroom door and back at me. "Yeah," came out slowly. "Maybe that would work."

•   •   •

Three days later, the wedding dress hung in our closet all sewn to perfection, at least it looked perfect to me. Meanwhile, Mama's condition stabilized, so she was able to hold herself together and make it through Maureen's wedding day. She never mentioned her episode with the dress, nor did she say a word to Auntie for repairing it.

•   •   •

After their marriage, Maureen and John Bailey moved to Bridgeport, leaving me alone in the house with Daddy. Mama landed in the hospital after the wedding, and her visits home became fewer and fewer. Auntie wanted me to stay with her and Uncle again, but I was reluctant to leave Daddy. One Sunday after Mass they came for a visit. "It's not fair, Mac. Betty's a smart girl and needs to study. She shouldn't be a housekeeper for you."

"I don't mind, Auntie." I sat beside her on the couch. "I have plenty of time for schoolwork."

The living room was smoky from Uncle's and Daddy's pipes.

"My opinion is Betty should stay here, but if she wants to go with you, she can," Daddy said. "Up to her."

Content to stay in my own room and cook and clean, I lived at home until I graduated from high school.

John enlisted in the Army, despite Maureen's protests. "I gotta do my part for our country. Look at Dennis and all the others."

Like veterans everywhere, neither Dennis nor John would ever be the same.

CHAPTER 22

1947

The war ended at long last, and Dennis was discharged in the summer of 1945. He never lived in our house again and settled in nearby Archer Heights. We saw little of him, and when we did, he didn't talk about the war or anything else for that matter. Private and moody, he managed to find a job at Midway Airport doing some sort of mechanical work. After a year or so, he married a girl named Sue from Cicero and found a small house to rent. How often did Dennis think about Joey? Did he still carry the heavy burden of blame on his shoulders?

Maureen's husband, John, was stationed in Germany for over a year after VE Day, involved in the American occupation in Munich. He finally came home in the summer of 1946 and reunited with Maureen in their Bridgeport house on Pershing Road. The following spring, he and Maureen welcomed a baby boy, Tommy. I was so tickled to have a nephew, and I spent as much time as I could visiting them. I hadn't been around babies, and I loved holding Tommy and taking him for strolls in his pram around the neighborhood. I adored his tiny hands and chubby arms and legs. Just think. He was related to me by blood. Daddy was so thrilled, you'd think Tommy was born of the Virgin. Mama's reaction would remain a mystery for now. She was in Elgin at the time, and Maureen visited her a few months later. "Mama nodded at me when I told her about John's return and her first grandchild. I showed her a picture of Tommy, and she just said, 'gee, a baby' and that was it."

•   •   •

My four years at Mercy High School would end in a couple months. I didn't enjoy those years like Maureen had. Without a circle of friends, I felt more like an outsider than at St. Basil's. My friendship with Joan continued, but I didn't participate in dances and parties. Painfully shy around boys, I avoided meeting them at occasional youth groups and chose instead to blend in like a wallflower. I kept mostly to myself and admired other girls who laughed and yakked away as they clustered in the school hallways. Why were they so happy? Girls like Brenda and Dolores were poorer than us and lived in tiny flats, but they still laughed and constantly babbled. *You're a sweet girl, Betty, but why are you so quiet?* I'd smile and mutter, *I dunno. I've always been that way.*

Most days after school, I'd come home, plop onto my bed, and turn on my music. By then I owned a small radio, a gift from Auntie and Uncle. I could ease the unhappiness of life as the Andrews Sisters carried me away with "Near You" or with the mournful lyrics of Frank Sinatra pining for a lady he called "Mam'selle." I found comfort and protection in music and poetry as well. *I wandered lonely as a cloud, That floats on high o'er vales and hills.* The cloud, a perfect description.

Eager for my high school graduation, I yearned to break free of the house and neighborhood, but I had no definite plans. The idea of college hadn't entered my mind, mainly because most girls got married after graduation or found jobs. Besides, we couldn't afford college tuition.

My English teacher, Sister Noreen, thought I should further my education and one day invited me to stop by her office. "Your work is excellent, Betty. I think you'd do well in college." She sat at her desk and shuffled a stack of papers. "I know it's expensive, but Loyola offers scholarships. And nearby Mundelein College for girls is excellent. Or there are quite a few junior colleges like Joliet or Oakton.".

I felt a blush rise on my cheeks. "Yes, we really can't—ah, we haven't decided about—"

Her kind brown eyes seemed sympathetic. "Why don't you stop by Miss Land's desk on your way out and pick up some brochures. Just look through and choose a few that look interesting." She straightened the gold crucifix around her neck. "You're a special student, Betty. One of the best I've had in recent years."

I stammered. "Um, really? I don't—" I was tongue tied. I wanted to dash away. "Thank you, Sister." I almost tripped over my feet hurrying out the door. What a dummy I was. Why was I so dumbstruck around teachers? I scurried down the hall and out the front entry, forgetting the brochures.

Auntie offered to lend Daddy the money for college, but Daddy wouldn't hear of it. "Girls don't need college. If they don't marry a man with a good job, they can go to secretarial school and make a decent living."

"But Betty's so smart, Mac. Women are even becoming doctors these days," Auntie said when she and Uncle visited one evening.

"Harrumph. Betty's place is having a husband and children and a nice house like Maureen." Daddy took a puff from his pipe.

"Good Lord, Mac, have you heard of Eleanor Roosevelt? And Susan B. Anthony?"

I couldn't suppress a laugh. Daddy looked so serious.

"For your information, I've heard of Rosie the Riveter. Thank God the war ended so she could go back to her husband and children where she belongs."

"Mac, you're absolutely impossible. No wonder Nora—" Auntie caught herself. "Your cousin Len's boy got a scholarship to Loyola, and Betty's just as smart as he is. He's in his third year there. And there's Northwe—"

"Agnes, no offense, but mind your own bee's wax. Betty's gonna do fine. She'll get a job, maybe at Goldblatt's with Maureen, and then find a husband and settle down."

They didn't seem to realize I was sitting there. No one knew what I wanted, or bothered to ask. But then, still ingrained in my brain like carved stone were the words, 'children should be seen and not heard.' Never mind I was seventeen; I remained forever a child in Daddy's eyes.

Tempted to raise my hand to speak, I said, "I met with Sister Noreen, and she said I could go to a junior college. They aren't as expensive."

"That's true," Auntie said. She sipped coffee from a pink Depression glass cup. "But I don't know what job they'd offer. Secretarial school might be the best, honey. DePaul has a good school, and after a year you could get a job maybe in a courtroom or fancy office somewhere, like Ford or US Steel."

I remembered that Maureen knew girls who went to DePaul and liked it. "I'll think about that," I said. I looked at Daddy.

"I dunno. I guess you'd get paid more than Goldblatt's." He tapped his pipe on the ashtray. "There should be plenty of men around from the war. Ask your sister if she knows anyone. Maybe John has some friends."

I sighed. "I'm not interested in getting married now, Daddy. Maybe some day."

He puffed his pipe. "You don't wanna end up an old maid like your Aunt Gladys."

"Mac, for pete's sake. There are worse things." Auntie shook her head as if defeated.

Uncle chuckled.

I just wanted to be anywhere but in that living room.

.　　.　　.

After graduation I enrolled at DePaul's Secretarial School along with Joan. I felt less nervous since I knew at least one person. Our classes were easy enough. I learned typing and could soon type seventy words a minute with no errors. Shorthand, taught from Gregg's manual, also came easy for me. The school had acquired new dictaphones, and I learned how to use the machines to take dictation from an imaginary boss's voice while using earphones. I marveled at the idea that the future had arrived.

In its effort to contribute to the welfare of community, DePaul held a benefit to fight the polio epidemic. It was a huge event, and that night, Joan and I got all gussied up in our Sunday best. I borrowed a dress from Maureen that Auntie had taken in for me because, to my secret pleasure, Maureen had put on a few pounds since Tommy's birth.

Flowers and pastel balloons colored the large dining hall. A huge cake sat in the center of the main table, and after dinner, students gathered around while a photographer snapped pictures. Several formally dressed men and women gave short speeches about finding a cure for polio and encouraging our contributions. They cited FDR as an example of a brave soul who lived to overcome the disease.

I knew a lady from St. Basil's Church who had polio and used crutches. She never missed Mass, even in winter when snow and ice blanketed the sidewalks. How could she always have a smile on her face?

.　　.　　.

During the year I visited Maureen once a week, and sometimes at night I watched Tommy. He was a good-natured boy and grew like a weed. Maureen confided in me once that John had nightmares and would call out German words. His army unit witnessed the Dachau camp and set it free. He said it was terrible and wouldn't say exactly what happened. *You don't wanna know what it was like. Nobody would. So don't ask me again.* Maureen didn't come out and say it, but John wasn't the same after the war. I could tell something was missing in the carefree, talkative man I once knew.

I lost track of Mama's hospital stays, but for the past eight years or so, it had become normal for her as a part-time presence. Auntie said many times that I grew up without a mother, but that's not true. I had a mother until I was eight, so it wasn't that bad.

·   ·   ·

The winter of 1948 thawed into an early spring. I began checking the want ads in the *Chicago Tribune*, scanning job opportunities for secretaries and clerks from companies of all sizes, and universities as well.

Maureen and Auntie encouraged me to apply for out-of-town jobs. *It would be good for you to move away and be independent.* Auntie thought smart women were better off with a career and living away from home. I sent several applications for court reporting and other office jobs.

One mild spring day in early May, I marked a post for a position as secretary to the president of a small liberal arts college in Milton, Wisconsin. I'd never heard of the place, nor had Joan or Mrs. Nelson, DePaul's women's dean. The thought of working in an academic environment appealed to me. Maybe people would talk about poetry and books.

When I got home that evening, I checked the map and found Milton, a small town north of Janesville, Wisconsin, south of Madison. I figured out it was almost 120 miles from Chicago. Disappointment overcame me. That was too far. When would I see my family? I'd never visit them except maybe Christmas.

But it wouldn't hurt to apply. I probably wouldn't get the job anyway.

CHAPTER 23

Autumn, 1948, Milton, Wisconsin

The day before I moved to Milton, I visited Mama in the hospital. Uncle and Auntie picked me up, as usual. Daddy stayed home claiming he had neighborhood council business of utmost importance. Auntie warned me about Mama's nonsensical talk and word rhyming, but I hoped she'd be lucid enough to understand a normal conversation.

The hospital hadn't changed in the last decade. The hallways and patient areas reeked of Lysol and despondency, with pea green walls bare of decoration.

Mama sat alone in the activity room, her hair unkempt, hanging in strings around her pale face. She gazed into space, her lips moving as if in deep conversation. When I approached her, she was singing "In the Gloaming," a melancholy favorite from childhood. *When the winds are sobbing faintly, With a gentle unknown woe.* I looked for the Satan lady, but she was not in sight. Several woebegone-looking men and women slumped in chairs, most staring into nothingness.

When I bent to kiss Mama's cheek, I caught a breeze of Ponds cold cream. At least she made a little effort. Colorless eyes gazed vacantly at me from a hollowed face. I sat beside her on the worn brown couch while Auntie and Uncle remained standing. "We'll leave you with Betty now, Nora. She has some news."

Mama's expression did not change as they left the room. She had aged in the last several months, as if the past ten years of grief had climbed on her shoulders and permanently stayed. When did so many liver spots begin dotting her hands?

"Guess what, Mama. I got a job as a secretary at a college in Wisconsin. I leave tomorrow on the bus."

" Leave on a bus, don't make a fuss," she murmured. "Tell Joey. He'll be here later on."

"Wha—what?" I was tongue tied. No one had said she had delusions. It must be something new. I'd hoped to catch Auntie, but they'd left the room. Should I tell the nurse's assistant sitting with two patients playing cards? Then Mama clasped my arm and said, "Is it time to go yet? Wanna bet? Take a nap?"

I'd repeated my news, saying I was leaving tomorrow and may not see her until Christmas. "Have a nice trip. On the ship. Break a hip. I had blueberry pie for dessert."

And so the conversation continued until Auntie rejoined us. "Nora, what do you think of Betty going off into the world?"

Mama's lips twitched from side to side. "The world. Unfurled. Till it hurled."

We said our goodbyes, and on the way out, the Satan woman approached us, her faded housedress hanging to her ankles. "Watch out, he's clever. Very clever. Beware." She glared at Uncle. "Maybe him." Ignoring her curses, we aimed ourselves toward the exit.

Driving home, I mentioned Mama's talking about Joey. Auntie tsked. "She's talked about him several times, as if he were alive. A shame what those shock treatments did to her. She'll never be the same."

A foreboding shadow lurked above my head. Last month I'd had a feeling of other-worldliness, an indescribable sensation with no warning. Like I was lifted from this life and then put back. For an unknown reason, I felt a connection with the Satan woman. I pushed the thought away because it terrified me.

•　　•　　•

The fall quarter had begun at the college, with students settling into dorms and campus housing. My transition to the new position and location had gone more smoothly than I'd dared hope. The bus ride to Milton took three hours with stops along the way. The scenery captured my interest as I took in red barns and white farm houses dotting the landscape, with trees spreading shade across green grass. My first time away from the big city.

Mona Sanders from the dean's office met me at the station in a Chrysler sedan she'd borrowed from Matthew James, the president. I would replace his secretary who recently resigned. Mona, a hefty, young woman with dark wavy hair, had secured a small apartment for me on the second story of a house two blocks from the Main Hall where I'd be working.

"I think you'll love it, Betty," Mona said as we drove to a residential area near the town center. "The landlady, Mrs. Adams, is really warm and friendly."

"That's good. Did ever you stay there?"

Mona laughed. "Oh no, you'll find that everyone knows everyone in town, it's that small. Of course, the students change from year to year."

Feeling anxious, I hoped I'd made the right decision. I'd heard people in small towns are busybodies, but I'd stick to myself as usual.

A charming, tidy little town, Milton boasted a population under 1,600, a far cry from 75,000 people in my Back of the Yards. In my eyes, Milton was cozy and safe, with its well-kept light-colored clapboard and red brick houses with long sidewalks connecting them to shady tree-lined streets.

Over fifteen buildings made up the college campus, almost twenty-five acres of green, hilly land. Milton College identified itself as a private liberal arts school, attracting a good number of foreign students.

As Mona promised, my upstairs apartment was roomy, clean, and comfortable with one bedroom, living room, and kitchen. The bathroom across the hall was large, but I was confused by a miniature porcelain tub on the floor beside the commode near the bathtub. Perhaps girls washed their underwear in it. Pretty fancy for someone like me. I felt like a queen. All this was mine. No sharing with anyone.

I unpacked my meager belongings from a large suitcase borrowed from Auntie and a smaller satchel. The place was furnished with ample seating, lamps, and a double sized bed.

"The washing machine is in the basement," Mrs. Adams said. "It's almost brand new, fully automatic. You can use it any time. Clothes lines are in the back yard and in the basement as well."

That sounded exciting. Our old wringer machine was still in our basement at home. I thought of Daddy. How often did he use it?

The last item I pulled from my satchel was Joey's red model car. My throat tightened into a knot as I placed it under my pillow. "I'm sorry, Joey," I said aloud. "I should've tattled to Mama. Then you'd be here with us."

I sat on my bed and let the tears flow. Did my moving far away from home move me further away from Joey?

CHAPTER 24

The days and weeks vanished into one another as I began my position as Dr. Matthew James's secretary. A man of generous proportions, his voice boomed with the timbre of an operatic baritone. My anxiety level was sky high, but his reassuring and congenial manner immediately put me at ease. Mona showed me around the offices in the Main Hall, introducing me to more clerks and deans than I could remember. Luckily, I was comfortable with typing and dictation, which I used each day quite proficiently, thanks to my secretarial training.

My social life was limited to an occasional football game, during which the Wildcats showed their tenacity against larger schools. I had Friday night dinners with Mona and a couple other women from our office. They'd chatter and gossip about eligible men and how they rated in looks and personality.

"I think Dr. Hall would be a good catch," Peggy said one night.

Mona gasped. "My goodness, he's too fat and has that greasy hair."

I'd never really dated, except twice in high school when Maureen had arranged a blind date in a small group. Even with the security of several people, my tongue tied in knots when confronted with the prospect of conversation with boys who I felt were *stuck with me*. I can't even recall their names and have always longed for the self-assuredness of Maureen and other girls like her.

So, when I met Phil for the first time, I amazed myself at how easily words came.

Sitting at my typewriter, fingers flying across the keyboard, I didn't notice two men walking toward my desk until Dr. James said, "Betty, I'd like you to meet one of our new English instructors, Philip Lundgren, or 'Phil' I should say."

I looked up at a tall, husky man who towered above Dr. James. He bent down and extended his hand. "Hi, Betty. I've heard exceptional things about you from Matthew here."

I smiled, noticing his watercolor blue eyes and polished white teeth. I took his hand, and he shook mine firmly. "Glad to meet you, Mr. Lundgren."

"Call me Phil." He patted my hand.

"Betty's told me she's a poetry fan, Dickinson and Whitman in particular," Dr. James said.

Oh no. Why did he say that? He'll ask me a question, and I won't know the answer.

Phil nodded, locking his eyes with mine. "Ah, tell all the truth but tell it slant—"

"Success in Circuit lies," I said, relieved I knew the quote.

"Too bright for our inform Delight—" Phil continued.

"The Truth's superb surprise." I tried to subdue the flush rising to my cheeks, for I felt I'd passed a difficult test.

Dr. James chuckled. "Whoa, I know when I'm lone man on the totem pole. We'll leave you to your work, Betty."

"Good to meet you." Phil said and followed Dr. James into his office.

My heart thumped. Golly, what a nice man. But an instructor? I wouldn't have a chance, I figured, but our shared lines of poetry had titillated me. I'd have to read through *America's Most Treasured Poems* again. Since Auntie had given me the book for Christmas several years ago, I'd devoured it on lonely nights, its pages a comfort and refuge for my troubled mind.

CHAPTER 25

I floated through the next two months in rainbows of vibrant colors. I was a normal person with what I guessed were love-struck emotions. But how would I know? People fell in love in movies. Maureen had fallen in love. But me? Romantic love was a fairy tale I'd only dreamed of. The morning after we'd met, Phil stopped by my desk and invited me for coffee at the B's Café in town, a couple blocks from campus. I hid my trembling fingers under the desk, and of course, I accepted. I later thought of something Maureen had advised me. *Don't be too available, Betty. It makes you seem desperate. Let a man wait a while.*

We'd strolled to the café late afternoon. Reds, yellows, and golds splashed the trees, and leaves crinkled under our feet in the cool refreshing air. Our conversation flowed smoothly, effortlessly. This was not the Betty O'Leary I knew. Maybe this was my bluebird flying over the rainbow. My brain told me to slow down, be careful. But my heart did not listen.

I thought of Scrooge's transformation. *"I am as light as a feather, I am as happy as an angel, I am as merry as a schoolboy. I am as giddy as a drunken man. A merry Christmas to everybody!* How long would this last? Was Phil too good to be true?

We soon became a couple, meeting for lunch at the college union, going to the movies in Janesville, and attending football games. Hesitant to tell Mona and other friends about Phil, I was forced to confess after I'd declined their invitations for dinner two times in a row.

"What's going on, Betty?" Mona had queried. "Got a secret man? I think you're getting awfully chummy with Phil Lundgren."

I'm sure my cheeks flamed red. "We're just friends. I like poetry." I was uncomfortable that they had infringed upon my privacy.

"Golly gee, she likes poetry." Peggy pretended to swoon.

"Yes, 'Roses are red, Violets are blue, Betty and Phil—um—"

"Oh stop," I said. "He's nice. That's it." These women were acting like Maureen's high school friends, giggling about boys and dates. But secretly, I took pleasure in my good fortune.

My friendship with Phil had grown beyond what I had experienced, and I no longer worried I'd put my foot in my mouth as I had done in the past. I tried not to think of the gap between our positions, he as instructor and I, a lowly secretary.

"Tell me all about yourself, Betty," Phil said at our first coffee date.

I folded my napkin in squares. "There's not much to tell. I'm from Chicago, but you knew that."

"Where exactly? It's a big city." He stirred his coffee.

His soft, smooth voice put me at ease. I told him all about the yards, Daddy's job, my schools.

Phil looked impressed. "That's something. After I read *The Jungle*, I swore I'd never eat another wiener or hamburger again." He grinned. "But that lasted about a week."

"What about your life in Duluth?" I wanted to know all about him as well. His dark blond hair fell over his forehead now and then. I liked how he'd brush it away.

I listened intently as he recalled his college years at Duluth State Teacher's College, majoring in English and German. Then to the University of Minnesota in Minneapolis for his Master's in English. His parents were Gus and Ida, his older sister, Carole. "All four grandparents came over from Sweden, two lived near Stockholm and the others in Borlange. I've always wanted to travel there."

"I've dreamed of going to Ireland to see our people who are still there. They say it's so beautiful, but they've had a hard time—" I let my voice trail off.

"Yes, we're fulfilling their dream of a better life."

Indeed, I thought. My life is certainly better, but not in the way Phil meant.

•　　•　　•

I took the train back to Chicago for Christmas. I was keen to see the family again, including Mama, who had been home from the hospital for several weeks. Maybe she'd hang on until I arrived. I couldn't wait to tell them about Phil. I'd written Maureen about him, and she wrote back saying he sounded like a good catch. What would Mama and Daddy think, me courting a Lutheran man? Since the Accident, they had fallen away from the Church, and I hoped my beau's religion wouldn't matter. Most people from home, though, wouldn't dream of marrying a Protestant. Since John was Catholic, Maureen's marriage was fine with everyone.

I still hadn't told Phil about Joey's death and Mama's mental illness. When he'd asked about my family, I couldn't bring myself to deny Joey's existence, so I said I had a sister and brother, and another brother was killed in an accident. I'd choked and looked down. Phil placed his hand on my shoulder. "I'm sorry." And we said no more.

That year, I enjoyed Christmas more than I'd expected. Maureen, John, and Tommy showed up Christmas Eve, Maureen's belly protruding under her loose maternity dress. She'd written me in August about her good news. Tommy ran about the room playing with the wrapped packages. "Open. Open," he squealed a dozen times. John paced the room until he and Daddy retired to the kitchen to drink Guinness.

Mama's face had the usual haunted, concave look, and she sat, shoulders slumped, speaking softly now and then. Auntie and Uncle joined us for coffee and a visit before Mass. They both had aged since I'd seen them in August. More wrinkles etched Auntie's cheeks, and Uncle's silver hair circling his shiny noggin was thinner.

Auntie was first to notice a change in me. "Betty, you look brighter, more energetic somehow. Maybe it's my imagination." Did she wink at me?

I cleared my throat. "Well, you'll be surprised to hear I have a beau."

Mama gasped. "Honey, that's wonderful. Tell us all about it."

The interrogation suddenly came from all corners of the room. "How old is he?" "Where's he from?" "Is he first generation?" "What kinda fancy degree does the guy have?" "Is he stuffy?"

Maureen and I couldn't suppress our giggles. "Leave Betty alone, for crying out loud. She hasn't married him yet."

"Now you'll both be too big for your britches," Mama said.

In the end, I tried to make them understand that Phil was a kind, decent person, regardless of his education. "He's a very good man, and we're always kind to each other."

John harrumphed. "Yeah, easy to do when you're not hitched." He poked at Maureen.

"Very funny." She gave him a quick kiss on the cheek. I was relieved that John's nerves were relaxed enough for him to crack a joke. I hoped he treated her well.

I didn't dare bring Dennis's name up around Mama. Maureen said she still won't talk to him and agreed with Auntie that the shock treatments affected Mama's brain.

After Mass, I asked Maureen privately about Dennis. "He's still in Archer Heights, working at Midway. We dropped by once, John, me and Tommy. His wife, Sue is friendly. Soft-spoken like you, Betty. No kids yet."

"I'd like to call him. He probably isn't interested, but I still—"

"I know," Maureen finished my thought. "I'll give you his number."

I guess it was no surprise that I could not reach Dennis. After three attempts at calling with no answer, I decided to let it be. I hated to admit that he had long become a stranger.

· · ·

Auntie and Uncle drove me to the train station to leave for Milton several days after Christmas. Snow gently fell as we drove up Halsted. "The neighborhood has changed, but I can't pinpoint why."

"You probably heard your father talk about some old timers moving away, and more Negros moving in," Auntie said. "Yes, the yards aren't what they used to be. People say they've laid off more workers."

"Really," I said. "I hope Daddy's job is okay. He's not ready to retire yet, he says."

"I think his job is secure, honey," Auntie said. "There are even some Mexican families who've moved in. Some moved just down the street from us, and they seem friendly."

I saw the changes in my Back of the Yards and realized that I was merely a visitor now. But I knew in my heart no matter where I may wind up in life, my neighborhood would be part of who I am.

The outdoors was covered with a white softness when I hugged Auntie and Uncle goodbye at the massive Northwestern depot. I joined the throng of travelers scurrying here and there to their own corners of the world.

Later, as the train puffed along, singing its song on the tracks past the city skyscrapers and then the Illinois countryside, I thought of my new stage of life. Phil and I planned to celebrate the new year together at The Crown restaurant, where he'd made reservations. My first real new year's celebration. What would 1949 bring?

CHAPTER 26

1949

As we celebrated the new year, I knew this was what I'd been missing all these years. I felt older, although I would turn nineteen in June.

Maureen had lent me a black sleeveless dress to wear on the big night. *This fit me when I was thin; it looks perfect on you, Betty. Remember, you'll never go wrong with black.*

She had learned about fashion from experienced clerks and buyers at Goldblatt's. She gave me a single strand faux pearl choker necklace to complement the dress. *You never want too much jewelry. Looks cheap. Keep it simple and elegant. Remember that, Betty, if you ever meet Phil's family.* I tried not to think about that possibility. The thought frightened me.

•   •   •

I wished for the umpteenth time that I could relax when facing new people, new experiences. I wanted Joan here to help me get gussied up, as she'd say. She'd been hired as an assistant for three attorneys in Winnetka, and she'd welcomed the chance to work in the affluent suburb. We exchanged letters once or twice a month. Of course, she wanted to know about Phil, and I found her comments less intrusive than Mona's.

I examined myself in the mirror. The dress, black satin with a v-neck, the most revealing dress I'd ever worn. I had no cleavage to speak of, which was fine with me. Black lace overlaid the waist, and the skirt fell several inches below my knees.

When Phil knocked on the door at seven o'clock, I was ready and fidgeting. "Wow," he said when I opened the door. "You look like a movie star."

I laughed. "Of course, I do." He always knew what to say. "I bet you say that to all the girls."

"No, just one." He helped me on with my wrap, a sable stole that Mrs. Adams insisted I wear. I protested, but she was resolute: "I only wear it to church, and it looks so lovely on you with your clear skin and pretty hazel eyes."

I'd smoothed the long, silky fur. "I could spend all day feeling this softness."

I felt a bit like an imposter with Maureen's dress and jewelry and the borrowed fur stole. At least the shoes were mine.

"You look very elegant, all in black except the pearls and your red lipstick." Phil took my chin in his hand. "Do I dare kiss you without smudging?"

I laughed and gave him a peck on his mouth. He smelled of sandalwood and musk. I wanted to bury my face in his neck and felt a flutter in the pit of my stomach.

He opened the car door for me, and I climbed in as delicately as I could. His dark, moss green Chevrolet was several years old, but always clean and shiny. He'd offered to teach me to drive, but I was hesitant to accept the suggestion.

We arrived at the large, stone restaurant, blazing with colorful lights, a huge Happy New Year's 1949 banner flashing above the door.

The valet helped me from the car, and Phil and I entered the front arched doorway. A touch of seasoned meat and charcoal wafted in the air. The maître d' seated us in a far corner, thankfully away from crowded tables. Men in black suits and women in dressy or cocktail attire mingled about. Phil waved at a history professor as we ordered our drinks.

An air of excitement was palpable throughout the place. I looked around at the pillars and a cherub fountain spewing red and green water in the center of the room. The tables were covered in white linen surrounded by white upholstered dining chairs with wooden legs and armrests. A brass ensemble played a variety of Miller, Ellington, Shaw, and other big band tunes. A young black man sat at a grand piano, his fingers skimming over the keys as couples danced to "A' Train."

"We'll have to get out on the dance floor after dinner," Phil said as the waiter placed a bottle of wine and glasses on our table. He uncorked the wine, poured an inch in Phil's glass. He tasted, gave a nod of approval, and our glasses were filled. The thought of dancing in front of everyone petrified me. Perhaps I could dream up an excuse.

Roast duck was featured as a special entrée, which appealed to both of us. I'd never eaten duck, but figuring it tasted like chicken, I took a chance. I studied the place setting and thought of Auntie's advice. *Remember, when you have several forks and spoons, always start from the outside and go in.*

Later as we finished our desserts of strawberry chiffon cake and coffee, two couples stopped by our table. "Hi, Phil. Betty." Tom Haven, history professor, patted Phil's shoulder. "This is my wife, Dorothy. Dear, meet Betty O'Leary, our secretary par excellence."

Dorothy looked me over. "How lovely to meet you, Betty. I see you're in enviable company." She looked at Phil. "Enjoying your evening?" Her face wore a permanent expression of disapproval.

Bert Noland, also from the history department introduced himself and his wife, Ginny.

"Betty, good to meet you. Are you settling in well?" she asked.

Flustered at the interruption and new names to remember, I fought my desire to bolt. "Yes, it's a splendid town and everyone on campus has been very helpful." I looked at Phil for reassurance.

"Betty's from Chicago, so quite a contrast. But she's done a terrific job, and seems to take to the town, like I did."

I could tell they wanted to stick around, but Phil wiped his mouth and reached for my hand. "We're about to trip the light fantastic. Anyone else?" Thank heavens. Wishing to fend off Dorothy, I figured dancing was the lesser of two evils.

"Nah, I have two left feet, just ask Dorothy," Tom said.

Dorothy hesitated and took note of my necklace as if she wanted to give me a final once-over. "Maybe we'll see you again sometime soon." Her red lips curved into an insincere smile. Her hard, marble eyes, like icebergs.

Bert and Ginny echoed their goodbyes as they all headed wherever they were going.

Thankfully, the band played "Tenderly," so we could slow dance. I had practiced swing and slow dancing with Maureen and Joan, but I felt unsteady, both in body and mind.

Phil twirled me around on the floor, and I melted into his arms. All so natural, effortless, how could I be this radiant? Except I just detected that Dorothy woman in the corner of my eye. I disliked her from the minute she looked at me. Judging me. Looking like she smelled cooked cabbage.

We danced around in time to the song. "Were you surprised to run into your friends tonight?" I tried to sound casual, like it didn't matter.

"Not really. A small town like this, and an established restaurant, bound to happen." He held me close. "What did you think?"

"Of them? Too soon to say, but they were friendly enough." I nuzzled into his shoulder. "Except—never mind."

Phil brushed my hair with his lips. "Except what? You can say anything to me, Betty."

"Um, there was something about Dorothy. The way she said 'enviable company' made me wonder."

Phil pressed my back closer to him. "Yes, she can be scathing, is what I've heard. Don't let her bother you. You're twice the woman she'll ever be."

I laughed. "Phil, you've known me for what? Four months?"

"I know gold when I see it."

Frost's poem, "Nothing Gold Can Stay" popped into my mind. I shooed away a moment of doubt.

"You're too kind," I said. I'd heard Ingrid Bergman say that in a movie. I felt more confident. Or maybe it was the Pinot Chardonnay.

I commanded myself not to think of Dorothy and her superior attitude. Maureen would assure me that the woman's too heavy and not as pretty as me, so she's a fine one to put on airs. Maureen always knew how to stand up for herself.

The evening rushed by. The band took several breaks, and shortly before midnight, as if reading my mind, they played "Near Me." I took Phil's hand, and I glided to the floor and floated in his arms.

"I love this song. It's special." I recalled listening to the Andrews Sisters on my radio and finding comfort in the lyrics.

"I think it was written for us," Phil said. "Let's make it our song." My eyes moistened, and I buried my face in his chest.

Was this too good to be true?

CHAPTER 27

Several weeks sailed by, a warm cloud of joy surrounding me. Phil and I saw each other several times a week. He lived in a tidy brick bungalow half a mile from the town center. Once a week or so, he cooked a simple dinner of spaghetti and ground beef and served it with a green salad and a glass or two of Chianti. I'd never thought much about wine or liquor and associated it with over-indulgence, like Daddy and his corner pals. I had no interest after tasting a beer once with Maureen.

One night at Phil's we finished our dinner and sat in his comfortable living room sipping a second glass of wine. "You know, I never thought I'd like wine. I'm realizing you can enjoy it without getting plastered. Just normal enjoyment."

"All in moderation," Phil said. "It's been a problem with a few people in my family. My uncle's an alcoholic and has a tough time staying on the wagon."

"I'm not sure about Daddy. He gets loaded on the weekends and did almost every night after my brother—"

"What happened to him, Betty?" Phil's voice soft.

I decided it was time to tell Phil about Joey, so for the first time in many months, I told my brother's story, and included Mama's as well. I tried to stop the tears, but they'd been buried too long and needed release.

Phil said little, but I knew he grieved right along with me, for that little freckled boy, forever unchanged in my memory, never growing older with the winds of vanished years.

"Every year in December, I think of his grave. This is the first year I haven't visited. I hope someone gave him flowers, but I didn't ask. We never—"

"I know, Betty." Phil rubbed my shoulder. "People need to talk about loved ones who have passed away. They're afraid it's too sad, but didn't their life mean something? Why act like they never existed?"

"I think so too. I'm still sad, but I feel a relief inside after telling you about him." I snuggled into his arms, and for the first time, I spent the night in Phil's bed.

. . .

Unlike some men I'd heard about, Phil always respected my physical wishes. Although I lacked experience with men, it was easy and natural to be close to him and spoon or make out, or whatever it was called these days. It was ingrained in this good Catholic girl to wait until marriage to "go all the way." Truthfully, I was afraid of the act, and even Maureen hadn't told me much. I had the impression she was not pure as the driven snow on her wedding day, but I wouldn't dream of asking.

"You know I want you, honey, but we can wait till you're ready." Phil's words so often repeated, gave me relief and hope we'd have a future together. We fit together like two hands slipping into silk gloves.

That night we kissed and cuddled off and on. I'd shed my clothes and wore a pajama top of Phil's. I pressed the collar against my face, inhaling the woodsy, leather scent of him. A couple times he left for the bathroom when things started getting 'hot and heavy,' as Maureen would say. Probably best to not spend the night any more.

The next morning, I felt like a teenager sneaking out the kitchen door and through the alley to the next corner. Phil pulled his car around and picked me up as if I'd been walking home alone.

"This is pure nonsense," Phil grumbled. "Here we are, two adults, and we're supposed to follow Victorian rules. One thing I hate about a small town."

"We shouldn't need to," I said.

"Trouble is, this college was religious based. Used to be associated with the Baptists. They required chapel attendance before the war too. I'm sure I wouldn't get fired, but I could get called in."

One way to solve that would be to get married, but I didn't voice the opinion.

. . .

In February, Maureen welcomed another baby boy into their family. Looking forward to meeting little Andrew, I'd needed to wait until my summer vacation in June. Like most women I knew, I assumed I would marry and have a family. It was a scattered, cloudy thought until I met Phil. I think he loved me, but I would let him take the lead and follow Maureen's advice. *Don't be too available. Men don't want pressure.*

As our courtship progressed over the months, I felt a distant coldness from Mona and the other single women. Conversations with them became awkward, and I avoided meeting with them as I once had.

"We never see you any more, Betty," Mona said one morning. "How about dinner some time this week?"

"Yes, we should do that," I'd answered with little enthusiasm. I hoped she wouldn't pin me down on a night.

"You and Phil getting serious? Maybe we'll hear wedding bells soon."

I laughed. "Ha, that's news to me." I tried to hide my discomfort. "We're just having a nice time now."

Later, Peggy showed up. "I hear you're having more fun with Mr. Lundgren than your old girlfriends." She pretended to joke, but she didn't fool me.

"Don't be silly. We're not married, you know."

"You sure lucked out nabbing him. About the handsomest man on the faculty. What's your secret?"

I could visualize her fangs. "No secret. Just be yourself," was all I could think of. Her comments transcended envy. Downright jealousy. I'd have to write Maureen about it. See what she thought.

I wondered how many co-workers harbored the same opinion about Phil and me. That I was the lucky one. What about him? Wasn't he lucky as well?

I told myself to quit worrying what others thought, advice Maureen and Auntie used to drum into me. I needed to relish these blissful days and embrace my long-awaited normalcy. However, now and again, a small voice niggled in my mind. *You don't deserve him. You're not good enough, not educated, too working class.*

The following weekend, we drove to Madison for a movie. A fresh layer of snow carpeted the countryside, and the spindly branches of the maples and elms cast inky shadows over the landscape. Phil suggested I come to Duluth with him in June before summer session.

"By then the snow should be gone if we're lucky. Just kidding. You'd like the city, honey. It's a port city, right on the shores of Lake Superior."

He didn't mention his family. "It sounds fun, but it's an awfully long way. And where would I stay?"

He slowed down for a railroad crossing. "My folks have plenty of room in the house, especially since Carole and I are gone. They may sell it after Pop retires."

"Phil, I'm sorry but I'm a little nervous meeting your parents. They're going to wonder who I am."

He chuckled. "What do you mean, who you are? You're Betty, that's who."

"You know what I mean. Besides, I—I come from a different—"

"Betty, I think I know what you're getting at, but you know me by now. I put no stock in where anybody comes from. I like folks for what they are, how they act, how they treat others, and all that."

"I know, but—"

"Besides, I'm keen to meet your family and take in the sights of Chicago. I've only been there once, and that was years ago."

I figured that idea wouldn't work. Phil would need to stay in a hotel. He couldn't possibly stay in our tiny house or Auntie's.

Plenty of time to worry about that.

CHAPTER 28

The long frigid winter laden with ice and blizzards melted into spring. I always felt a renewal in the air, and this season held the promise of poets. Phil lent me several books on Dickinson and Keats, as well as novels like *Jane Eyre* and *My Antonia*. After I'd complete them, we would discuss their meanings and significance.

"You should be an English teacher someday," he said one evening.

"I'd have to go to college, and I'd be the oldest student there." I wasn't serious, even though my love of books was forever instilled in my bones.

By the time spring quarter ended in early June, we'd set our plans to travel to Duluth. Still anxious Phil's parents would disapprove of my background, I resolved to believe I was a good person and worthy of their son.

I wrote Maureen that I would delay my family visit until later in July. She sent pictures of Tommy and Andy, who were growing fast. I was more eager to see them than anyone else.

. . .

One morning in early June, we packed Phil's used Studebaker with suitcases and a picnic lunch. We hoped to cover the 350-mile drive to Duluth in seven hours plus stops on the way.

Rain poured down the day before we left and threatened to repeat itself, but by noon the sun swept away gray clouds. I enjoyed the scenery, rusty barns and yellow farmhouses. Who lived inside, and what were their lives like? Later, we pulled into a rest stop near Wisconsin Dells, a vast resort area with sandstone formations carved from glaciers. "People have toured here since the eighteen-hundreds," Phil said. "Lots of folks from Chicago vacation here."

Not my family, I thought, but said nothing. We found a picnic table and ate our tuna sandwiches, apples, and peanut butter cookies as we swished the flies away. We drank lukewarm coffee from a large thermos, using melamine cups we'd brought. The spectacular sites were invisible to us, since we were on the outskirts near the highway. "Someday we'll vacation here, maybe a weekend next fall."

"I'd love that." I munched my cookie. I didn't dare hope for such a thing.

The leisurely hours faded by as we drove north on Highway 53 toward Duluth. I fell in love with picture book lakes, their clear blue waters and peaceful songs they sang. Phil said some day we could buy a house on a lake. We'd mentioned a future together, but he had not proposed. Perhaps he was waiting to see if I passed the test of his parents' approval.

The landscape grew dense with pine trees and rivers as we neared Eau Claire. "What a lovely town," I exclaimed. "It looks like a movie."

"Another place to visit," Phil said as he drove across one of many rivers flowing through the city.

We parked at another rest area near Chetek. The air was warm, but invigorating. After a short walk around foot paths shaded by elms and pines, we climbed back in the car and made our way toward Superior.

"You'll see the shores of Gitche Gumee soon, but not exactly in the forest. That'll come later," Phil said as we reached the outskirts of the city named for the big lake.

"Tell me again about the name."

"Gitche Gumee means big sea or huge water like the poem. It's from the Ojibwe Indian language, also called Chippewa by most white people."

I loved learning about cultures and places I'd never seen and was determined to travel extensively someday. We passed small homes, stores, bars, gas stations, until we approached a wooden bridge stretching over the bay.

"There it is, Lake Superior," Phil said as we crossed the bridge leading into Duluth.

I marveled at the cobalt-gray water shimmering in the sunlight. "Wow, I can't believe it. The second great lake I've seen."

We passed railroads, factories with smoke billowing from chimneys and then drove up a hill through residential sections. Some homes reminded me of houses in Milton, purple and yellow flowers and shrubs planted in yards. Phil explained about the east and west ends of town as we meandered through the neighborhoods. I noted the houses became larger as we drove on. Phil slowed and parked in front of a two-story white Victorian-looking house with bay windows, covered front veranda, and pointed dormers. I thought of my shoebox-size house in the yards.

Butterflies danced the Charleston in my stomach as Phil took my hand and led me up the sidewalk past tidy beds of red and pink roses, their fragrance perfuming the air. Lilac bushes bloomed along the front in both lavender and white blossoms. Large black iron pots with geraniums and ivy spilling out surrounded the front porch.

We approached the shiny wood door with beveled glass panes, and as Phil touched the knob, the door opened. "Phil, welcome, come on in." A tall, brown-haired man with brow-line glasses, flashed a wide grin, showcasing white teeth. His blue eyes matched his son's.

"Hi, Dad." Phil took his hand as he ushered me into the foyer. "I'd like you to meet Betty O'Leary."

His eyes locked with mine as he held out his hand. "Hello, Betty. I'm Gus. Welcome to our home."

As I took in the winding staircase and elaborate furnishings, a sculptured-like middle-aged woman joined us. She gave her son a hug.

Phil put his hand on my back. "Mother, this is Betty."

She acknowledged me as an afterthought. "Yes, I'm glad to meet you."

"Good to meet you too, Mrs. Lundgren." Her steel blue eyes were icy as she seemed to appraise my Sears catalog pedal pushers without blatantly looking me up and down.

"You may call me Ida." Her pink lips curved up, but it wasn't a smile. She wore her bleach blond hair in a twist in the back, and her white sleeveless blouse and tan linen slacks reminded me of Maureen's fashion mantra of understated elegance.

It was plain to see why Phil stood over six feet tall as my neck strained to look at his parents. "You must be exhausted," Ida said. "We'll show you your rooms, and then we can have drinks and dinner."

"Mom—"

"Don't worry, son. You said a light dinner, and it'll be very light." She laughed and blinked at me. "Carole will be here any minute." I'd forgotten about his sister.

Phil led me up the stairway and down the hall to a door at the end. "This is your room." He put my suitcase at the bottom of the double bed, a green and white floral bedspread on top.

White furniture and a small green upholstered easy chair accessorized the room. "Your home is really breathtaking, Phil." I was not used to such luxury. He showed me the bathroom next door.

"My room's right across the hall here. I may sneak in at midnight tonight." He chuckled.

"Naughty boy," I said, but I felt a little devilish excitement at the idea.

Phil left me alone to unpack and freshen up. I lay down on the bed and dreaded his coming back when we'd join his family downstairs.

My Shadows would visit me that night.

CHAPTER 29

In ten minutes, five of us gathered in Phil's spacious living room going through the motions of getting to know each other. I tried not to gape at the tastefully decorated room with its velvet maroon and beige striped sofa and ivory chairs on either side of a white brick fireplace. Several other occasional chairs adorned the place with the same rolled arms and tufted backs. Needless to say, I felt out of place.

Phil indicated the sofa, where we both sat. "Your furniture is gorgeous, Mrs. Lu— I mean, Ida." I tried not to gush.

Her smile obviously forced. "Thank you, Betty. I've always liked French provincial, and we had the fireplace re—"

"Mother, please. That's too long a story for—"

She arched her penciled eyebrows. "All right. I know you're not interested, son, but," she let her voice trail off.

"Time for drinks," Gus said. "Betty, what's your pleasure? Manhattan? Martini? Jim Beam and soda's my choice."

I looked at Phil for help. "She may prefer wine, Dad. Betty, what do you think?"

"Yes, white wine sounds swell." I really preferred iced tea, but I wanted to join in.

Carole, the older sister, sat next to her mother. "I'll have the same, Dad." She had a kindly smile. "I appreciate that you made the trip, Betty. Phil said I could show you around tomorrow. Duluth is tiny compared to Chicago, but I'm sure you'll enjoy the canal and the rose garden."

"Thank you," I said. "I'd like that." I hoped Phil would come too, although Carole seemed friendly and down to earth.

Gus stood at a wooden bar cart against the wall next to a large bay window. After mixing, shaking, and pouring, he said, "We're ready, Phil. Come help."

After we were situated with drinks, Ida pointed out a tray of cheese, crackers, and something I couldn't identify. "Help yourself, everyone."

Phil apparently noted my glance at the tray. "We like creamed herring, Betty, like all good Swedes." He helped himself to the fish using a tiny fork. I hoped no one would notice if I stuck to cheese. The slithery appetizer was anything but appetizing.

Ida sipped her Manhattan and took me in. "What part of Chicago are you from, Betty? It's such a huge city."

"I grew up in South Chicago," I said, hoping she wouldn't ask more.

"Oh." She raised her pointy chin. "Do you have trouble with colored people?"

"Trouble?" I pretended to be confused.

"You know, they're mostly in southern cities, but—"

"Mother," Phil said. That's not—"

"We have good friends who moved there a few years ago. In Lake Forest, but it's all white, so their schools are excellent. I wonder if that's near the south part where you lived."

"Mother, you know where it is," Phil said. "Betty likes Milton and has really adjusted well." He looked at me. "Sorry, hon, don't mean to speak for you." I loved his consideration, how he stifled his mother's questions.

"That's wonderful you're liking Milton," said Carole. "Sometimes I think a small town would be preferable."

Ida pursed her perfectly lined lips, pried a cigarette from a leather box on an end table, and reached for a silver lighter, soon puffing furiously away.

•   •   •

At long last, dinner was served in the dining room. The décor echoed the living room's, with a colorful Persian rug in reds and golds. Thankfully, the meal was casual, with only a salad, green beans, and chicken hotdish, as Ida called it. A second glass of wine helped ease my discomfort.

Afterward, Ida directed us to a large screened-in porch where French doors separated it from a wing in the back. The room overlooked a rolling, landscaped back yard, with lilac bushes, geraniums, and blue hydrangeas. A large glass-top table resting upon wrought iron legs and frame held a stack of blue cloth napkins, silverware, and china plates, coffee cups, and saucers.

"Really, Mother, you didn't have to do all this just for me and Betty." Phil clenched his jaw.

Carole spoke up. "You'll have to forgive our mother, Betty. Gustav and Victoria just left yesterday, so everyone's royalty."

My face apparently showed confusion. Phil said, "Never mind, hon. He's the king of Sweden, and—aw, forget it, let's have dessert already."

"Really, how you do exaggerate. I'll get the pie." Ida left in a huff, or so it seemed.

When would the evening end?

•   •   •

Several hours later, I crept into the hallway and eyed the tub in the bathroom, anticipating a relaxing soak. Phil joined me.

"How 'bout if we sneak out early tomorrow, say around seven. I know a cozy little café for breakfast."

I readily agreed. I couldn't wait to be alone with Phil, and after my bath, I settled into the comfortable bed, exhausted. Sleep eluded me. Instead, the Shadows came.

•   •   •

I shut my eyes and saw them. Three black, blurry forms lurking above me to my right. Like three cane-shaped leeches, the tallest one in the middle. I opened my eyes. Was it the wine? I closed my eyes again. The Shadows still hovered, black, against the night. How were they visible in the night? Dear God. I was afraid. Afraid. Of what, I didn't know. Just afraid.

•   •   •

After a night of waking and dozing, with fragments of forgotten dreams, a muffled tapping came at the door. "Come in," I called softly.

"Ready for coffee?" Phil peeked in.

I jiggled the cobwebs out of my head. "Yes, just a few minutes."

Ten minutes later I met him in the entry, and we tiptoed out the door.

As we rode to the café, Phil slowed down at a corner. "I'd like to leave for Milton early, hon. I know we planned to stay three nights, but I have a lot of preparation for summer session, and I'd like an earlier start."

"That's okay." I felt instant relief, then suspicion. "Is that the only reason?"

He drove slowly up a hilly street lined with trees. "Look, let's be honest. I sense you're not enjoying yourself, and I don't want you to—"

"Phil, to tell the truth, your mother doesn't like me—"

"Now wait a minute—" He stopped in front of a small café with 'Lorna's' written across the front window.

"It's okay. I understand why she'd rather have you with someone who—who—" I tried to stifle the catch in my throat. Damn, my eyes welled up.

"Come here, honey." He reached for me across the seat and drew me close. "My mother has problems. Kind of like delusions of grandeur. I don't know why, because Dad isn't like that at all. So if you can see it as her flaw and not take it personally." He paused. "Because no one could be a better person than you, honey. And I want you to remember that."

We sat silently for a minute. "That's good to hear. You must've told her I'm Catholic since she didn't ask me about my religion."

Phil cleared his throat. "Yes, she knows. It's important to their generation, but not to me or Carole either."

I shuddered. "My folks would've been horrified if Maureen had married a Protestant."

"Maybe they'll change their minds about me," Phil said.

I rubbed his arm. "I'm ready for coffee."

•   •   •

When we reached Phil's house, Gus and Ida were sitting on the back porch drinking coffee. "I thought you might be at Lorna's," Ida glared at me. "It's a favorite spot of Phil's."

"Sit and have another cup with us," Gus said. He indicated the cushioned love seat.

"No time, Dad. Carole and I are giving Betty the city tour, and this afternoon I'm taking her up the shore to Two Harbors and Gooseberry Falls."

"All right, dear, but don't forget dinner at the club tonight. Reservations at seven." Ida took a sip from a pink flowered china cup. "It's not a formal event, just dinner. So, an attractive dress will be fine." She pierced me with feline eyes.

Phil cast his eyes upward. "Mother, we're not in junior high."

"See you two later," Gus said as adjusted his glasses.

CHAPTER 30

Another bright lemony day was in store for us as we picked up Carole at her house about a mile from Phil's parents. The neighborhood was landscaped with abundant trees and shrubbery. Flowers bloomed in nearly every yard. Carole hurried out the front door and Phil opened the back-seat door for her. "Hi, Betty. Hope you slept well." She wore a white cap sleeve blouse and red plaid pedal pushers, her brown hair tied in a pony tail.

"Yes, the bed is really comfortable." I straightened my new pair of navy slacks I'd bought at Bostwick's in Janesville. Not everything I owned came from Sears catalog.

I enjoyed driving around the neighborhoods, past interesting stone churches, Forest Hill Cemetery, and Northland Country club where we'd dine tonight. Phil's family had belonged for years, and Phil and Carole grew up swimming at the pool and later learned golf. A world apart from Back of the Yards.

We reached the town area and headed for Canal Park on Lake Superior. Its famous aerial lift bridge and ship canal's metallic blue water was a sight to behold, as Auntie would say. Phil parked alongside the retaining wall near the water, and we emerged from the car and roamed around.

"If we're lucky, a ship will come through," Carole said. "At night it looks spectacular with lights."

Phil explained how the ships carrying iron ore, coal, or grain go through the canal in Lake Superior to Duluth harbor. The bottom part of the bridge raises to allow the ships to pass under. He discussed technical industrial and shipping details, but I'm afraid I found it tedious.

"Phil, we're not engineering students. You're putting us to sleep," Carole said.

I laughed. "I'm sorry, but I agree, hon." I nudged his arm.

"Guess I'm outnumbered." We walked in comfortable silence and were heading back to the car when a sudden boom made me jump. Carole and Phil chuckled. "That's the ship horn," Phil said. "We'll see one come through."

The horn kept blaring; I covered my ears. The bridge slowly made its ascent to the top; then a huge steamship leisurely glided through and passed us as we waved back to several men on board.

Afterward we drove to Glensheen mansion, a large brick estate with a carriage house and ornate gardens. Phil said the Congdon family lived there since the early 1900s. The owner had been a lawyer and entrepreneur and acquired wealth in mining and railroad companies.

We stopped at a small diner on the way home for a light lunch of sandwiches and ice tea.

I appreciated getting to know Phil's sister. "Thanks for coming along, Carole," I said. "It was fun."

"For sure. Next time you can meet my perfect kids, who are away at camp."

Phil had told me about his niece and nephew, and said he liked being an uncle. I'm sure he'd make a wonderful father. I convinced myself not to get too hopeful.

We dropped Carole off and rode back to Phil's house. After freshening up, we left for the North Shore before Ida could trap us with more conversation. Phil seemed a little anxious, but I dismissed the thought. We'd be alone, which was fine with me.

. . .

We headed southeast, picked up Highway 61, and drove north along the shores of Lake Superior. It looked like an ocean, or as I'd imagined one. No end to the blue water; just the horizon beneath a swirl of puffy clouds and sky the color of bluebirds. I caught glimpses of the lake through pines and maples, breathtaking scenery. "Gee, Phil, this brings the 'shores of Gitche Gumee' to life. I can't believe I'm actually seeing it."

He grinned. "I knew you'd like it."

"Like it? I love it." To be this joyous all the time. I thought of my favorite stanza in the epic poem I'd memorized, how the baby Hiawatha learns of life in the forest from his wise grandmother.

"I love the words of Longfellow when he describes the rainbow. In fact, I know that stanza by heart." I kept gazing out the window.

"Let's hear it," Phil said.

After protesting a couple times, I nervously began. After the first two lines, I became absorbed in the beauty of the words.

"...Saw the rainbow in the heaven,
In the eastern sky, the rainbow,
Whispered, "What is that, Nokomis? "
And the good Nokomis answered:
" 'Tis the heaven of flowers you see there;
All the wild flowers of the forest,
All the lilies of the prairie,
When on earth they fade and perish
Blossom in that heaven above us."

"That's charming, honey. Just like you." Phil patted my shoulder. "Literary types look down their noses at Longfellow, but he had more depth and intelligence than given credit for."

"It seems to me if people can actually understand a poet, they're not considered as good as poets like Keats and Byron. That's what my English teacher said, and I agree." We studied British literature in senior English, my most memorable class.

"Yes, he certainly was the people's poet." Phil slowed down as we approached the quaint town of Two Harbors.

"This looks like a picture postcard, with all the trees, shops, and the 'shining big sea water,'" I said. "So much beauty."

"Yeah, you're seeing the best of it. Dreary in winter, though." Phil made his way through town, and soon we drove in the open land of trees. "We're coming to Gooseberry Falls State Park in a few minutes. We'll stop and walk around the falls."

I'd never seen a waterfall, and after we parked the car and wound through a path in the woods and down stone stairs, there it was. What a sight! The falls cascaded over rock formations and splashed into pools of boulders. The sound of gushing water filled the air, like ambient chanting or a distant pipe organ. We sat on a huge boulder as kids and adults alike hopped from rock to rock in the swirling, foaming water. The falls blew a faint breeze of mist our way, cooling the warm sun on our faces.

"This must be what paradise is like," I said.

Phil put his arm around my shoulder. "It sure is, hon."

After we hiked to a lower level of the falls and relaxed on another boulder, we sauntered our way up the winding stone stairway to the parking area. I was reluctant to leave, but I knew there was another place Phil had in mind.

He stayed on Highway 61 and continued north. "We're coming to Split Rock Lighthouse, another state park."

"Oh Phil, I've never seen a lighthouse. My brain can't take all this in."

He laughed. "Sure it can. The place has an interesting history. If I remember right, in the early nineteen-hundreds, there was a huge storm and almost thirty ships were lost on Lake Superior. I think the lighthouse was built in 1910."

We veered right onto a road through pines and wound our way to a parking lot near the lighthouse. We climbed up concrete stairs to the red stone fortress-like building at the edge of a rocky cliff. I felt dizzy when I looked down over the vast blue waters and tree-lined shore.

"This is unbelievable," I said. "What's that building?" I pointed to a smaller structure next to the light tower.

"That's the fog signal house," Phil said. "Much louder than the horn for the aerial bridge." He pointed out another dwelling place where the staff lived in later years. Then we climbed to the top of the tower and looked through a telescope available for tourists. The view was dramatic, breathtaking, scary. Once again, I felt light-headed, and took Phil's arm. "I think we better get you on solid land," he said.

We reached the ground, and he led me around the side facing the lake. "The path over here goes down to the water. I wanted to show you that before we go back."

He took my hand and led me down a path zigzagging through the trees until we reached the rocky shore. The lighthouse looked spectacular against the azure sky and silvery clouds. I wished I had a camera.

I leaned against Phil, mesmerized by the lapping waves.

"I'm thinking of our song, honey. There's just one place for me, near you."

He half-sang, off-key.

"You sound just like Sinatra." I laughed.

He continued his faux-singing. "Make my life worthwhile, by telling me that I'll, spend the rest of my days near you."

My throat formed a knot. "Hon, that's so sweet."

"I mean it, Betty."

He took my hand and kneeled down on one knee, reaching in his back pocket. He held out a tiny white box. "What? What's this?" I thought it can't be.

"Open it." He beamed, still on his knee.

My hands trembled as I fumbled with the box. When it opened, embedded in a blue velvet tuck lay a sparkling oval diamond on a gold ring with two small oval diamonds on the sides. I felt breathless. "Oh Phil. I don't know what to say. It's—it's absolutely gorgeous."

"Let's see if it fits." He lifted the ring and slowly slid it on my waiting finger. A perfect fit. "I told the jeweler my little finger was a little bigger than your— he guessed it right." He stood, brushing sand off his pants leg.

I hugged him close and we kissed, long and fervently. We drew apart. "Will you marry me, Betty?"

"Absolutely, yes, yes, I can't believe it." I couldn't wait to tell Maureen and Auntie. "How long have you planned this?"

"A long time, and I had this spot in mind."

I sighed. "I'll always remember we were engaged on the shores of Gitchee Gumee. Oh Phil, you're the best thing that's ever happened to me."

•   •   •

Driving back to Duluth, we debated whether to announce our exciting news at dinner with Phil's family or to wait. "Your mother won't be overjoyed," I said.

"Like I said, we'll just ignore her, but maybe we should wait."

"I think so. I'll hide the ring and we can tell everyone tomorrow." I knew Ida would disapprove no matter when she found out, but at least she wouldn't spoil our dinner tonight.

CHAPTER 31

The next morning, Phil and I packed our bags, impatient to drive back to Milton. He'd told his parents we needed to leave earlier than planned because of summer session preparation.

We ate breakfast in the dining room and gathered on the porch for more coffee. One thing I'd learned about the Swedes: they love their coffee, morning, noon, and night. After we took our last sips, Phil rose. "We have some news for you. Mother, Dad." He put his hands on my shoulders. "Betty and I are engaged to be married."

"Congratulations," Gus said and sprang to his feet. "Betty, welcome to the family." He came around the table, bent down, and gave me a hug.

"Really?" Ida's mouth twisted in displeasure. "Son, this is pretty sudden, isn't it?" She snapped her snakeskin cigarette case open, took out a Chesterfield, and lit it with her silver flip-top lighter. She inhaled and blasted out swirls of white smoke.

"No, Mother. Betty and I have been seeing each other all year, and we just made it official." He touched my arm. "Show them your ring, honey."

I rotated the ring around in my finger and held out my hand. "Yes, isn't it stunning?"

"Indeed it is," said Gus with a wide grin.

Ida puffed and exhaled more trails of vapor. "Hmm. Did it come from Norden's?"

"Yup." Phil said. "Joe helped pick it out and he sized it."

"How many carats is it? It seems a little under one."

"I don't remember," Phil said, teeth clenched. "All that matters is it's perfect, and Betty loves it."

Before I could agree, Ida piped in, "Does Carole know?"

"Yeah, we told her after dinner when we were mingling 'with the old-time throng'." Phil grinned.

Gus took a Chesterfield and lit it. "Have you set a date yet?"

"Yes," Ida said. "Where will it be? Will there be a problem with churches?" She inspected me. "I didn't think Catholics allowed Protestants in the wedding party."

Phil harrumphed. "Since I'm the groom, they'll have to."

The conversation was getting away from me. I chimed in, "We haven't decided when or where. If there are problems with that, we could get married in the church rectory or office with just a few people."

Ida looked as if a mouse just scurried across the room. "Heavens, you must have a church wedding. Carole's was so—"

"Now, dear," Gus broke in, "it's their wedding, their decision. We'll agree with whatever you decide."

Ida crushed out her cigarette with a vengeance on a green ceramic ashtray. "I'm sure Carole will be glad to help you out, Phil. We'll—"

"Please, Mother. We'll do just fine. We're adults in case you hadn't noticed. And now, we need to hit the road. It's a long trip."

Ida looked like she wanted to say more, but controlled herself. She'd barely given me a second glance, other than to scrutinize my ring. I'm sure she was dying to know how much it cost, and was I worthy of her son. I knew the answer already.

• • •

By late morning we were on the road, driving over the swing bridge into Superior, headed south for Milton. Two days had raced past, other than the tedious dinner at the country club last night. Gus and Ida had greeted friends and rambled on about their golf handicaps, the Yankees, communism in China, and other grave matters. Carole's warmth and conversation made the evening bearable. I thought once again how thankful I was we lived far away from the Lundgrens.

• • •

When we reached Milton, we had discussed nearly every aspect of our upcoming wedding, marriage, and children. "I'd like at least two kids, maybe more," I said. I enjoyed Maureen's two little ones and had always assumed I'd have a husband and family like most women.

"Yes, definitely two," Phil said. "We can see how it goes; they may drive us nuts, who knows."

I wasn't sure what restrictions would take place if we wanted to marry at St. Basil's. I could ask Maureen to find out. But I didn't want a huge church wedding, and we'd considered marrying in a Justice of the Peace office. We thought our parents would disapprove, so we decided I'd see if we could marry in the priest's office with only a few guests like Maureen and Auntie. Of course, Daddy and Mama if she was home.

"I can't see your family coming to Chicago. I don't think your mother would agree," I'd said.

"I'm sorry to say, but she'd stick out like a sore thumb. I want our wedding to be as private and intimate as possible." Phil, the voice of reason.

I agreed, and set our sights on an August wedding before the start of fall quarter.

•   •   •

The following week we returned to campus for summer session. Matthew James was first to congratulate us with a bear hug. "That's wonderful news, Phil, Betty. Somehow I knew you two would hit it off when you quoted Keats to each other."

"Actually, it was Dickinson, but we like Keats too," Phil said. "A thing of beauty, and all that."

Later, Mona and Peggy buzzed over to my desk. "Betty, what's this we hear about your engagement?"

"Let's see the huge rock," Mona said as she reached for my left hand. "Gosh, it's positively glamorous. You're so lucky."

They continued with questions: When and where will the wedding be? How were his parents and family? How was Duluth?

I think all I did was grin and blush. I'd never attracted attention like that, and didn't like it. I preferred to blend into the fringes of whatever group I found myself.

As I went to bed that night, I thought of the Shadows.

CHAPTER 32

Summer, 1949

The weeks rushed by in a flurry of plans and arrangements, including a bridal shower hosted by the wife of the English department chairman. A plump woman with white hair in a bun, Margaret Olstaad warmly welcomed everyone as they entered her charming red brick house with elm trees shading the yard. We sat in traditional, pleasant surroundings, sipping coffee with teacake, a dense, large cookie Margaret's mother used to bake.

I was overwhelmed meeting new women, and thankfully, Mona, Peggy, and several others from Dr. James's office were invited. Mona and Peggy beamed and whispered impressively while taking in the gathering.

Dorothy Haven was holding court with three ladies. She gaped at me. "We were wondering where the wedding will be, Betty."

"We're not sure yet. Maybe in Chicago, we're still planning."

"Where in Chicago are you from?" said a blond woman whose name I forgot. "I have cousins in Oak Park."

"I was south of there, near Bridgeport, close to Midway Airport." I'd become Mama, not mentioning Back of the Yards.

They bobbed their collective heads, as if they knew all about Chicago.

"Betty, you're really a lucky girl. Phil is such a good man, handsome too of course," Dorothy gabbed on. "He's from a good background too." She seemed to study my green cotton shift, no doubt wondering where it bought it.

I said nothing, but was curious how she knew about Phil's family.

The afternoon finally came to a grinding close. Although Margaret was a gracious hostess, small talk with mostly strangers exhausted me. However, I received many useful gifts, like highball glasses, everyday drinking glasses, Pyrex mixing bowls, and the requisite Tupperware.

That night I phoned Maureen and told her about my day. "It was wonderful except this snooty woman I don't like and she doesn't like me."

"Betty," Maureen said, "there are always people who are gonna be jealous of a young attractive girl like you who doesn't put on airs. She probably can't stand how a girl without a college degree could bag a man like Phil."

I harrumphed. "I asked him once, and he said I was more interesting and fun and genuine than most of the girls he'd met."

"You're a sweet girl, Betty. If only you'd believe it."

"I know, I guess."

"There you go again. You'll need to buy thank-you notes to write to everyone. I hope you remember who gave you what. Look at the cards again and jot down their gift." Maureen had learned these things from her own wedding and her supervisor at Goldblatt's.

. . .

After much discussion, Phil and I decided we would marry in a small ceremony at St. Basil's. We would tell his parents after the fact. We knew they would not approve of a Catholic wedding, nor would Ida be comfortable meeting my family and would look down her aristocratic nose on my neighborhood. We could do nothing to change her opinions, so we simply accepted the situation.

. . .

The day finally dawned. Swollen gray clouds crowded the sky, hiding the sun. I hoped it wasn't an omen. As if by magic, an hour later the outdoors emerged shiny and golden. Phil and I drove to Chicago; he stayed one night at the Ashland Hotel not far from our neighborhood. The next morning he drove to my house and met Daddy. Phil was friendly, and they chatted about the lakes and fishing in Wisconsin and Minnesota. After our coffee, Auntie, Uncle, Maureen, and John dropped in. Everyone was introduced and cordially chewed the fat, as Uncle said. Maureen joked about our childhood shenanigans. "You should've seen Betty when we snuck into the stockyards, Phil. Poor kid got scared, and then she fell and bit her tongue. What a mess."

None of us mentioned Joey or Mama, who was back in the hospital.

Maureen and I excused ourselves and went into our old bedroom to change my clothes. I'd selected an ivory satin suit with a peplum jacket and calf-length straight skirt. I'd ordered it from Sears catalog, along with a matching pillbox hat with a net veil.

After I was dressed, Maureen applied my mascara, rouge, and pink lipstick. "Look at yourself, Betty." She guided me to the wall mirror. "Who's that movie star?"

"She looks like Rita Hayworth." I admitted to myself that I looked pretty.

"Let's go get married," Maureen said.

.   .   .

The ceremony was simple with six guests: Maureen and John served as our maid of honor and best man, and Daddy, Auntie, Uncle, and Joan were guests. I'd called Dennis last month to ask him if he'd be our best man, but he declined with a vague excuse. I tried not to think of my hurt at his and Mama's absence.

After the service, Father Timothy blessed us as we left the altar and proudly grinned at our guests as man and wife. I was sorry Father John had died last year. He'd seen our family through abundant joy and tears.

A comforting whiff of incense followed me as we met outside and drove several cars to an old neighborhood restaurant where Phil would treat our guests for lunch. We rode north on Western Avenue toward Pilsen, an area rich with Tuscan immigrants. We reached Bruna's, a neighborhood favorite since the early thirties.

I'm not sure Daddy had been to such a fancy restaurant, and he took in the white table clothes, napkins, paintings of Tuscan scenes. Our waiter helped with menu selection and explained the various dishes like Linguine Con Calamari and Spaghetti Alla Carbonara.

Everyone seemed to enjoy the food and wine. John and Phil appeared to get on, perhaps because Phil showed interest in his job at the Dodge plant, which John had resumed following the war. After our meal, we said our goodbyes outside, shaded by Bruna's white canopy.

When would I see my family again?

.   .   .

Still in our wedding clothes, Phil and I drove north toward the Edgewater Beach Hotel, where Phil had reserved a room for three nights. The famous resort hotel complex on Lake Michigan was a favored spot of celebrities, politicians, and other affluent folks. A good thing Phil's parents sent us a generous check, an early wedding gift.

The hotel and grounds boasted ornate architecture and landscaped lawns. We registered in the massive lobby, and a bellhop rode with us in the elevator to the fifth floor. Phil dismissed him with a tip outside the door.

"Gotta do this right," he said as he swooped me up and carried me across the threshold. "You're so romantic, hon. I feel like a princess."

I was struck by the room's spaciousness, tufted furniture, and blue and white décor.

I'll always have warm memories of our time in the lavish surroundings, including the four-poster bed with a white canopy overhead.

We spent most of the days and nights exploring each other's bodies in passion and delight. I was even more in love, with hope of a brilliant future ahead of us. Of course, I knew it wouldn't be perfect, but I felt ready to face any obstacle in our paths.

Including the Shadows.

CHAPTER 33

Two years later, 1951

The morning after our son was born, the nurse placed him in my arms. I looked down at him, eyes squinted shut, tufts of black hair sticking out. Panic punched my gut. Raw fear gripped my chest. What was wrong? I looked at Phil, who sat by my bedside seemingly tired, but gratified.

"Isn't he something, honey?" He leaned in to see the baby bundled in a blue blanket. "Just think, we created this little human being. At a whopping eight pounds, twelve ounces." He beamed at me. "You did all the work though."

The nurse said, "I'll let you have a couple minutes, then I'll be back with his bottle so you can feed him." She marched out the door.

I wanted to run away. Anywhere but here. "How long have I slept, Phil? Have you been here all night?"

"No, I went home for a few hours sleep." The hospital was in Edgerton, a small town about nine miles from Milton. "I called my folks and Carole. They're thrilled." He touched the baby's ruddy cheek with his finger. "You said you wanted to tell your family today."

Still groggy, I nodded, unease enveloping me. "Yeah, I'll call them later. Should we name him David like we decided?"

Phil grinned. "David it is, and we'll go with Joseph as his middle name after your brother."

I felt the tears spill. I couldn't restrain the dam bursting. "Oh Phil, what's wrong with me? I'm so tired and nervous, and I don't know why." David grunted. I didn't want to look at him.

"It'll be okay, hon. I've heard of 'the baby blues' where new mothers feel down and overwhelmed. You'll be fine. Don't worry."

But I did worry. The Shadows had been back the past months. More foreboding than ever.

The door opened. "Are we ready for baby's breakfast?" A chipper nurse handed me a small, warm bottle with ivory colored liquid. "Similac is good for him. He'll stay strong and healthy." She unwrapped the blanket around the baby and handed me the bottle.

"I know this is your first, and I'm going to show you how to tilt the bottle. Make sure the liquid covers the opening completely. We don't want him to suck in air, now do we?"

She sounded like Sister Ambrose from second grade.

The nurse studied me. "Are you feeling all right, dear? Don't worry, it takes at least a week or two to be yourself again."

"She's tired," Phil said. "But I'm sure after five days of hospital rest, she'll feel stronger."

I looked at my husband. "Ah, the voice of experience."

He chuckled as we both watched our son sucking away on the bottle's long brown nipple.

The nurse said, "When he's halfway through, then we need to burp him."

I'd seen Maureen do that several times, but had forgotten it in the feeding process.

When all was done, nurse and baby departed for the nursery and David's morning nap.

Still tired and edgy, I yearned for solitude. "You don't need to hang around here, hon. I'll just doze off, and let you get some work done."

I knew Phil was agreeable with whatever I wanted, so he left for home. I lay back and lowered the bed to a flatter position. My thoughts carried me back to the past two school years, when I continued working for Dr. James. Phil had encouraged me to audit a class in Renaissance poetry taught by Harold Olstaad, English chairman. I enjoyed the course and studied poets I'd never heard of, like Robert Herrick and John Donne. I planned to sign up for another class, but when morning sickness arose, I needed to postpone my plans.

I noticed a distance from friends like Mona. Those single girls now seemed to have no use for me, but I made a new friend whose husband taught math. I met Bonnie McCormick at a faculty wives autumn tea party to welcome new members, including me. I was reluctant because of my usual bashfulness and lack of confidence, but Phil convinced me to attend. "Matt won't mind if you go to the tea. In fact, he'd want you to meet the other faculty wives, now that you're one too, Mrs. Lundgren." I still wasn't used to my new name, but wore it proudly.

I found an empty chair next to Bonnie, and we chatted easily. I noted her Irish name. "I'm Irish too, but maybe just your husband is," I said.

"Actually, I'm a Murphy, so our poor kids are Irish through and through, don't 'cha know."

I learned Bonnie and her husband Jeff had two children under five. They lived in Edgerton, and we exchanged phone numbers to keep in touch. One night, Phil and I went to their house for dinner, and we enjoyed the evening. Their two little girls were boisterous, but settled down without much difficulty.

Bonnie was the only person who knew about Joey and how his death still lingered in my mind.

•   •   •

Lying in my hospital bed, I recalled the ether during labor. "No, take it away." I visualized myself at age six, the nurse forcing the ether mask over my nose and mouth. I've heard women forget labor pains. I couldn't forget ether. I didn't want more children. Not after this.

•   •   •

As the days inched by, I pretended all was well. Visitors came and went with flowers and candy. Nurses brought baby David in to be fed, thinking I'd like time with him after the bottle. But I did not want to be with him, so I rang for the nurse. "He's done now and ready to go back."

I didn't dare tell Phil how I really felt. Anxious, fearful, wanting to run away. Other women loved their babies, holding them, playing, feeding. I wanted a baby. I always had. Why couldn't I feel anything but fear and anxiety?

What would I do when Phil went to work and I was home alone with the baby? I wished Maureen could come and stay for a week or so. But with her two boys, that was impossible.

Phil said Ida and Carole had both called, offering to come and help after I was home. But how would I tolerate Ida's disapproving attitude? I think she offered, knowing full well I'd turn her down. As for Carole, pleasant as she was, I'd feel beholden to her.

I knew I needed to be an adult, forge ahead, and promise myself things would improve.

CHAPTER 34

They won't release me. The Shadows come mostly at night or early dawn when I'm still shrouded in darkness. Fear grips me as I choke and gasp my way into the real world. My eyes widen as I try to obliterate the three specters from my mind. Always skulking overhead, worming closer, closer. I'm sore in body and spirit. I carry a pillow around the house to sit on, whether the couch, kitchen chair, anywhere. I soak in a warm tub like the doctor advised, but the soreness remains. My breasts leak milk despite medication I was given to suppress the flow, since I am not breastfeeding. I wrap squares of tissue in plastic cling wrap to put in my bra so the leakage won't show.

Yesterday when Bonnie dropped by with a chicken casserole, I looked down and two circles of stains highlighted my blue blouse. Thankfully, we could laugh it off, since we were good friends, and Bonnie had experienced similar embarrassments. "I was almost ready to nurse the second one to avoid leaking like a cow," Bonnie said. "As for your other end, keep doing the warm sitz bath. Another trick is spray your bum with warm water after you piddle. Helps with the burning."

I moaned. "Dear God, why did I do this?"

"I know, but it'll get better. And the milk dries up too."

I looked at my friend. "I'm having a worse time than most new mothers. I can't believe women have been giving birth since Adam and Eve."

"Betty, it's the hormones. I was a basket case too, but you'll be fine in another month or so. If not, ask Dr. Myer for pills. My sister got Miltown and that calmed her down."

I thought of Mama's treatments in Elgin and meds she'd taken. Anyway, it was a glimmer of hope.

Bonnie tucked her blond hair behind her ears. "Just thought of this. After my first baby, at our check-up, Dr. Myer said 'no relations for six weeks.' Does that mean I can tell my mother-in-law not to come help?"

We both laughed. "Ugh," I said. "Sex is the last thing on my mind. Ouch!"

David started to fuss. A flash of dread chilled me. "Damn, I was hoping he'd nap longer."

Bonnie chuckled. "Honey, they never do. Go get the little guy and let me see him again."

A minute later, I held David as I gingerly sat on my pillow beside Bonnie. Something sour hit my nose. "Oh crap, he spit up." I went to the nursery for a clean snap suit.

"A burp rag over my shoulder was a permanent fixture for me in those days," Bonnie said.

Back with a clean outfit, I sat and removed the soiled clothing. Bonnie cooed over him. "Hello, blue eyes. What do you see? When's your first doctor appointment?"

"Next week," I said as I smoothed David's cornsilk hair on top. "I'll see about those pills."

Bonnie left shortly, promising another visit soon. I hoped she was right. I'd feel better one of these weeks.

•　　•　　•

The days limped by, inch by inch, as if they carried my millstone of lead around their necks. Phil helped with David, getting up during the night to feed him. I felt guilty, knowing he needed to work every day. "It's all right, honey. He's my son too."

He even helped cook dinner several nights a week. I had no reason to feel tired and miserable, but I was. I wouldn't dare tell anyone I didn't really love my baby like I should. His cries jangled my nerves; I didn't know how to handle him or make him stop squalling during the long afternoons. I called Maureen one day in tears. I rarely used long distance during the day; I waited until evening for lower rates. "I don't know what's wrong with me. Why aren't I like other mothers?"

Maureen, now expecting her third child, said calmly. "Listen, Betty. One thing to do is make sure he's not wet or hungry, and put him in the crib. Close the door and walk outside for a few minutes. Or if it's bad weather, go in your room or basement, put the radio or phonograph on full blast, and wait ten minutes. He'll be asleep by then and you'll save your sanity."

I wasn't sure about that advice, but that afternoon I tried it. It worked, and I felt calmer afterwards.

The next day, I bundled up David and took him to Dr. Myer. Phil had taught me to drive right after we married. He'd bought a new Chevrolet dark red sedan with automatic transmission, making learning easy. He encouraged me to drive during the day; he usually rode to campus with a colleague.

Nervous driving the baby for the first time alone, I placed his infant seat beside me. The nine-mile trip to Edgerton was an easy one, with little traffic and warm weather. Five minutes from the doctor's office, David started howling and flailing his arms. Damn, I'd left my bag in the back seat. I pulled into a gas station, stopped the car, reached in the bag. I fumbled around while he screamed, beads of sweat popping out on my forehead. "Oh crap, hush. Hush." I dug deeper into the bag and finally pulled out my lifesaver, his pacifier with a blue guard and ring. I stuck it in his mouth. Mercifully, he quieted and began sucking.

David's eyes drifted closed as I parked outside the clinic. Thank God that ride is over, I thought as I gently carried him into the reception area and took a seat.

After twenty minutes, Dr. Myer strolled in the exam room and proceeded with a routine check. "David's perfectly normal, Betty. He's gained five ounces from birth weight, so he's right on target. He'll get his DTP vaccination when you bring him back in three weeks."

I nodded as if I knew what the initials stood for. I'd ask Bonnie.

The doctor called for his nurse, who came in and held David while I undressed and awkwardly wrapped a white opened gown around myself.

After I climbed onto the exam table, Dr. Myer said, "Let's take a look here. Has your bleeding gotten lighter?"

"Yes," I murmured. At least I didn't go through so many pads.

"Let's see how you're healing," he said, guiding my feet into the metal stirrups. Will I ever get over the humiliation? "Still a little red. Taking the sitz baths?"

"Yes," I said. "And sitting on a pillow."

"Right. I'll give you some cream to help. Now, we'll check up here. Still expelling milk?"

"Not much anymore." I wished he'd quit touching me.

"All right, young lady. I think we're done here." He helped me sit up. "You can get dressed and—"

"Um, excuse me, but I was going to ask something." I hesitated. "Um—"

Dr. Myer said, "Janice, I'll take young David here, and that'll be all."

The nurse left the room, and I said, "I don't feel right. I'm so high strung all the time, and I know I shouldn't, but I have a hard time—"

The doctor smiled, his kind brown eyes edged with lines. "You're not the only one who feels like that, Betty. Your hormones are still out of whack, and it takes two to three months to get back to normal. I give all my nervous mothers Miltown. I'll write you a prescription, and you take as directed."

Elated, I said, "Thank you. I thought I was going crazy."

"No, Betty. It's perfectly normal to have the jitters and the blues."

I left the office, knowing my emotions went far deeper than the blues and jitters. I'd stop at the drugstore for my prescription. I'd need to take David inside with me, but it would be worth the effort, even if he screamed his head off.

I had to take that Miltown as soon as possible.

Chapter 35

The call about Mama came a week later in the evening. Maureen's voice was raspy.

"They found her in her hospital room lying on the floor. It could be her heart—she's getting better, but they don't know much. I just thought you'd—"

"Do you think I should come down there?" I almost hoped for an excuse to leave.

"I don't know, Betty. It's hard to say how serious it is, and with your new baby and everything…" her voice faded off.

"Let me talk to Phil. I'll call you tomorrow." I needed to think.

"All right. By the way, I wanted to tell you that Dennis and his wife split up. He moved into an apartment. Don't know details, but I'd guess it had to do with his drinking."

"Really? I didn't know he drank that much." I felt distanced from my family.

"Yeah, like Daddy." Maureen cleared her throat. "We'll talk tomorrow."

I hung up the phone and crept into the nursery where Phil was trying to settle David. "Here, fella, take this." Phil nudged the pacifier in the baby's mouth.

We left the room, and I hoped David would give us peace for a while. We snuggled into the sofa. The Miltown helped me feel slightly more relaxed, but underlying fear and despair still floated in the corners of my brain. The thought of going to Chicago was tempting, but I wanted to stay with Phil, yet felt a need to take off.

I told him about Maureen's call and debated if I should go. "I'd feel terrible if Mama doesn't make it and I wasn't there," I said.

"I think you should go if you feel the need." Phil rubbed my shoulders. "I'm sure Carole would be game to come help."

"What about her kids?"

"They could stay with my folks during the day. Or Carole has friends who trade off watching each other's kids."

It sounded promising. Exciting. Selfish. The idea of taking the train back home and leaving my baby behind. Maybe it could work out.

. . .

Five days later, I sat on Auntie's couch sipping coffee and nibbling a slice of cherry pie. Mama had improved, but was still under close watch in the hospital. Auntie invited me to stay with them indefinitely. "It'll be so good to have you back, Betty," she'd said when she and Uncle met me at the train station earlier. "But you look so thin for just having a baby."

"I don't eat much. I'm just not hungry." David's birth had robbed me of my appetite, but I kept it from Auntie.

I felt a sense of release and freedom returning to my home city and neighborhood. It felt that way because I didn't think of Milton as home. Not yet.

"Your mama's quite fragile," Auntie said. "Maureen and I think we should visit her tomorrow morning so we can talk to her doctor."

Later I called Phil. "Hi, honey. How is everything there?"

He assured me all was fine, and David was letting Carole feed him. Maybe the baby would become attached to Carole. I hoped not. If so, I'd really feel guilty.

. . .

I awoke the next morning wondering where I was. Dawn filtered through the curtains of the homey room where I once stayed years ago. Feelings of abandonment hovered in my mind. Would other mothers have sent a child away for so long? I must be unworthy somehow. Maureen and Phil tried to convince me otherwise, but my self-disdain, ebbing and flowing, had cemented itself in my mind, refusing to liberate me. Last night when the Shadows appeared, I wondered if they were my inner self, dark and threatening, or perhaps a warning of something evil.

A flavor of bacon drifted through Auntie's apartment as I went in the bathroom and took a pill. I'd bring them along today in case I needed to chase away any agitation. I'd never tell anyone that my fear of inheriting Mama's illness had become stronger in the past summer. One day I'd asked Phil if he thought her sickness could be genetic. "I don't know, hon. Not that I've heard. If you want, I can ask Chuck Lang, the psych professor. He's not a psychiatrist of course, but he must keep up with the latest research."

"Yes, but don't tell him it's about me." I didn't want anyone to know about Mama.

Auntie's voice interrupted my thoughts. "We'll leave right after breakfast, Betty. Maureen just called."

My stomach tightened. Why was I getting jumpy? Come on pill, do your work.

• • •

When Maureen opened Auntie's door and saw me, she said, "Betty, you're so skinny. How did you lose your baby weight?"

"I don't have much appetite." I brushed my bangs from my forehead.

"Auntie, you'll have to fatten her up on cake and ice cream."

As we drove through the neighborhood and headed north to Elgin, I observed small changes in houses and stores here and there. Alice's house was torn down, and a dry cleaner had replaced Maud's Café.

"Ah, the rancid stink of the yards is still sweetening the air. Some things never change." I rolled up the back window of Maureen's old Plymouth.

"A few changes though. More Mexicans are moving in," Maureen said as she drove onto Western Avenue. "Of course, Daddy isn't pleased about that or the Negroes either. Lots of stuff going on down south with them. Guess they want to escape up here."

"There's been talk of getting rid of segregated schools all over," Auntie said.

"Our kids'll attend Nativity, so they'll be okay," Maureen said. "By the way," she glanced back at me, then Auntie in the front passenger seat. "Auntie knows already, but we're having another baby in February, maybe March."

How could Maureen cope with three kids? "Really? Are you all right with it?" I said. A flash of guilt scolded me for my non nurturing attitude.

"Of course, silly, why wouldn't I be?"

I forced a chuckle. "Um, let's see, because I have my hands full taking care of one."

"Seems you've got the baby blues, but you'll feel better any time now."

"Yeah, that's what people tell me, but—"

Auntie looked back at me. "Some women take to it easier at first. Not every woman has the motherly instinct."

"Auntie," Maureen said in surprise. "I think they must. Maybe it takes some longer."

"Perhaps I shouldn't say this, Betty, but your mama had a hard time after you were born. I mean at home afterwards. She went through a period of—" Auntie's lips closed.

"Of what?" I hadn't heard this.

She straightened her hair around the bun at her neck. "You know, kinda like after Joey. She'd stay in her room and expected Mac to do a lot of the baby care. But she got over it, and so will you."

I wanted to agree with Auntie. So far, I had no mother's instinct, no desire to nurture. I hoped someday I would. I was more convinced than ever there was something wrong with me. Something I inherited from Mama?

CHAPTER 36

An hour later we parked near the center building of the formerly named Elgin Hospital and Asylum for the Insane. The gothic-looking façade hadn't changed in atmosphere since I'd visited Mama several years ago.

"Watch out for the Satan lady, Betty. She's out to getcha," Maureen said.

"Hush, Maureen. Don't tease," Auntie said.

Actually, I welcomed a little well-placed humor. "Don't worry, Auntie. I'll fend her off."

The gray-haired lady at the receiving desk signed us in, and soon an aide dressed in a white tunic and calf-length skirt led us through the dingy, half-lit passageway. The odor of medicine and mold reminded me of the long-ago day I tramped up darkened stairs to have my tonsils out.

"She's still in the infirmary," the aide said as we reached a dreary lobby area and approached a nurse's station. "They're O'Leary's family," she told the nurse at the desk.

A hefty woman, rounded bosom resting on the desk, looked up, her smile tight. "Oh yes. Take them down to Room Six. She might be awake by now." She bent her head, returning to her paper work.

When we entered her stuffy room, Mama lay with her eyes closed. The aide gently joggled Mama's bony shoulders. "I'll leave you be. She should wake up any time now, and I'll tell the doctor you're here." She closed the door on her way out.

"I'm sure the doc will come any minute." Maureen rolled her eyes. "Last time it took ages to talk to anyone."

"Nora," Auntie said softly, bending over Mama. "It's me, Agnes. Maureen's here and guess who else? Betty came all the way from—"

Mama's eyes flashed open, darted back and forth, as if trying to settle on one person. "Who—who…" her voice faded away.

"It's me, Mama. Betty." Her eyes were sunken pools of black, her face a shriveled apple, like someone had pinched the skin away, leaving only the bone. A mustiness arose from her blanket. She brushed her unwashed gray-streaked hair from her face. Mama had just turned fifty. She looked eighty.

Her eyes rested on me. "Oh—I forgot where—"

Maureen touched Mama's arm. "You're still groggy from sleep. You'll wake up in a minute. You know, Mama, Betty had a baby boy. Now you have three grandsons, isn't that something?"

"Yes. Yes." Mama's eyes wandered in confusion.

Maureen went on, "And you'll have another grandchild next winter. From me. Maybe you forgot that. I hope it'll be a girl this time, but who knows."

Mama dozed from time to time during our conversation. Finally, Auntie said, "I'm going to see if that doctor is ever gonna get here." She left the door open a crack on her way out.

After what seemed an hour, Auntie returned, followed by Dr. Rice, one of several who had treated Mama. "Good morning, everyone," he said. His black hair was Brylcreemed to a shine, and pouches weighed his eyes downward, giving him a forlorn expression.

He went to Mama's side. "How are we today, Nora? Lovely to have your family visit." A whisper of Old Spice hung in the room. The doctor listened to her heart and lungs. "Almost back to normal." He straightened his stethoscope around his neck.

"Nora, we'll just step outside for a minute so I can talk to these ladies. They'll be right back."

"No—no, don't go. Don't leave me." Mama's words slow and raspy. "Stay here for good cheer, the gang's all here. Hail, hail—"

"It's all right, Mama," Maureen said. "You rest some more and we'll be back in a jiffy."

Mama gave a soft groan and lay back as we followed Dr. Rice out the door.

He led us down the hallway toward the nurse's station and gathered around the doctor. "Your mother is physically improving. I may have told you that we suspect she tried to take too many medications, which caused—"

"You mean she tried to—to—" Maureen broke in.

Dr. Rice's lips stiffened into a line. "I'm afraid so. We think she somehow stockpiled her medications or was able to pilfer some. We try and—"

"Excuse me," Auntie interrupted. "But I don't see how—isn't she supervised?"

Stunned, I remained speechless. Attempted suicide? Our mama? I guess I shouldn't be that shocked, given her history, but I felt like someone punched the air out of me.

"I'm sorry, Mrs.—Mrs.—"

"Casey." Auntie's voice sharp.

"Yes, Mrs. Casey, we try our best to assure the safety of all our patients and staff, but sometimes things can slip past us. She is on special watch now." Dr. Rice wiped his brow.

"Mentally she hasn't gotten better," Maureen said. "In fact, she's gotten worse."

Dr. Rice shook his head. "Some days are better than others, but there are patients who have shown improvement from certain treatments like surgery."

"Yes," Maureen said, "but you said Mama isn't right for that."

"Hmm, yes, that's true. She's not the right candidate for a lobotomy since she doesn't present as manic a good deal of the time. However, if she continues to worsen, we may consider it."

Auntie's eyes widened. "I don't like that idea, Doctor, but of course I'm not a blood relative." She eyed Maureen and me.

"Meanwhile," Dr. Rice continued, "we'll keep on with the—let's see." He flipped a page on his clipboard. "Yes, Amytal, we'll stay with that. And they've improved the convulsive treatments, so we may try that again."

The doctor checked his wristwatch. "Now if you'll excuse me, I need to leave. It was good to see you again. We'll be in touch." With a nod, he hurried away.

"Let's get back to Mama," Maureen sighed. "Not wonderful news, as usual."

Deflated, I said, "I don't understand why nothing has worked. Don't other people get better, or isn't there a cure for melancholia or depressive whatever she's supposed to have?"

"I don't know," Maureen said. "And seems like nobody else knows either."

We returned to Mama's room where she lay dozing, breathing heavily.

Suddenly I wanted to crawl into a corner and sleep. "Should we wake her up before we leave?"

"Of course," said Auntie. "She'd be upset if we left without saying goodbye."

"Does she ever mention Joey?" I said.

Maureen wet her lower lip. "No, or Dennis either. When I mention Dennis, she acts like she doesn't know who I'm talking about."

At the small window, I watched people walking to and from their cars. "Should we tell Daddy about Mama's suicide attempt?"

He's better off not knowing," said Auntie. "Dennis too. But I suppose you'll want to tell Phil."

"Oh for God's sake. Why does someone's health have to be so hush hush." I could feel my cheeks burning. "We couldn't even talk about Grandpa's cancer, as if it was his fault. And then Aunt Doris had a hysterectomy, but everyone said it was female troubles. Oh yeah," I ranted on, "and Lord forbid we talk about someone who died, like Joey."

"Settle down, Betty. I've never seen you like this." Maureen reached for my arm.

"Yes, what's come over you?" Auntie said. "That's the way things are. I know you're learning highfalutin ideas at that college, but remember where you came from."

I huffed. "Oh Auntie, I'm just trying to—never mind. I'm just upset that Mama would want to kill herself and leave us."

Auntie came and put her arms around my shoulders. "I know, honey. I think it's eaten away at you that your mama sent you to live with us those years ago."

I forced myself not to cry. "I still don't understand—"

"You know I can hear you. I'm not dead yet," Mama said.

The three of us startled; almost jolted toward her, lying on her yellowing sheets.

"Goodness, we're sorry, Mama." Maureen sat beside her and took her hand. "We're so worried about you. We don't want to lose you. Why on earth did you take those pills?"

"What pills?" Mama frowned. "I dunno. I'm tired all the time. I wanna sleep, sleep in the deep, sleep in the deep."

"Do you want to come home again?" Auntie reached for her other hand.

"I dunno. I wanna sleep." She half-sang. "Sleep my child and peace attend thee all through the night. He's waiting."

"Who's waiting, Nora?"

"Why, Joey. I told you that. Why don't you listen to me?" Mama rolled on her side facing the wall. "Soft the drowsy hours are creeping…Hill and dale in slumber sleeping…" Her voice faded into a low, soft moan.

"Should we ask her about Joey?" I whispered to Maureen.

"No, I'll tell the doctor she mentioned him again." She looked at Auntie as if for approval.

"Yes, and now we should go. She's groggy from the drugs." Auntie bent toward Mama and lightly kissed her forehead. "Bye, Nora. We'll visit again soon."

Maureen and I each gave Mama a kiss on her wizened cheek and we left the room. Maureen wrote a note for Dr. Rice at the nurses' station, and we silently made our way out of the building and toward the car.

Maureen and Auntie babbled on, repeating the doctor's comments and Mama's state of mind. I rolled down my back window so fresh air could ease the stuffiness in the car.

I hadn't settled on how long to stay with Auntie. I knew I should return to Phil and baby David. But I'd felt better since I arrived, which was most likely due to the Miltown and escaping the baby. If I stayed a couple more days I could call Joan and perhaps have lunch or dinner at Bruna's in Pilsen. And I wanted to visit my nephews, Tommy and Andy. Maybe David would be easier when he was their age.

That evening, Phil said I should stay as long as I wanted, that Carole was enjoying David, but they missed me. I knew I didn't deserve Phil. What other husband would put up with his wife leaving him and their baby for almost a week? I shuddered to think what Ida said about me leaving Phil in the lurch. Another reason for her to look down her blue-blooded nose at me.

I needed to remind myself of Eleanor Roosevelt's quotation I read in high school, *No one can make you feel inferior without your consent.*

How I wish it were true.

CHAPTER 37

After three more days, I returned to Milton. Maureen had consulted Dr. Rice, who assured her that physically Mama was on the mend and was gradually increasing her appetite. I thought of Auntie's words. *Your mama had a hard time when you were born.* Maybe that's why Mama wasn't available all the time. Could she have sent me away after Joey because I was too much trouble? I was lucky Phil didn't think I was unworthy. Otherwise, he would've found someone else.

Carole met me at the train station, and we chattered on about David. "He's fussy in late afternoons, but most babies are. He'll grow out of it." It seemed like I was always waiting for things to end: my so-called baby blues, David's crying, then it'll be his teething, and the list goes on.

Impatient to see Phil, I hurried into the house, greeted by him holding a squalling, red-faced David. "Oops, must have the wrong house."

Carole said, "Here, let me take him so you two can have a minute of peace." Phil handed David over to his sister and gave me a hug.

I happily melted into his embrace, but David's wails made my jaw clench. "It's so great to be home. I missed you."

"Welcome back, honey. We missed you too and glad Nora's a little better." Phil took my arm. "Let's go in the kitchen. Carole has dinner cooking."

After freshening up and walking around with David to hush him, I attempted to eat supper. The baby finally settled down in a new infant seat structured to lightly swing back and forth.

"This is delicious, Carole," I said after taking a bite of beef stroganoff. I took a sip of Chianti that Phil had opened. Here I sat again, enjoying food and wine while someone else had tended to the baby. Was I abandoning him?

"Thanks," Carole said. "By the way, the drugstore called and your prescription for Miltown is ready. He assumed I was you when I answered the phone, and before I could say anything, he told me."

Embarrassed, I said, "That's all right. No secret I suppose. But I'd appreciate it if you didn't say anything to your mother."

"No, I wouldn't. Mother doesn't understand that young women these days might need a boost. I have a couple friends who take Miltown, and they swear by it." Carole straightened her napkin.

Phil said, "Mom's the one who needs something to relax besides her Manhattans."

I had doubled up on the pills a couple times, but I hoped Dr. Myer would write me a refill, even if I reached the "you should feel better by now" time.

My trip to Chicago and talking to Maureen, Auntie, and Joan, had helped renew my lagging spirits. I felt I could carry on as long as I had those pink pills nearby.

•   •   •

The days and months passed with deepening shadows, but I managed to keep afloat in my sea of pretense. I wore the mask others expected, a smiling face of a young wife and mother, following a script of complacence and quiet resignation. I carefully doled out my thoughts to Phil, who patiently listened. He'd met with Chuck Lang from the college, asking him if insanity could be inherited. According to Lang, *research indicates the cause of mental illness can be both environmental and genetic. In other words, no one knows for sure.* Phil also explained that a genetic disposition most likely passes down such illnesses, but again, nothing certain. He doubted I'd inherited anything from Mama, but he was no doctor. However, he couldn't explain why I had improved little in the months since childbirth.

Phil, my friends, and acquaintances commented on my weight. *Betty, you need to get some meat on your bones.* I was never hungry, and I'd lost pleasure in food I used to enjoy, like roast chicken, mashed potatoes, and even ice cream and cookies. I caught myself in the mirror one night after my bath and thought of the last time I saw Mama, looking as if her bones were trying to break free from her body.

When I told Dr. Myer I couldn't sleep, he prescribed Nembutal, warning me not to take more than the dosage on the bottle. I convinced him I still needed Miltown, and he reluctantly refilled them, saying this was the last time. *You're way past the postpartum time frame, Betty. You should get a hobby like gardening or bridge perhaps.* My lips formed a tight smile.

I desperately longed for normalcy and hated the person I'd become. I avoided people who complained and whined, yet I had become one of them. But more than that, although grateful for Phil and a healthy child, I could not rid myself of feelings of impending doom, fear, and immobility.

I would soon learn of one more family link to insanity.

Chapter 38

One autumn evening, Maureen called. "I'm sorry, Betty. It's Uncle. He—he had a heart attack and—"

"Did he—" My heart pounded.

"Yeah, he did." Maureen tearfully gave the details. "He'd been raking leaves in the back and came in saying he was tired. He went upstairs and collapsed on the bedroom floor, clutching his left arm. Auntie was right there and called the police. By the time they came, he was gone."

"When did this happen?" I hoped I hadn't missed a call when I was out earlier.

"Yesterday afternoon," Maureen said. "I should've called earlier, but it's been so—"

"It's all right." Once again, I was left out of a family crisis, but I knew Maureen had her hands full with three little boys. Jack was born last winter, vigorous and healthy like his two brothers.

Maureen said she'd call tomorrow with the final arrangements. I wanted to attend Uncle's funeral. He was like a grandfather to me, especially since I'd lived with him and Auntie for almost a year.

At seventy-two, Uncle had declined with the usual hallmarks of aging, but as far as anyone knew, he had no heart problems.

Phil hugged me. "I'm sorry, honey. I know how much he meant to you."

I was longing to see my family again. Perhaps Carole could care for David, even though the drive from Duluth was tedious and bus and train connections poor. I didn't want to press my luck because she helped last year.

David sat in his high chair nibbling a Graham cracker. He had turned one year old a couple months ago and had walked at ten months. Still robust, his hair had paled to a dusty blond, and his blue eyes matched Phil's. Thankfully, I grew to love our round-faced son and was less anxious caring for him, enjoying him more as he matured. Although he was rambunctious and into everything, I beamed with pride when friends told me how advanced he was. "He's a busy little boy," Bonnie commented the last time we visited her. She'd invited another friend with a boy David's age, and David had zoomed around while the other boy sat docile, playing with a toy truck.

Looking at his chubby cheeks and clear, watchful eyes, I felt a stab of guilt for wanting to attend Uncle's funeral. "We'll work something out," Phil said. "Maybe Bonnie could help."

In the end he was right. Bonnie offered to take David during the two days Phil would be at work. Then he'd be home on the weekend. I planned to stay three nights, so I hurriedly packed my suitcase, along with instructions for David's care. Since Bonnie's kids were long out of diapers, she'd be stuck with that task. "Don't worry," she said, "I still have my old diaper pail. I'll drag it out for soaking."

. . .

Two days later, I sat in St. Basil's Church beside Maureen, John, and Daddy. Auntie was in the first pew ahead of us, along with several relatives of Uncle's. I hadn't attended Mass since I moved to Milton. Because Phil was Lutheran, we had not joined a church and planned to wait until David was older.

The familiar fragrance of incense and nostalgia brought comfort and warmth to my heart. Father Timothy celebrated the Mass, and later we rode to the cemetery where Uncle would rest near Joey and other O'Leary kin. I managed to keep my feelings in check, perhaps because of my meds.

A crisp October day, trees painted in lively reds, yellows, oranges. After the interment ceremony, Daddy, Maureen, John, and I strolled over to Joey's headstone, as if it were waiting amongst the fallen leaves. I'd forgotten to bring flowers for his grave. I kneeled beside the stone marker and felt my throat tightening. "You'd love your nephew, my boy David. His middle name is Joseph after you. I'm—so sorry, Joey. I love you." No one heard my words as I stood and hung my head before we trudged away, leaving Joey and Uncle in peace and reflection.

. . .

I stayed beside Auntie as people meandered toward their cars along the dirt road winding through the cemetery. "Auntie, you know how I felt about Uncle. I'm sorry."

She wiped her watery red eyes with a hanky. "Betty, dear, I'm glad you came. Your uncle loved you so much. But you're so thin. Are you all right?"

"Yes, I'm all right." Was I sick of that question.

She raised her eyebrows doubtfully. "Will I see you before you go back? You can stop in any time."

"I hope so." I didn't think that would happen. She had out-of-town relatives staying with her, and I didn't want to intrude. Besides, I still found it difficult to converse with new people.

We hugged our goodbyes, her soothing gardenia fragrance sweet on her neck. I joined Maureen and the rest as we headed for John's car.

"Daddy, you and Betty can stop in to see the boys. I'll rustle up some lunch." Maureen opened the car door.

I knew Daddy would've preferred Kerry's Bar, but he agreed.

Maureen's neighbor had taken care of the boys, who would've ruined the funeral for everyone else, according to my sister.

Ten minutes later, we sat in the Bailey's Bridgeport living room cluttered with toys, a wooden playpen on one side. Daddy played with Tommy, who at age five had begun kindergarten. Andy busied himself with a toy train, and Jack, at eight months, held onto the railing in the playpen and looked around at all the activity, emitting a grunt now and then.

"Jack started crawling at six months and just pulled himself up in his crib," Maureen bragged.

"Brilliant kid," said Daddy. "Got the O'Leary brains."

"Says you," John scoffed.

Soon Maureen called from the kitchen, "Sandwiches are almost ready. Come get a plate and we'll eat in the living room so the boys will stay put."

Unlike my own home, chaos reigned over Maureen's. How could she cope with three boys and still talk about trying for a girl? Of course, she'd always had a more relaxed temperament than me.

After lunch, Daddy wanted to leave, and Maureen came along so she and I could spend time without the boys around. John agreed to hold down the fort for a couple hours.

Later, Maureen and I sat on the couch in our old house where I was staying for two more days.

Maureen's hair, still wavy, reached her shoulders in a pageboy style. "Betty, I didn't say anything, but you're absolutely scrawny. Are you sick?"

I sniffed. "You and Auntie. You're exaggerating. I just don't have much appetite."

"I know. You didn't finish your tuna sandwich. Left half of it."

"Did not. I want to hear about Mama. You said you had something to tell me earlier." Had she gotten worse?

Maureen leaned in, lowering her voice even though Daddy was at the corner. "A couple weeks ago I took some food to Daddy and stayed to visit. He just opened a beer and the phone rang and he went in the kitchen to answer. I got the idea it was Aunt Johanna calling from Pittsburgh. I snuck closer to hear, and they were talking about Mama." Maureen cleared her throat, while I listened impatiently.

"Daddy was saying things about Dublin and Alma and stuff I didn't know about. I snuck back to the couch when Daddy started to end the call."

"What then?" I couldn't imagine what I'd hear.

"He looked kinda mad or upset, and when I pressed him, he said it was nothing, and to never mind. I couldn't let it go, and you know me. I begged and insisted he tell me. I said I was an adult now with kids, and what was the secret? I finally wore him down, and he said for me never to tell a soul."

"What? What?" I was ready to grab Maureen by her red hair.

"All right, but you have to promise never to tell anyone. Even Phil."

Now I was afraid.

CHAPTER 39

"All right already. Cross my heart and hope to die, stick a needle in my eye."

I recited the silly childhood rhyme to hurry her on.

"Okay, here goes. Years ago Mama told this to Daddy, swearing him to secrecy. You may know Mama's grandmother was Alma Byrne from near Dublin back in the eighteen hundreds. They survived the potato famine and lived on a farm. Alma got married and had three kids, but her husband, was mean and would beat her. One night when he was passed out drunk, she took a butcher knife and stabbed him to death."

I gasped, speechless.

"He kinda woke up, but she kept on with the knife, maybe ten stab wounds. So she ended up in the—let's see—the Criminal Lunatic Asylum for Ireland in or near Dublin. She was locked up there for the rest of her life."

"Wha— I can't believe that. She was in an asylum too. Was she crazy?"

"I guess they thought that. Daddy said even in those days they wanted to separate regular prisoners from crazy people."

I dropped my jaw, still stunned. "Do you think Mama inherited something from her?"

"I don't know, but it reminds me of Lizzie Borden, except our great-grandmother used a knife instead of an ax."

I burst out laughing. I visualized the woman wielding a knife over her head and whacking away. "Must be a nervous reaction. It's not funny." That set off another wave of laughter.

"Yeah, the sickness is in the family, Betty. Mama's side. You know about her cousin Peter in the asylum in New York."

"Um, I remember something about him, but was he really in a mental hospital too?"

"Yup. For years, I think. He had depression like Mama."

I still couldn't believe the story of Alma. Murdered her husband. Of course, if he drank and beat her all the time, who knew what I'd do.

"Can you imagine what asylums were like back then?" Maureen said. "And we think Elgin is bad."

"I wonder about me sometimes," I said.

"You mean the baby blues you had?"

I shifted position on the couch. "I think it was worse than that. And don't tell anybody, but I'm still taking the Miltown." I didn't mention the Nembutal.

Maureen grimaced. "I'm sorry. I didn't realize. You know, a friend of mine said her mother was going to a psychiatrist because she had such highs and lows."

"I don't know if I'd qualify for that," I said. "I think you have to really be bad off like Mama to see a psychiatrist."

I tried to stifle the sense of unease that crept in me. "Can we visit Mama before I go back?"

Maureen hesitated. "I don't think so. We don't have much time, and I'd have to leave the boys again. She's really about the same."

I felt she wasn't telling me everything. "I guess I assumed I'd see her this time."

"Ah, I'm sorry, but I don't know how—"

"It's okay. Just let me know if there's any change." I didn't trust Maureen to keep me posted. Were there more skeletons in the family closet?

•   •   •

Two days later, Phil and David met me at the train station in Milton. I gave them both hugs and said to David, "You've grown in the last four days." It seemed I'd been away longer.

That evening after David was asleep, I told Phil about Alma Byrne. Maureen would be angry at me for breaking her confidence, but I never wanted to keep secrets from Phil. "That's unbelievable," he said. "I wonder how accurate it is. I mean, there must've been records, but I guess a story like that would stay in the family for generations."

I snuggled against Phil on our new blue velvet sofa. "Yeah, not something to be proud of, but certainly mysterious. I wonder if they thought she was insane because it's more unusual for females to commit murders."

"Hard to say in those days. I know you've been worried about family genes from your mother, but I can't believe it's inherited. After all, look at Maureen. She's doing fine, and your brother is, as far as we know."

"I don't know about Dennis," I said. "He didn't come to Uncle's funeral. He gave Maureen some vague excuse. He really changed after Joey died. Got quieter for sure."

In some ways I was relieved to live far from the family, most likely the source of my depression. It would take me many months for Alma Byrne's story to sink into my very essence and become a permanent fixture.

Right now, I was glad to be home with a loving husband and healthy son. What more could a woman like me want?

CHAPTER 40

1953-54

The next couple years rolled by, seasons vanishing into one another. Time marches on regardless, captured only in our memories. Some we choose, others choose us.

As David grew, our house seemed to shrink, so rather than move to a larger home, we hired a contracting company to build an addition in the back, adjoining the dining and kitchen areas. We called it the family room which included a small bathroom and shower. A sofa bed added guest accommodations, and the space housed most of David's toys, helping me keep the living room tidy.

Shortly after construction, Phil's parents drove down to visit us on their way to Chicago and the Ozarks. Too bad Carole wasn't coming instead. The prospect of Ida seeing our house for the first time set my heart racing. "Just try to ignore what she says. I know it's easy to say, but she has a problem, not you, hon." Phil, always to the rescue.

The Shadows had kept their distance the past months but appeared more frequently as their visit approached. "What will I serve for dinner? They can have our bedroom; we'll sleep on the sofa bed. What if David has a tantrum?"

"Whoa, one problem at a time. I don't like to give up our bedroom, but since they're older, I guess we should," Phil said as we were at the sink rinsing dinner dishes. "As for dinner, they're only staying a couple nights, and we'll take them to the Crown one night. Friday I'll make steak or hamburgers outside. The Weber grill to the rescue. I need practice to become a master backyard chef."

That helped my anxiety, for I would just need to make a salad and baked beans or potato salad. Then a dessert. I wished I enjoyed cooking and baking like Maureen and Bonnie. I don't think Mama ever liked it much either. I realized she and I had more and more in common.

The afternoon arrived for the visit, and Phil was still at the college. Damn, he'd promised to come home early. How could he stick me alone with his parents? I took a deep calming breath as David and I plodded down the sidewalk and greeted Gus and Ida at the curb. "Oh, look at that handsome boy," Ida gushed. "Just like Phil was." Nearly age three, David was shy with strangers and hid behind my leg.

"Betty, so good to see you," Gus said and gave me a hug.

"Yes, dear, good to see you." Ida's words sounded like an afterthought. "I hope you didn't fuss too much. I told Phil, don't—"

"I'm sure she didn't break her neck," Gus said. "I'll take the suitcases in."

After a flurry of objections of not wanting to put us out of our own rightful bedroom, they acquiesced, freshened up, and joined me and David in the living room. "Can we see the rest of the house?" Ida gushed. "Carole's told me how cozy it is."

Did she think I didn't understand her euphemism for small? I forced a smile. "Of course. We have more space now with the new addition."

Ida tilted her chin. "Yes, we heard about that. Why didn't you just move to a roomier house?"

"Dear, it's none of our business—"

"It's okay," I interrupted. "We both like the basic structure of the house. High quality workmanship and the back yard and location." I chastised myself for defending our decision.

We took the grand tour, David in tow, and ended up in the basement where the washer and new dryer sat. Phil had strung clotheslines across a part of the large room. Ida brushed aside a pair of denim jeans hanging in her way. "My, I haven't had clotheslines for years."

Did she mean hanging clothes was passe?

She scrutinized the dryer. "Yes, this is nice. Smaller than ours, but nice."

When we climbed the stairs to the kitchen, I heard Phil open the garage door. Thank God he's home. I was tempted to chew him out for being late, but decided not to supply Ida with more ammunition to use against me.

·   ·   ·

We sat in the living room sipping cocktails. I'd bought ingredients for Manhattans and martinis. Phil drank a Schlitz, and I chose my usual Chablis.

"I think you'll like the Crown," Phil was saying. "Betty and I go there every New Year's. Then tomorrow you'll get a taste of my expertly grilled steak."

Ida's perfectly shaped nose lifted a bit. "Yes, it'll be good to have a home-cooked meal."

"Right, and Betty's potato salad and dessert are wonderful." Phil meant well, but I didn't need defending. I'd steeled myself not to let Ida get under my skin.

We chattered on about Carole's family, briefly touching on mine. "I'm sorry about your uncle passing," Gus said. "But good you went to the funeral."

I nodded in agreement. I wasn't about to explain he was my great uncle and how I'd lived with him for a while years ago.

"Anyone need a refill?" Phil got up. Everyone but me said yes.

He returned with drinks on a tray. Ida took a sip and leaned toward a plant on the coffee table. "It looks like that wandering Jew hasn't been anywhere for a while." She laughed.

It took me a second to catch on. "Yes, it's a little skimpy looking."

"You need to give it more light. It's too dim here. Moving it over by the window would help."

I'd remember to tell Bonnie that my mother-in-law insulted her recent gift to me.

"On second thought, I think I will have a refill." I headed for the kitchen.

●   ●   ●

The next evening, we sat on our outdoor patio enjoying, I hoped, a grilled steak dinner with garden salad, potato salad, and thankfully, plenty of wine. David sat in his blue plastic booster chair devouring a wiener Phil grilled for him. "The steak is delicious, son," Gus said. "Just the way I like it, nice and rare."

A flash of the stockyards struck my mind. I almost commented that, no doubt, Gus hadn't seen what Daddy had.

"Yes, very good, Phil." Ida poked at the small amount of potato salad she'd taken.

Gus took a drink of Chianti. "Very tasty salads too, Betty."

"Yes indeed," said Phil.

Thankfully they were leaving in the morning. I don't think I could have endured another day of Ida Lundgren.

Later, we "repaired" to the living room for dessert, as Phil said. His love of British literature, especially Charles Dickens and George Eliot, never left him.

I had made an apple cake recipe from Bonnie and refrigerated it until that evening. Ida reluctantly agreed it was acceptable. "Yes, very good, dear."

An hour later, we said good night to David, who was up past his bedtime. He'd been a typical toddler in his demands, but Phil and I managed his deportment, as he would say.

Ida had only chastised her grandson once or twice, asking him where his manners were.

After tucking David into bed, I headed toward the kitchen where Phil and Ida were straightening up. I heard Ida say "…saw Barbara at the club last month, and thought you'd be—"

"What makes you think I want to hear about her husband and kids? I don't care." Phil's voice harsh.

"It's still awkward when I run into her mother. You know—"

"You've gotta drop it. And drop her."

"And really, Phil, do you do most of the cooking? It seems Betty—"

"Stop it right—" Phil's voice lowered. "I've had enough of you interfering—"

My heart thumping, I tiptoed into the living room. How could that woman be so damn nasty? At least Phil stood up for me. I knew Barbara was his former girlfriend, so leave it to Ida to bring it up. I sank into an easy chair and picked up my library copy of *Witness for the Prosecution* and opened it to the bookmarked page. Gus was in the family room watching sports on TV.

"There you are." Phil came in the room. "The boy asleep?"

"Yup. You wanna take a walk?"

"Sure. I'll tell the folks. They can listen for David."

Warm night air breezed around us, carrying whiffs of smoky wood in our midst.

We strolled hand in hand along the cracked sidewalk past well-kept houses, dim lights filtering through curtained windows.

I slowed my pace. "I thought you'd come home early today, Phil. I really didn't want to—"

"I know, honey, but Olstaad called me into his office at the last minute and I couldn't leave."

"I guess I'll forgive you this time." I squeezed his hand. "But I overheard Ida in the kitchen talking about Barbara."

Phil scoffed. "Jeez, the woman never lets up. Wanted to tell me all about her husband, what he did, her kids. I had to tell Ma to knock it off."

"I'm sure your mother wished you would've ended up with her—"

"Now, don't get paranoid. We've been over this."

"Just how serious were you?" I knew I should shut up, but didn't.

"Just so you know, we were almost engaged, but before you get upset, I broke it off." Phil slowed down. "I didn't love her the way you should, and our mothers kept pushing us. Later when I got the Milton offer, and ran into Barbara at the club, she said it was best we broke up because she'd never move to a small town like that anyway."

"Sounds like sour grapes." I reminded myself not to let Ida's damaging words damage me.

"That's for sure," Phil said. "And let's be thankful for you and me. 'If you were coming in the Fall, I'd brush the Summer by.'"

"I know, hon. I know." I was one lucky lady, especially since I knew the Dickinson quote.

· · ·

In March 1954, we welcomed our second son, Steven Eric, a nine-pound healthy boy. When I called Maureen from my hospital bed, she said, "Gee, Betty, we have five boys between us. We gotta get a girl one of these times."

I had secretly hoped for a girl, but a healthy baby was most important. When Dr. Myer said, "You have another robust boy," I groggily answered, "Two boys are a great family."

"A good *start* for a family." Was he correcting me?

I knew all along we'd stop at two children. I lacked the emotional strength for more, along with an easy-going temperament like Maureen.

My Miltown prescription was long gone, but I still took Nembutal for sleeping. When Stevie came home, I craved Miltown again to help my anxiety, although it wasn't as severe this time. My second childbirth was easier, and I was better prepared for the demands of a new baby. Stevie was more relaxed than David, but since babies sense their mothers' moods, it seemed logical that my second baby was calmer.

Once again, Carole came to the rescue, driving down shortly before my labor began. She said it helped her to get away from it all, and I didn't know if it were true or a well-intentioned lie to alleviate my guilt at her leaving her own family for a week. Regardless, I could never repay her.

"Just accept her help, hon. She wouldn't do it if she didn't want to," Phil said.

· · ·

We had visited St. John's Lutheran Church on High Street after David was born. Since I had fallen away from the Catholic faith along with my family, I agreed to join the Lutheran Church. Of course, Ida had been distraught over Phil's marrying a Catholic, but soon realized the souls of her future grandchildren would be assured of salvation through a Protestant pathway. "When the boys are old enough for Sunday School, I'll start going to services," I told Phil, and he agreed.

Stevie was baptized at six weeks old, after which I could go forward, the last of our newborn parental obligations fulfilled.

· · ·

I continued to live life as an ordinary wife and mother of small children. The months following Stevie's birth passed quickly with occasional bouts of darkness when the Shadows surfaced and haunted me for one or two days. I would again visualize my own head popping out of one end of an iron lung, my body immobilized, imprisoned in that machine, essential to the life and breath of the polio patient.

The beginning of my downfall was yet to come.

CHAPTER 41

It began with a sore jaw. I ignored it at first, but the pain worsened, and my back teeth ached. I took a few aspirins with no relief. "I think I need to see Dr. Hanson," I finally told Phil. He knew how I felt about dentists.

After hearing my tale of woe, Phil said, "Call right away tomorrow morning, hon. You shouldn't have to suffer like that."

"I know, but—"

"They've improved over the years, and now they use Novocain all the time, you don't feel a thing. When Dad had a tooth pulled awhile back, he got laughing gas."

"I can't imagine laughing in the dentist chair," I said. "What's the real name of it?"

"Something oxide, I can't remember. But Hanson's up on the latest, I'm sure," Phil assured me.

• • •

The next morning, I sat in Jay Hanson's dental chair trying to make sense of the X-rays he'd taken of my mouth. "You can see how the wisdom teeth on the bottom are coming in at a sharp angle, and they have no room to—" his voice droned on, "impacted and could cause infection that could—"

I held onto the armrests so I wouldn't float into the air. "They need to be extracted, Betty. The sooner the better so you can feel well again."

I'd heard of wisdom teeth, but what were they? Why did we have them if we don't need them? I tried to hide my sudden dread. A pit formed in my stomach. "I guess I don't have a choice."

"I know lots of folks are afraid of extractions, but we're not in the Dark Ages anymore. You'll get plenty of Novocain and the nitrous oxide if you want.

You'll be so relaxed it'll be over in no time." Dr. Hanson shut off the fluorescent light panel behind the X-rays. Salt and pepper hair framed his kind face. "I can clear time tomorrow morning for you."

"So soon?" I said, alarmed.

"I think it would be best. I'll give you a prescription for the pain starting today. That'll get you through until tomorrow."

After more discussion of details I immediately forgot, I left the office, prescription in hand. I'd stop by Rexall Drugs on my way home. The boys were across the street at my neighbor, Mrs. Kowalski's house. A sixty-year-old widow, she had been a frequent babysitter for us as well as for several young families in the neighborhood.

By the time I waited for my prescription, picked up the kids, and arrived home, my mouth throbbed. Before settling the boys with lunch and tending to Stevie's soiled diaper, I headed for the bathroom and took a newly prescribed pill called Percodan. I'd ice the area later with a bag of frozen peas.

After the boys ate lunch of open-faced spam sandwiches, they watched cartoons until nap time. My pain had miraculously disappeared except a shadow of an ache. I felt a sense of well-being with added energy to return to the kitchen to wash and dry the dishes rather than wait until after supper.

I lay down, hoping the boys would sleep longer and let me bask in my newfound joy.

"Mama, can I go swing in the back?" David whined.

I must've dozed off. I squinted into my son's penetrating eyes.

"Yeah, lemme get up. Is Stevie awake?"

"I dunno."

I rose, unlocked the back door, and let David out to play. A tall picket fence surrounding our spacious yard built a couple years ago was a godsent to ensure he didn't run off. In another year or two, Stevie could play unsupervised as well. I could easily keep an eye on them from the sliding glass door in the TV room.

Later when Phil came home, I was pleased to report that my pain had all but disappeared.

"Let's have happy hour like your parents do, and I'll tell you all about my poor wisdom teeth," I said, putting my arms around his neck.

"Yeah, let me get out of this suit. Be right back."

"Daddy, daddy," screamed the boys, running in from the TV room.

"How are my best guys?" Phil tousled with them, their daily routine. He seldom grew impatient with the kids, unlike me. I knew I could never cope with more children.

I'd arranged for Mrs. Kowalski to take the boys again for my dental appointment the next day. The pill had eased my fear of the extractions and boosted my optimism about the procedure.

• • •

According to Dr. Hanson, the extractions went well. I had taken another Percodan in the morning, so I felt little pain except when the foot-long needle penetrated my jaw on both sides.

Minutes later, numbed with Novocain, and added nitrous oxide, I felt like I was flying high above the events in the dental chair. I wouldn't call it laughing gas, but it was a true extrasensory experience. I actually sang aloud, 'there's just one place for me, near you.' Embarrassed, I later apologized to Dr. Hanson and his assistant, who both chuckled.

"Don't worry, Betty. We enjoyed the song. Nothing new to us."

Mrs. Kowalski had offered to keep the boys until mid-afternoon, so I drove home, took another Percodan and leisurely dropped off to sleep.

• • •

My extraction gum sites slowly healed, and I managed the pain with Percodan. Dr. Hanson refilled the prescription. Along with Miltown and Nembutal, I found myself in a pleasant state of relaxation and well-being.

Last month Bonnie had organized a canasta group, and four of us played cards in each other's homes, trading off every week. Our young kids played together and of course interrupted us now and then, but I looked forward to our Thursday mornings of friendship and conversation.

I gradually went to bed earlier, at times an hour after the boys. Phil said I seemed more tired than usual. "Are you feeling all right, honey? Your teeth bothering you?"

"No, they're almost healed by now." I hadn't let Phil know I was still taking the Percodan, thinking he'd object and wonder why I needed them.

"Getting enough sleep then?" His questions annoyed me.

"Yes, I think so." I tried to hide my irritation.

I had to admit that sleepiness and exhaustion now described my days. Twice I'd fallen asleep on the sofa, and David woke me up. *Mama, can we have a snack?* And later, *The TV isn't working. Come and fix it.* I felt like I'd been in a coma. Was I taking too many meds?

Then came the day at our Thursday canasta group. I'd forgotten to change Stevie's diaper, and he'd dirtied it by the time we got to Bonnie's. Even more embarrassing, I hadn't remembered to pack spare diapers, so I had to borrow one of Bonnie's old diapers she'd saved for rags.

Standing in her spare bedroom, my hands trembled as I changed Stevie's diaper. Bonnie seemed to scrutinize me. "Betty, what's going on? You're not yourself."

My cheeks flushed with heat, no doubt turning red. "I haven't been sleeping worth a darn."

"Are you still taking the Nembutal?"

"Yeah. Think I should cut back?" I didn't tell her I was still on Percodan and Miltown.

"I think I would. Do it gradually though. Here, gimme that thing." She took the soiled diaper. "I'll soak this in the other toilet. Yuck. What did that kid have for breakfast?"

I laughed, glad to think about something else.

After our coffee and cinnamon rolls, we were well into our game. When I discarded a ten of hearts, Bonnie made a half-gasp. Lorraine, our opponent grabbed it up. "Thanks, Betty, we got the game."

Confused, Bonnie told me what I should've discarded, but by then, my head was spinning and I felt my chair lift me up above the others and coast toward the door. I held onto the seat with both hands, hoping I wouldn't float away on my own. I heard her distant voice. *You usually notice what they don't discard, what they keep—"*

Suddenly I found myself back in the present, chair secured on the floor. I stared vacantly at the cards arranged on the table.

"Who wants more coffee? Or water?" Bonnie gaped at me.

I scooched out of my chair. "Um, I'm so sorry—I have a splitting headache. I should've said something. I covered my forehead with my hand. I hate to spoil the—"

"It's all right, Betty," everyone seemed to say at once.

In a daze, I gathered my purse and went in the family room to get the boys. Captain Kangaroo chatted with Mr. Green Jeans on the TV, and dolls and trucks cluttered the floor. "Come on, boys, we need to go home." I couldn't wait to get out of there.

CHAPTER 42

"Aw, no. I wanna watch this," David whined. "Why do we have to go?"

"We can watch it at home." I retrieved the diaper bag and stuffed the boys' sweaters inside.

They grumbled and fussed as I hurried them through the living room. "I'm sorry, I'm sorry," I said over and over to my friends.

"Are you gonna be able to make the drive home?" Bonnie frowned.

"Yeah. I'll be all right." I wasn't sure, but if I had problems, I'd have sense enough to stop the car.

"Drive slowly then," Bonnie said.

I got the boys into the back seat and tossed the diaper bag in the trunk. Driving down the street, I could almost hear the girls gossiping about me. Crap, I really spoiled things. Now they'd think I was crazy. I thought about Mama. I trusted Bonnie not to say anything.

I drove at a snail's pace on a back road, and we reached the house in one piece. I made peanut butter and jelly sandwiches for the boys. Damn, almost out of milk, so I poured them grape juice. I wasn't hungry but forced down half a banana.

I'd planned a chicken casserole for dinner but didn't have the gumption to fix it. Thank God for TV dinners. I looked in the freezer and found a Hungry-Man Country-fried chicken dinner, perfect for Phil. The boys and I would share a couple turkey dinners, complete with mashed potatoes, gravy, and peas. Good thing Ida wasn't around.

Later when Phil asked how my card group went, I said it was fine. I'd tell him the truth tonight after tucking in the boys.

• • •

We sat on the couch in the family room, and Phil paged through the TV Guide with Ed Sullivan on the cover. "What should we watch, hon?" he said.

"I wanted to talk about something first." Phil put the magazine down and looked at me.

I told him about my recent fatigue, difficulty concentrating. "I messed up our canasta game today by a stupid mistake…just wasn't thinking. I should've known better."

"Sorry, honey." He held out his arms, and I scooched close to him, rested my head on his shoulder. "I've been worried about how tired you are. Maybe you should have Dr. Myer give you a checkup."

"Yeah, I guess. If I don't feel better soon, I will." I knew I wouldn't call the doctor. I didn't have the energy to call anyone.

In the next few days, I became more lethargic. Phil noticed I lost my balance a couple times. "Hon, you could've fallen," he said after I tripped over a stuffed bear on the floor. "You need to call Myer tomorrow, or I'll have to."

"I'm telling you Phil, I can't. I just can't." I sat on the living room chair and buried my face in my hands. "I can't— can't do anything."

Stevie waddled in from the TV room. "Mama, possa, possa." He leaned against my legs and gazed at me with round hazel eyes tinged with green, his light brown hair like mine. I saw myself mirrored in this sweet boy. I leaned over and hugged him, breathing in his No More Tears baby shampoo.

"My precious boy, yes. Have Daddy give you a popsicle." My eyes filled as I gently released Stevie from my arms. I looked at Phil. "Go with Daddy now."

"Come on, buddy," Phil said, taking Stevie's hand. "Let's give your brother a popsicle too. We'll let Mommy rest."

I didn't try to stop the river of tears. I sniffed, wiped my nose on the back of my hand, too tired to get a tissue. Too tired to move. Too tired to think.

•   •   •

Days filled with dusty memories, images of Shadows fading in and out. I can only sit. I cannot talk. I have lockjaw. I don't know what that is, but I must've heard of it. Because that's how I am. My jaw can't move. I remain wordless.

Phil told me later that he and the boys drove me to the hospital the next day. I could barely move, so he called Dr. Myer, who directed us to the emergency room at Edgerton. An hour later, I was admitted to the hospital in a single room in the main unit. Time flew in fragments, visions of needles, sweating, throwing up, all hazy.

It could've been a day or a week. I felt slightly better. Slightly more aware. Things more in focus. What had I done? What happened to me? I'm ending up like Mama.

"No, you aren't crazy, Betty, like you kept saying," Phil told me the evening after I was discharged from the hospital. We lay in bed, my head propped on pillows. "You took too many medications that interacted with each other. Your body got dependent on the Percodan. It helps the pain, but you craved the euphoria they can give you, and after a while, they no longer work."

"Crap. I can't believe it. Addicted to drugs." I was ashamed. A weak person. "I'm sorry, honey. I just wanted to feel happy. Just happy like other people."

"I know, hon. I mean, I don't know, but those medications can be so dangerous. We didn't know that, but Myer explained it."

"Then why did Dr. Hanson give me the Percodan if it's so bad for you?"

Phil cleared his throat. "I doubt if he knew you were taking the Nembutal for sleeping and the other one—"

"Miltown," I said. "But I had cut down on that." At least I had intended to.

"Yes, now you're on a new regimen. Myer cut the dosage of the sleeping pill, and gradually you're stopping the Miltown altogether." He switched off the lamp on his nightstand.

"Yeah, I have the directions." I worried that I'd feel worse without Miltown. I needed something to get by, to help me hang on. The Rolling Stones wrote a song called "Mother's Little Helper" that could've been written about me. If only Mick Jagger had been around to warn me about "tranquilizing my mind."

"What did you tell Mrs. Kowalski?" I hoped Phil was discreet. Thankfully, she kept the boys during the two days I was gone.

"Don't worry, she's had her share of problems, I think. I said you had a bad reaction to some medication and left it at that. And Bonnie called one night, concerned about you."

I hoped Kowalski wouldn't blab, yet I had a feeling she wouldn't gossip. I would be mortified if anyone discovered my instability. Insanity even.

.   .   .

A week passed, and I felt almost normal. At least I could think straighter and could cook dinner and complete other tasks without messing up. One day Lorraine from the card group called. "Hi, Betty. Are you feeling better?"

I'd obviously missed the last gathering and could imagine what people thought. "Yes, the headaches are much better. Sorry I missed last time."

"That's all right. I hope you're better. I've heard those drugs can really hurt people if they're not careful." I detected a false tone in her voice. How did she know about my drugs?

"Yeah, I'm all right now. Just wasn't sleeping. You know what it's like with little kids all day." I gave a forced chuckle.

"True, kids can drive you—We hope to see you next week, and take care of yourself, Betty. We were worried about you, being in the hospital and all."

"Thanks, Lorraine." I couldn't hang up fast enough.

A wave of betrayal punched me in the stomach. Bonnie obviously told the others about my taking meds. And the hospital. How could she? She was my best friend, or so I thought. I felt exposed, humiliated. How could I face those so-called friends?

I decided I would no longer belong to that group. I couldn't see them again. I'd find something else to do, maybe audit another class at the college. I needed some kind of retreat from the ordinary. A way to use the brains Sister Cecile said I had.

The next morning as I wiped up spilled milk and Alpha-Bits from the kitchen table, the phone rang. I hurried to the living room, and when I picked up the receiver and heard Bonnie's voice, I was tempted to hang up. "Hi, gal. How are you feeling?"

"Fine," I said, still hurt that she broke my confidence.

"That's good. Can you make it Thursday? We missed you."

I hesitated. "Um, no, I can't make it. Stevie has an appointment."

Silence on the other end. I knew she sensed my displeasure. None of the usual small talk.

"You sure you're, all right?" Did Bonnie sound different? Hard to tell.

"Yes. I gotta go. David is into something. Bye." I didn't give her a chance to speak.

My heart pounded. Angry at her betrayal, I stormed off to the kitchen to finish cleaning up. I could not be with those women again. Lord only knew what Bonnie had blabbed.

That evening after supper, we let the boys watch *Disneyland* while we sat in the living room. I told Phil about Bonnie's divulging my private business.

"I'm sure she meant well. They're all worried about you," Phil said.

"Meant well? She knew better than to tell about my drugs and landing in the hospital."

Phil hesitated. "I don't remember if I told her to keep it a secret."

"Even if you didn't, I assumed she'd know not to tell. She knew how embarrassed I was about the Miltown." I couldn't believe Phil was taking her side.

"I don't know, hon. It's probably not worth risking your friendship over."

"Phil, you don't understand," my voice rising, "my problems aren't anyone else's business. I'm not gonna air my dirty linen in public."

"Is that what you are? Dirty linen? Do you hear yourself, Betty?"

I leaped from the sofa. "I can't believe I'm hearing you. How can you be on their side? Bonnie betrayed me. Don't you get that?" I stomped away.

Standing, Phil said, "Don't go off mad, honey. I just don't want you to—"

"I want to be alone." I slammed the bedroom door and sank onto the bed. Phil and I rarely had words. I needed a Miltown, regardless of my dwindling supply, so I got up and headed for the bathroom.

The pill calmed me down, and soon I was in the TV room telling the boys to get ready for bed. Phil had joined them on the couch. "Feeling better?"

I sure wished people would quit asking me that. "Yeah, sorry I blew up."

"I'm sorry too," Phil said as he gave me a hug. "Come on, guys, race you to the bedroom. Last one in is a rotten egg." That ploy worked on Stevie, but David had grown wise to it.

The next morning when the phone rang, I didn't answer. I knew it wasn't Phil because we had an arrangement: if he called and I didn't answer, he'd call right back, let it ring twice, and hang up. Then I'd call him. We were so clever.

I was afraid it was Bonnie calling again, and I couldn't tolerate talking to her. I just hoped she'd take the hint and realize what she'd done.

I sat on the living room sofa staring at the window as if something remarkable were outside. My thoughts strayed back to my old school at St. Basil's. The church and the neighborhood changing, people losing jobs at the stockyards. I didn't know how accurate Daddy's reports were about the decline of the whole meatpacking industry. I yearned for those growing up days. Days of blurred, cozy memories of Dionne dolls, library trips. Days before the Accident when everything changed.

CHAPTER 43

1957

It had been two years since we'd last visited my family in Chicago. Phil's parents gave him money for his birthday, so he suggested we stay at the Edgewater Beach resort, where we spent our honeymoon. The boys' eyes lit up at the prospect of swimming in the hotel's pool and building sand castles at the beach.

Last summer when we visited Phil's family in Duluth, Gus gave us a good deal on a new Chevy blue and white station wagon right off his dealership's lot. As the boys grew larger, so did our cars.

The day was hot, the air plump with humidity as we drove southwest from Milton on 26 and picked up 90 going to Chicago. We rolled down the windows which helped cool off the car, and I took in the scenery along the countryside. "Those farmhouses look so peaceful. I wonder who lives there," I said as we traveled past barns and steel grain silos amongst clumps of trees washed in sunshine.

After an hour, the boys were restless in spite of claiming the back of the station wagon as their own car room. "Mama, I'm hungry. Can I have a snack?" Stevie, usually easy-going, sounded cranky.

"We're gonna stop for lunch soon," said Phil.

"But I—" Stevie started

"I have to stop at a gas station," David said. He started kindergarten last year and learned modesty about bathroom needs.

Phil groaned, but slowed down after several minutes and pulled into a Texaco station outside of Cherry Valley near Rockford. A service man came out and filled up the tank and checked the oil. "Looks good," he said, and took Phil's five dollars. "You folks ready for lunch, there's Gert's Café down the way here. Good grub."

"Thanks," Phil said. "We'll give it a try."

Gert's Café lived up to its recommendation, and we ordered chocolate malts with either hamburgers or wieners. The place was small, crowded with tourists on their way to larger, more exciting destinations. "All Shook Up" blared from a jukebox.

"I like Elvis Presley," David said. "He's cool." He looked at Stevie as if to impress his kid brother.

Soon we were on our way, less than an hour's drive from the Edgewater. I couldn't wait to relax in our suite and browse around the shops. But first, we'd see Maureen and her family in Bridgeport, then Daddy. I'd called Auntie last week, and she had scheduled a trip to Beloit, so I'd miss seeing her.

I hadn't told Maureen, but I planned to see Mama in Elgin by myself. For several months, I'd been slipping into darkness again. The Shadows had lurked in my brain, several times a week, usually in the black early hours of morning. I no longer had Percodan to ease my despair and had to beg Dr. Myer to continue my Miltown. I hid these feelings from Phil.

Determined to talk to Mama alone, I wanted to discover if she had experienced instability before Joey. Auntie had said that after my birth, Mama had a hard time. Maybe the sickness was inherited in some, like me, but not others. Maureen, lucky as usual, avoided that fate.

• • •

Traffic thickened as we drew near the suburb of West Dundee. My stomach tightened when I saw the sign for Elgin. The boys gawked at the industrial areas with their concrete buildings, brick apartments, and glimpses of homes and store fronts. "What's that building, Daddy?" David called out.

"I can't look, son, gotta keep my eyes on the road." Phil was better at reading maps than me, so I'd lean over and steer the car so he could consult the fold-out highway map.

"There's the airport, boys," I said as we reached the massive O'Hare complex. Phil exited 90 onto Devon Avenue and somehow got onto 14 going east toward Edgewater. We approached the hotel, and Stevie cried, "Wow. How tall is it, Daddy?"

Phil laughed. "It's twenty stories high, and there are about six hundred rooms, I think."

"When can we go on the roller coaster?" David rested his head on Phil's seat.

"I've told you twenty times we'll go to Riverview in a day or two after we see Aunt Maureen. Remember, your cousins are going too." I hadn't been lucky enough to visit the iconic amusement park as a child.

I could tell David wasn't convinced he'd have fun with Maureen's boys since he barely remembered them. One thing about kids; they adapted better than adults. Better than me anyway.

After we settled in our hotel room and freshened up, we made the trip south to Bridgeport to see Maureen. She'd invited us for dinner, and I was eager to see how my nephews had grown.

• • •

Driving south on 41, we passed Wrigley Field and Lincoln Park, then west to 90 and south to Bridgeport. "Let's take Halsted, so the boys can see the Ramova Theater," I said to Phil.

"I'll tell them all about the *Wizard of Oz*."

"We've already heard it, Mama." David squirmed in his seat. "Remember when we saw it on TV, you—"

"I know, but this time you'll see the real theater." Hard to impress that kid these days.

Shortly after my Oz lecture, we reached Maureen's house on Morgan Street near Pershing. The dark green three-level house stood beyond a small front yard, a sidewalk leading to a three-step front entry. Lilac bushes bloomed on either side of the sidewalk, their fragrance scenting the air as we reached the door.

Maureen appeared in white pedal pushers and a green blouse. "Wow, look at these boys. So tall. So handsome."

The boys scrunched their noses, but tolerated Maureen's gushing and hugging. I noted an aroma of seafood as she led us into the living room where her boys sprawled on the floor watching TV. "Turn that off, Tommy. Your cousins are here."

The five boys shyly observed each other while Phil and I chatted with Maureen about the trip, hotel, more small talk. "Andy, why don't you take David and Stevie up to your room. Show 'em your new train."

The boys lumbered up the stairs, with five-year-old Jack hanging back. A handsome child with mischievous blue eyes, he had a mind of his own. "I don't wanna go."

Maureen pooh-poohed. "All right, but don't bother us. You sit here with Uncle Phil while I talk privately to Aunt Betty."

Curious what news awaited me, I followed my sister. She opened the oven door and checked the covered dish baking inside. "Tuna casserole, Friday you know. Hope Phil doesn't mind," Maureen joked.

"Of course not. I've strayed from the church, you know, so we're both sinners."

Maureen paused. "Yeah, you and Dennis. Daddy too. Guess me and Auntie are the last family Catholics standing."

Once again, I envied her easy-going, non-judgmental temperament.

Maureen cleared her throat as she joined me at the table. "I wanted to tell you about Dennis."

"Oh, oh, here it comes," I said.

"You knew he'd been drinking more, sometimes with Daddy. He got a warning from his supervisor at Midway about showing up hung over. Then a few weeks later, he showed up drunk and an hour late. So instead of firing him on the spot, the guy told him to sign himself into the Conway House or he'd lose his job." Maureen poured two cups of coffee.

"What's the Conway House, a mental hospital?"

"No, it's like a drug and alcohol center where you live for a month and sober up. Then you go to AA meetings. They used to be called sober houses." Maureen placed the cups on the table. "The clinic is in Skokie."

"Can they have visitors?" I really wanted to talk to Dennis. We're both adults now.

"No visitors, no calls to anyone, just meetings and groups and stuff. I have a brochure around here some place."

I took a sip of coffee. "I never knew what Dennis's job was at the airport."

Maureen shrugged. "It has something to do with employees and records. I'm not sure either, but he had an Army buddy who knew the boss. He's worked there over ten years, so hopefully he won't mess up."

I thought about alcoholism and how people laugh at jokes about drunks, the shows on television where bums stumble around and get laughs. I can't imagine Dennis that way. To me, there was no such thing as a funny drunk.

"Does Mama know about him?"

Maureen twisted her cup around. "No, she doesn't want to hear his name. After all these years."

"That's so heartbreaking." I felt my throat clutch. "I guess she's forgiven Daddy since he visits her, but why not Dennis?"

"I don't know, Betty. She's in her own world of whatever it is."

I was suddenly tired to the bone and wanted to curl up in a ball and become invisible.

"When's John coming home?" I stifled a yawn.

As if on cue, I heard the front door open. "Hey, Phil, how are ya?" John's voice rang out.

Maureen and I pushed back our chairs and I went to greet John. He gave me a hug. "Betty, good to see ya."

"What about me, Daddy?" Jack said, who resembled their father the most with his black hair and sturdy frame.

John swooped Jack up in the air as the boy squealed. "Airplane, airplane."

Maureen and I were lucky our husbands were caring fathers, even though Maureen recently confided that John had his demons from the war and he drank too much at times.

●   ●   ●

Later, all nine of us sat at the long table in the dining room off the kitchen and living room. Maureen and I set the table and put the steaming casserole dish and other food on her special linen tablecloth she ironed "just for you, Betty."

We passed our plates to Maureen and she spooned out the tuna casserole topped with crushed potato chips. A red jello mold with fruit cocktail made in a fluted bundt pan sat proudly in the middle. Warm dinner rolls completed the feast. "This is yummy, Aunt Maureen," said David. "Our jello is just in a pan."

"Thanks, David," I said. "Air the family food linen. See what you did, Maureen? Now I'll have to get a bundt pan." I actually had one, but never used it for jello.

And the conversation pattered on. I noted that John drank two beers with dinner and one after a dessert of chocolate cake with fudge icing.

We made plans for the next several days, which included taking the kids to Riverview. I had arranged my clandestine trip to Elgin with Phil for our last day when we'd stop at the hospital on the way home. He'd take the boys to a park or café while I visited a so-called friend. Even David was too young to hear the truth about his grandma. When Maureen suggested we visit Mama, I pretended I didn't have time and would wait until my next trip.

· · ·

The next two days were a blur of activity. We spent most of one day at the huge amusement park, Riverview. The fear of polio, especially in crowded places, had all but disappeared when the Salk vaccine became available in 1955. Maureen had been more concerned than me because of higher risk in cities. In Milton, we were complacent; perhaps too much so.

Despite intermittent rain, the kids had an exciting time on the roller coasters and Shoot the Chutes, a water ride I had to endure to hang onto Stevie. He screeched when we ended up sopping wet but wanted to go again. All the kids begged to go on the Bobs, the infamous wooden roller coaster, and finally I gave in and allowed David to go only if Phil accompanied him. On other rides, Maureen and I would scream along with the kids, laughing like we seldom did in our own childhoods.

For the first time, I understood the action-packed joy of youth that had eluded me. For a short time, all the pain within me was lifted, replaced with a freedom of spirit I couldn't explain. I hoped David and Stevie would never experience the inner turmoil and self-aversion that plagued me.

I half-expected the visit with Mama to fall through. Would I have the courage to sit with her alone for the first time in almost twenty years?

CHAPTER 44

We spent the next afternoon visiting Daddy. I left him and Phil in the living room and took the boys on a neighborhood walking tour. I showed them the library, St. Basil's school, the church, the park. "Are people who live here poor?" David asked.

Surprised, I said, "What do you mean by poor? It's where I grew up."

"Yeah, but I thought you were poor too."

I was taken aback by my six-year-old son saying such a thing. Did I detect a tad of judgment? "I guess I never thought about it since most people were poor during the Great Depression." Phil and I had explained to David about those lean years, although Phil's family was financially comfortable.

I had to admit the houses looked small and forlorn, but the place had been kept up fairly well. It wasn't a slum by any means. I felt defensive about my neighborhood.

"Why is it called Back of the Yards?" David kicked a stone off the sidewalk.

"You know why. I've told you a hundred times. Because of the stockyards. We went by there yesterday, remember?"

Stevie held his nose with his fingers. "Yeah, pee-eu. They stink."

"Good Lord, will you stop it?" Becoming fed up with their attitude, I didn't like being hurt by my own children.

"Just remember this, smarty pants. You're no better than anyone else. Luckier maybe. But no better. And don't you forget it." I grabbed Stevie's arm. "Come on, let's go home."

I felt deflated, wishing I could erase the pain from my childhood. Maybe some day my boys would realize their good fortune.

Daddy wasn't talkative, and I suspected he wanted us to leave so he could drink more. He commented his days were numbered at the yards. "The place has been declining since the war. Don't need the houses like we used to, ever since they got refrigerated train cars."

"Yeah, I've heard that for a long time," I said. I knew he meant they didn't need the slaughterhouses like they used to, and I didn't want to pursue the subject.

"Yup, things are getting more new-fangled. Bring back the good 'ol days."

Phil agreed, but I knew the old days weren't that good. I guess Daddy just remembered the days at the corner when neighbors looked out for one another.

We said our goodbyes with hugs and handshakes. I kept mum about Mama, and Daddy didn't mention her. Her absence, however, seemed to fill the room and beg for attention during the intermittent silences.

On the way home, I wanted Phil to drive past the old gate to the stockyards, still standing over Exchange Avenue. "Last time to look at the old gate, boys," I said. "Someday it might be in your history books. It's part of the original limestone gate from back in the eighteen hundreds."

"It's very imposing," said Phil.

We didn't discuss the yards much in the presence of the boys. I had always been squeamish about the details and found it appalling that until recently school children were given tours of the place. The grisly scenes they witnessed no doubt caused them nightmares for months. Growing up, I had been relieved Daddy's job was a watchman and not directly related to the animals.

·   ·   ·

The next morning the drive from Edgewater to Elgin was easy since we picked up 90 going west, taking the opposite route from last Friday. Phil located the hospital on State Street and let me out in front of the building.

I tried to feel optimistic as I strode into the somber-looking place and headed for the main desk. An unsmiling older woman looked at me. "Yes?"

After assuring her I was my mother's daughter, she directed me to the activities room where someone would unlock the door.

Over the years, Mama had "graduated" to the less restricted areas and was even allowed to go outdoors every day, weather permitting. According to Maureen, she had not received shock treatments for nearly ten years, even though the doc said there had been improvements in administering them in the last couple years.

An orderly unlocked a hall door leading to several open areas, including the activity room where I spotted Mama sitting alone in a blue occasional chair. She fiddled with knitting needles and a skein of red yarn on her lap and looked up as I approached her.

"Hi, Mama." I pulled another chair next to her and sat. "It's Betty. I came to—"

"I know who you are," Mama said. "You think I don't know my own daughter?" Her lavender pinstriped duster had coffee stains on the front. She held up her knitting, a few rows of a scarf perhaps. "See this? I got knitting permission." She cackled.

"That's wonderful, Mama." At one time, she was not allowed anything sharp or breakable. "Is that a winter scarf?"

"No, can't you see? It's a hat. A hat for Joey when it snows. Joe in the snow, Joe in the snow." She frowned. "No, I mean Tommy. Tommy, Maureen's boy. That hat is for him."

She stared at me. "You got boys too. How many? You should have a girl. A pearl of a girl. I knew a Pearl once. A nice girl, Pearl." Mama started a sing-song rhyme. "You can bring Pearl, she's a darn nice girl but—"

"Mama, that'll be a lovely hat. Would you like to take a little walk outside? It's really warm—"

"No. Wanna stay right here." She pursed her lips and puffed away a strand of gray hair from her forehead. "Where's Agnes? Not here?"

"No, Auntie Agnes couldn't come. She's living in—"

"Pooh, she never liked me. Never did, not a kid, never did." Mama looked at the ceiling as if waiting for approval.

"Mama, she never said that." A white lie, but my best response at the moment.

I reached in my purse and took out two photos of David and Stevie. "Here are my boys, your grandsons."

She set her knitting on an end table, took the pictures and held them close to her eyes. Squinting, she said, "This one's an O'Leary. What's his name?"

"Stevie, and David's the other—"

"He looks German, all blond and tall." She handed me the pictures and reached for her knitting.

"Actually, Swedish, Mama. Phil is Swedish."

"Humph," Mama said. "Guess Swedes are okay. They're a grumpy lot though."

"Mama, I've thought about our family—some of the family's hardships with—like me when I had my first baby, I had a very hard time—"

"What are you talking about, Betty? Can you help me with this?" She held out the knitting mess she'd created. "I had to pull this row out." She scanned the room "Can you find what's-her-name who helps with this stuff?"

So much for a meaningful conversation. Was she on too much medication or not enough? Or pretending not to understand my words?

I saw one aide in white working on a jigsaw puzzle with a thin stick of a man, but I wasn't willing to walk around trying to find what's-her-name.

"Maybe you can find her later. You know I live in Wisconsin, and I came to visit you. I just saw Maureen and—"

"She was here already. And Mac, he never comes, the drunk bastard."

"Mama," I cried. "You've never called him that before. Did—"

"Ha, you don't think I know what goes on? Maybe I'm stuck in this looney bin, but I'm no dumbbell, no ma'am." She snorted, scratched the outside of her nose, and regarded me closely.

"How did you get here? Why do you want to bother with me? Poor Betty. Poor Betty," Mama crooned. "Little Betty Nettie Gettie —" She laughed. "Okay, okay, you know what? The food here is terrible."

Determined to try again, I said, "Mama, you know problems like yours can run in families." I mustered all the courage I could. "Like your grandma, Alma, Alma Byrne."

"My grandma? Shoosh, she's been dead for years. Years." She tore a thread of yarn and pulled it off the needle. "This damn thing. She told me the wrong way, that woman did."

"Mama, your grandma Alma was in a hospital like this one in Ireland years ago."

She held her yarn and needles like a baby, rocking back and forth. "In the gloaming, oh my Darling, When the lights are soft and low—"

Mama quit rocking and motioned me closer. "Will you—"

I joined in, singing with her, ".. think of me, and love me As you did once long ago."

She nodded at me, indicating one more time as we sang the mournful words, "Will you think of me, and love me As you did once long ago."

I wiped my eyes, and Mama gave a small sniff. "It always makes me sad to hear that song," I said. "You have a beautiful voice, Mama." She suddenly seemed to change into her younger, normal self.

She perked up. "In the old days when our aunts and cousins would visit from Ireland, we'd sing and dance up a storm. Uncle Dan played his concertina, that's like a small accordion, and he could play any Irish jig or song you wanted." Mama looked toward the window as if a bluebird had sung her name.

I took her hands and freed them from the yarn. "I remember hearing "Danny Boy," and what was the other one?"

"Molly Malone," she said dreamlike. "Molly Malone. In Dublin's fair city, where the girls—"

"Are so pretty," I joined in. "I first set my eyes on sweet Molly Malone." I stumbled along while Mama sang the rest.

Then hands started clapping, just one or two, then several. "Encore, encore," called the skinny guy at the puzzle.

Mama gave a wide grin and looked around at the six or seven patients who applauded us.

"Ah, I sang that to Joey when he was just born and home from the hospital." She paused, looked at the ceiling. "He loved that song, he did. But he's gone now, isn't he?"

Mama seemed to talk to someone known only to her. She had a spark in her I hadn't seen since I was a child.

"Yes, Mama, Joey's gone, but maybe we'll all meet again someday."

She regarded me as if I'd just appeared. "Betty, you have to tell the people here the food is terrible. They're trying to poison me."

I squeezed her hand, knowing my visit was at an end. We would not talk about Joey or my Shadows or hurts or anything important in my world. Mama was somewhere I could not reach, but for a moment, she had surfaced from her world of darkness and through music, was transported to her younger, happier self.

And so I left with no answers of why I became who I was, nor did I penetrate Mama's protective veneer that guarded the gashes on our family tree, and most of all, the anguish named Joey that would never heal.

CHAPTER 45

1958

I never told Maureen I had visited Mama alone that summer. I realized the part of Mama I had once loved and depended upon was forever gone and could not be reclaimed. Did our family genes cause my own black periods, the Shadows surfacing unbidden for no apparent reason? And how had Maureen broken away unscathed, finding her place in the world with ease, equipped to cope with the hardships of life?

That fall the college offered several night classes for continuing education. Phil showed me the schedule, and I immediately noted Early 20th Century American Literature. I was drawn to Willa Cather and Edith Wharton on the course list. Wharton's *Ethan Frome* particularly resonated with me, reflecting poverty similar to my own as a child. "Yes, I'd love to take this class," I said. "What's Hazel Bishop like? She must be new."

"Right, she was hired this summer. Seems personable. Middle-aged lady. I'll tell her you'll be in her class."

"But what if I don't get an 'A?' I'll embarrass you." I was half-serious. I handed Phil a stack of four plates for the kitchen table.

"Hon, it would take more than that to embarrass me. You'll do terrific." He finished setting the table. "Spaghetti smells good. I'll get the boys."

•   •   •

The class proved to be as stimulating as I'd hoped. I especially connected with Cather's *My Antonia* and Lewis's *Main Street*. I also discovered it was all right not to care for Hemingway and Faulkner. Hazel Bishop encouraged group discussion, but I lacked the courage to speak up, even when I had an opinion. Who'd be interested in what I had to say?

After the last class ended, I mustered the nerve to stop at Bishop's desk on the way out. "I really enjoyed the class, Miss Bishop. I've always loved reading, and it was—ah—good to read these books." Jeez, what a dumb thing to say. I could visualize my crimson cheeks.

Miss Bishop smiled. "Thank you, Betty. Like I told Phil, I've enjoyed having you in class. Perhaps there will be another literature class you can take next year."

I mumbled something and slid out the door. At least she didn't comment on my lack of participation in class.

*   *   *

The months carried on with little noticeable change. When spring hinted its arrival, Phil wanted to plant vegetables since we'd had success the previous year. He had created a garden space by the back fence and was itching to begin work. "It's almost time for beets and onions, and in a couple weeks, tomatoes." For a city boy, he enjoyed living off the land, as he said more than once.

I had little interest in the idea and didn't care about planting pansies and snapdragons like I had last spring. "I can't explain it, honey, but I just can't work up any ambition for it. David's old enough to help you."

Besides that, my fingers itched, and tasks like peeling potatoes and carrots exacerbated the problem. The more I scratched and gouged my hands, the redder the skin became. I needed to make a doctor's appointment. I also needed more or different sleeping aids. I couldn't remember the last time I'd seen Dr. Myer, asking him to refill my Nembutal, but I had long run out. Tablets I bought from the drug store, like Sominex, didn't work unless I doubled the dose. Then grogginess would overcome me the next day.

The Shadows emerged, usually in my sleepless early dawn hours. My brain raced, spinning, circular thoughts going nowhere. I couldn't explain where the thoughts originated, like fractured dreams with no discernable meaning.

*   *   *

I saw Dr. Wall on a morning when Stevie attended a kindergarten round-up group. With David in second grade, I could come and go with ease.

Ray Wall was a graduate of Wayne State University School of Medicine in Detroit, according to the black-framed certificate on a wall in his shoebox-sized examining room. A man of ample girth, as Auntie would say, he studied my hands through thick bifocals perched at the end of his bulbous nose. "Looks like psoriasis. Or eczema. How long have you had this?" He peered at me over his glasses.

"About three or four months I think." I couldn't recall when the rash began.

"Did anything cause the flare-up that you can remember?"

I bit my lower lip. "I can't think of anything."

"I'll give you some steroid cream to use. Prednisone has worked well for different types of rashes. And use rubber gloves with lining for washing dishes and other housework. Come back if it doesn't clear up by next week."

"What can cause this?" I took the scribbled prescription he handed me.

"A number of things, like certain soaps or detergents, lotions, fabrics. And stress is another factor. So avoid stress if you can."

Stress meaning what exactly? Sinking downward into a heaviness of grief and fear for no apparent reason?

"I have trouble sleeping. I toss and turn half the night. Then I wake up at 5:00 or so and am wide awake."

After warning me about not drinking coffee or alcohol near bedtime, he said, "You said you took Nembutal for a few years. We'll try Doriden, which might be more effective." He tore another paper off his prescription pad and handed it to me. "Call me if there's no improvement in a couple weeks." He must say that to all his patients.

I thanked him, feeling hopeful for the first time in months.

•   •   •

Time passed, and my eczema improved, but would flare up again, the ugly redness stiffening my fingers until I could barely bend them. Dr. Wall called in a refill for the cream and said if it didn't help in another two weeks, he'd send me to a dermatologist. The new sleeping aids helped me fall asleep, but I'd still wake up before dawn, trying to lie still so I wouldn't wake Phil or the Shadows, my thoughts spinning like a top out of control.

During the days, I managed to wear my mask of normality and tend to ordinary tasks like cooking and laundry. Until the day I couldn't.

CHAPTER 46

I knew I was spiraling downhill the night Maureen called about her new baby. "Guess what, Betty. You won't believe it. It's a girl! We finally have a little girl. She's so beautiful, you must—" and on she went.

"Wow, Maureen. That's swell. Congratulations," I said with forced enthusiasm. Of course, I was glad for my sister. She'd wanted a girl since Tommy, and that's all she'd yammered about for the last six months. But I felt distanced from her and her words. My brain said I was pleased for Maureen, but I didn't feel it. An emptiness clouded my emotions; an unexplainable nothingness.

Maureen blithered on. "Her name is Jennifer Maureen, Jenny for short. She has the same dark hair and blue eyes as the others, especially Jack. Now I can get some pink outfits. I can't wait to go to Goldblatt's and get—they have such cute things, and in the catalogs too."

"Have you told Mama she finally has a granddaughter?" It was still beyond me how Maureen could be so cheerful with four children.

"No, Jenny was just born a few hours ago. I'm high as a kite, I can't sleep. Daddy and Auntie came by earlier. Daddy's about ready to retire. I sure wish you could come down and see your brand-new niece."

"Hmm, maybe I can. I'll order something from Sears and have it shipped to you. It'll be fun to pick out baby girl clothes."

"That'll be keen, but make sure she can grow into it. Don't get something too small just because it's cute. Listen to me babbling on. But I need to go now, Betty. This is costing me money."

We hung up, and I sat on the couch staring at the black telephone. I heard the TV playing in the family room, Phil's voice now and then.

The day had been miserable. The Faculty Wives Club hosted a goodbye luncheon for a woman whose husband took a position in Ann Arbor. I barely knew them, but felt obligated to attend. Of course, the first person I ran into was Bonnie.

"Hi, Betty, how have you been?" Her blond hair was styled in a sleek pageboy. Bright pink lipstick highlighted her white teeth as she fake-grinned.

"Fine, thanks." I knew the question went deeper than the casual formality. "And you?"

She gave a forced chuckle. "I'm fine. Busy with kids, you know what that's like."

We had never resumed our friendship since she'd broken my confidence. Phil thought I should forgive and forget, but I refused to let it go. Maybe pride? Who knows.

We awkwardly looked around as if we both sought a getaway route. "I guess I'll go sign the card," I said. We parted ways and Bonnie joined a small group of women standing around in their white gloves and pastel suits, laughing and gabbing.

Unfortunately, I ended up at the same table as Dorothy Haven, the one person I'd disliked since my first year at the college. The tables were round, making it impossible to avoid her critical eye. The minute I sat down I saw her mouth twist in disapproval. "Hello, Betty. It's wonderful you could come today." Her voice like ice.

"Hello. Why wouldn't I come?" I pasted a smile on my face.

Her lips curved in a wrenched grin. "I know you have small children."

"Yes, and they're in school, so I come and go as I please." I leaned toward the person next to me. I wasn't going to allow Dorothy to get under my skin.

The endless hour of lunch and chatter was torture. I spilled a dab of red jello on the white table cloth and nearly choked on my iced tea. Everyone babbled away with one another except me. The women on either side of me conversed with people on their other side. So there I sat, an island unto myself. I tried mentioning my American literature night class. This single attempt at conversation was met with polite nods and glued-on smiles.

After dessert, my misery transformed into anger as my apparent invisibility continued. I noted Bonnie talking with her friends or whoever they were. The room grew dim, the walls became shadows, blackness approached from all sides. I took a drink of watery tea and breathed in and out several times. I pushed my chair back and mumbled, "Excuse me." I'm not sure anyone heard me or cared to.

By then people were leaving their tables for the restrooms prior to the speaker or whatever the agenda was. The hell with this. I didn't give a damn anymore. I had the urge to run home, pack my bags, drive to Chicago and stay.

I made my way toward the bathrooms and kept walking until I was out the door and into the sunshine. I figured the old crows at my table wouldn't even notice I was gone. I visualized that shrew, Dorothy. "To hell with all of you," I said aloud, and headed for the car.

Funny, but I never told Phil I ditched the luncheon. He may have understood, but I didn't want to worry him. He knew I dreaded social occasions, and his efforts to boost my confidence were in vain.

That night the Shadows descended in full force.

CHAPTER 47

Saturday morning dawned gray and wet, the day I'd planned to grocery shop since I had lacked the energy to go Thursday, my usual time. The boys finished breakfast and had rooted themselves in front of the TV. I took my coffee in the living room and sat immobilized. I sipped and stared at the floor, then the furniture.

Phil ambled in and sat beside me on the sofa. "Whatcha doing?"

"I can't go. I'm sorry. I just can't."

"Go where? The grocery store?" He frowned, facing me.

"Yeah. I'm sorry. I know I said—"

"It's all right. I'll take the boys. We'll go." He grimaced. "The list on the counter?"

I moaned. "No list. I just can't. I don't know why. I can't do it." I set the mug on the end table.

"Are you tired? What is it now, Betty?" I heard his irritation.

"Excuse me for being a nuisance, but I'm exhausted. I'll go lay down. Get out of your hair."

Phil sighed deeply. "I just don't know what to do for you. Is it drugs again?"

"I don't think so. Just the new sleeping ones." I smoothed my robe over my knees.

"Go back to bed for a while." Phil bent down and patted my shoulder. "I'll make a list, and we'll see you later."

I felt awful. Guilty for burdening Phil with jobs I should be doing. Yes, I should do things, but I couldn't. I was incapable of thinking straight enough to write a grocery list. Food? What did we need? Who would fix it?

Phil and the boys left for the store, leaving dishes in the sink and drops of milk on the table. I added my coffee cup to the mess and went off to the bathroom to pop another Doriden before burying myself under the blankets on the unmade bed. Dear God, help me. Holy Mary, Mother of God, pray for us sinners—no, wrong prayer. What was wrong with me? Let me sleep. Let me sleep.

.　　.　　.

"I think we should go to the hospital, hon." Phil's voice. I sat in the living room still in my robe. How long had I been there? Was it supper time?

I must've dressed myself. I don't remember driving toward Edgerton with the boys in the back and reaching the emergency room. Phil told me later I refused to go through the door, saying there were too many scruffy-looking bums sitting in the waiting room, and I didn't want to go in. Did we go home and come back?

.　　.　　.

I sat on an examining table in the emergency room the next morning. I don't recall how I got there. Everything was sterile and white. Walls, curtains, sheets, doctors, nurses, orderlies. "You'll be going upstairs to a room, honey," Phil said and assured me the boys were with Mrs. Kowalski.

After my flash of memory in the white room, my mind was a blank canvas.

CHAPTER 48

A Month Later, Winter, 1959

Phil told me I had shock treatments. Or the preferred name, ECT. I stayed in the hospital in Madison for four days. I remembered none of it.

I'd been declining. I knew that. People noticed. *Are you okay, Betty? You don't seem like yourself. What can I do to help?* Only Phil knew the truth. It was easy to hide for a while. And then it wasn't. I can't say when it happened. A nervous breakdown is not a description that fits. It implies one staggering event, like a dam bursting. No, my episode, as they called it, was degenerative, gradual, subtle, prolonged.

The last night at home I'd sat in the living room chair, wrapped in my long chenille rose-colored bathrobe. I stared into nothingness. A puddle of nothingness. Not even of water like the Wicked Witch of the West. I recall Phil's voice. *We should go to the hospital, honey. We need to go.*

Time eludes me. Past or present? I'm visited by snippets of memory. Torn pictures flash in my mind. It's morning. I'm sitting on a bed in the emergency room of Edgerton Memorial. I'm waiting to be admitted. Phil is standing beside me.

I take his word for everything. After one night, an ambulance (no sirens, thank God) transferred me to Mendota State Hospital in Madison, formerly named Mendota Asylum for the Insane. Shades of Elgin's name changes over the decades.

As far as I know, things fell back into place when I came home. Those days and weeks remain blurry, like an eye chart when the optometrist purposely turns the black letters hazy.

Carole had come to the rescue and taken care of the boys. Later I begged her not to tell Ida or Gus the truth, but I'm sure she did.

I did not return to whatever passes for normal after leaving the hospital. I was told it takes a year or more. Continually amazed that my mind is a blank slate, as if someone told me I had been on a trip to California for a week. No memory of it. I am not certain, nor is my doctor, whether the memory loss was due to the depressive episode or the ECT. Perhaps it's good I don't remember. A nurse told me that, but I'm not sure I agree. She assumed that what happened was so horrible, it's best I don't remember. Thoughts of Elgin and Mama were constant reminders tucked in the corners of my mind.

Carole stayed on for a couple more days until I convinced her I could manage the family and house. "Carole, I can never repay you for everything. It's not right that you're away from your own family."

"Betty, the kids like it when I'm not around. Their dad lets them get by with murder. Besides, families help each other. That's what we do." She patted my arm. "It sounds like you're on the right track with this new doctor."

"Yes, she's really good, very smart of course, but she has a down-to-earth way." I'd told Carole about Dr. Myrna Woods, who was assigned to me when I was admitted to Mendota. She designed a treatment plan that I would follow indefinitely.

My thoughts still jumbled and flitted from one topic to another. I felt guilty for leaving the boys for several days and was aware I hadn't spent the time with them I should have.

Carole told me that Stevie's kindergarten teacher said his behavior had changed. "Betty, I don't want you to feel guilty, but it was after you went to the hospital, he started acting out a little. I guess he didn't listen to directions like he should." Carole rolled her eyes. "It didn't sound serious; I mean he didn't stab a kid or anything."

More guilt struck me. "I'll give him lots of attention now," I said and promised myself to follow through.

After Carole left, I felt better, probably because our family was alone again, and I didn't feel obligated to make conversation.

That evening after putting the boys to bed, Phil and I sat in the living room snuggled on the sofa. "You know I don't remember being in the hospital, and I want to know. I need you to tell me what happened, what doctors I saw, what they said about treatments, you know, everything."

"Okay, but of course, I wasn't in the hospital all the time." He stretched his legs under the coffee table.

"First of all, you'd been shuffling around the house and hardly talking at all. I was surprised you went to that faculty lunch, even though you didn't say much about it. The boys would ask you questions or talk to you, and you'd just mumble something or not talk at all. I kept urging you to call the doctor, but you refused."

Phil said what really scared him was when he found me sitting on the bed, rocking back and forth. I moaned and spoke. *My poor brain, poor brain. It'll be all right. I hope it'll be all right.* When Phil asked what I was doing, I told him my brain needed help and I was trying to soothe it. I kept looking down at my arms in front of me like I was cradling a baby and rocking. Phil nearly panicked. *Jesus, Betty, we gotta get you to the hospital.*

Riding in the car, I apparently kept saying, "my poor brain, my poor poor brain."

A doctor on call in the Edgerton emergency room examined me, and Phil signed admission papers. He told the doc about my history of depression and overdosing on Percodan, even though he hated to admit all that. It felt like violating my privacy, but he knew he needed to be truthful if I was to get well. After I settled in my hospital room, Phil and the boys left.

The next day, a psychiatrist and another doctor had met with me. Meanwhile, Phil took the boys to Mrs. Kowalski's house and called Carole. She drove here the next day to rescue us once more.

When Phil arrived at Edgerton around noon, the doctor wanted to transfer me to Mendota State Hospital in Madison, a hospital built in the 1800s, which like Elgin's hospital, had evolved over the decades and no longer had 'asylum' affixed to its name. It was reconstructed in the last few years, with its red brick square buildings set on hilly green land dotted with cedar and pine trees.

I rode in an ambulance, went through the intake process, and was assigned to a room with a roommate. Phil said I objected to that, but there were no private accommodations available. A privacy curtain hung between the beds. I had it drawn at all times even though my roommate was a pleasant middle-aged pudgy woman. I apparently didn't mind her company when forced to see her.

Phil went on that a male psychiatrist, whose name he forgot, sat with us and strongly recommended electroconvulsive therapy, or ECT; in other words, 'shock' treatments. He said many patients had success with them, and he was sympathetic when I had objected, saying the treatments had made my mother worse. Phil recalled the gist of the doctor's reassuring words: *I understand your reaction, Betty, but let me assure you, ECT has improved since the thirties and forties. Now patients receive a muscle relaxant and light anesthesia which prevent the intense seizures that prevailed back then.*

So, I received ECT on alternate days, along with an initial sleeping aide. Of course, I remembered nothing. I don't even recall meeting my new psychiatrist, Myrna Woods, who met me the second day. I vaguely remember driving to her office with Phil a week after my discharge, where we arranged a schedule of further treatment and maintenance, as she called it.

It was an hour's drive to her office in a clinic on the outskirts of Madison. She spent two or three days at Mendota Hospital and the remaining time at the outpatient facility. I was to continue ECT as an outpatient at the hospital twice a month, then taper down to once a month and then discontinue altogether.

Phil rearranged his class schedule so he could drive me to my morning ECT's, which I gradually remembered as time passed. I actually found them quite pleasant. A far cry from Mama's experience. I adapted to the simple routine with ease. After a nurse took my vitals, I donned a green cotton gown, and she escorted me into a small surgery room where I lay on a bed surrounded by an IV machine and other medical equipment unknown to me. A male doctor explained the type of anesthesia, and someone started an IV on my hand. A nurse stuck small rubber circles on my forehead and around my neck.

I rather liked being fussed over and nurtured. *Are you warm enough, Mrs. Lundgren? Would you like another blanket?*

Then the door opened, and Dr. Woods strode in dressed in a white lab coat. *Good morning, everyone. Betty, are we ready to start?* Someone put a band around my head with a nasal mask. *Close your mouth, take deep breaths, in, out, in*—the voice so gentle, like a wooly lamb.

Then I was back in the small room, Phil in a chair, handing me my clothes. "The doc said it went very well, Betty. Ready to go home?"

Ten minutes later, we were on the road south toward Milton as if we'd been to a movie or dinner. We had told no one except Carole the truth about why I was in the hospital. I didn't want to tell Maureen over the phone, my excuse for not disclosing my problems. "It would be better if I told her in person," I said to Phil. "Maybe I could take the train down for a weekend this fall." I still hadn't seen my new niece, Jenny, who was over a year old now.

Phil agreed. "Yeah, let's arrange that. First, we'll see if the doc approves."

"Why wouldn't she?" I said, irritated.

"I dunno, maybe she wouldn't advise traveling alone."

"For God's sake, Phil, we're not in the Victorian era. Women are capable of going out of town without a man." I didn't like feeling coddled.

"You know I didn't mean that. I'm sure it'll be all right."

I grimaced and stared out the window as we drove toward home. I also needed to dream up something to do this fall to occupy my mind. Maybe a morning class at the college. Another literature course. Anything to keep my brain active. I had few friends to invite for coffee. My one effort at joining a church circle had been a disappointment, similar to the abysmal faculty luncheon when I'd absconded early. You'd think church women would be welcoming and warm, but not the case. They all knew each other, and after several half-hearted introductions, they left me to my own devices. I should have been more outgoing and personable, but I've never been able to force those behaviors.

I needed to discuss my reserved personality with Dr. Woods. Could I ever change?

CHAPTER 49

During the following months, I gradually transitioned off ECT and began seeing Myrna Woods twice a month in her office. She advocated a program of medication and explorative psychotherapy to see what types of approaches were best for each patient. She briefly explained various psychological theories and how the field of psychiatry continued to evolve and improve.

Dr. Woods was the kindest, smartest woman I'd ever met. Perhaps in her sixties, she wore her white blond hair in a short, serious bob, tucked behind one or both ears, framing a pale, narrow face. Her eyes, the color of Wedgewood, suggested a Scandinavian heritage. Several black framed certificates punctuated one paneled wall, and a floor-to-ceiling bookshelf held the requisite manuals, journals, files, and pottery on the opposite side.

A mammoth teak desk sat under a row of windows, and a green and white brocade loveseat and three green armchairs were arranged alongside and facing the desk.

I had told her about the Shadows during my hospitalization, and we continued to speak of them at each meeting. Thankfully, they gradually diminished, perhaps a harbinger of my recovery.

When I was an inpatient in Mendota, Dr. Woods prescribed a new pill called Marplan. *This just came out, Betty, and it's the first MAOI, or isocarboxazid, used as an antidepressant, and not entirely as a tranquilizer. It's an inhibitor that—* I got lost in the scientific explanation, but was encouraged to hear, *it's often been successful with patients when other treatments failed.*

. On my second visit, this time without Phil, I chose the loveseat which became my permanent fixture for years to come.

"How is the Marplan working for you, Betty?" Dr. Woods sat in a nearby chair and smoothed her black skirt over her knees.

"Good. I'm sleeping better since you changed the dosage." I leaned back. "I'd like to visit my sister in Chicago. She had a baby a year ago, and I haven't seen her yet."

Dr. Woods agreed. "I think that sounds good. Would you see your mother?"

I'd told the doctor that Mama was in Elgin Hospital, that Joey had died at age eleven, and I'd been sent away. I had avoided talking further about it, but I knew I'd needed to. The Shadows still appeared.

"I'd probably visit her if Maureen could come too. I'm not sure how I really feel about Mama."

"How do you mean?" Dr. Woods tilted her head.

"I know most people love their mothers, like my boys love me, but I don't— I can't make those feelings materialize. For one thing, I still wonder why she— why she—"

"Sent you away? Abandoned you?"

I cleared my throat. "Ah, yes, even though I'm not a kid anymore. I know she was, is mentally unfit. And I don't think she'll ever get better."

"Maybe not," said Dr. Woods softly. "We need to decide what's best for you. Would it help you in any way to visit her? Or not visit her? Your mother clearly suffered from episodes of major depression before proper treatment was available. What kind of connection would you like with your mother?"

"I'd like a normal, loving feeling with her, a mother to visit with my boys, who will like, or love us." A lump formed in my throat.

We sat silently for a minute. "I just don't see how Maureen can be so lackadaisical and unaffected by Mama. She just goes on happy with her life."

"Think about this, Betty. Maureen wasn't sent away."

I felt a stab. "No, she was older. Could fend for herself."

"You know, Betty, it's all right to be angry with your mother. Even though you rationalize it and say she was mentally ill, and she couldn't help herself."

"That's true, isn't it? People kept saying it wasn't my fault. I didn't do anything bad."

"Yes, it's true. But to a little girl, it's impossible to fully understand that she's not to blame."

Damn, I felt the tears already welling in my eyes. Don't cry.

"Betty, even adults like us have trouble with that concept. Our emotions don't catch up with our intellect. We say we understand, but we don't feel it."

"My aunt always thought my mother should have been stronger, that she should have pulled herself up by the bootstraps." I sniffed and took a Kleenex from the coffee table.

"Some folks don't have bootstraps to pull, Betty. They lack that part of their mind or character. I don't know your mother, and even if I did, I couldn't pass judgement."

I thought about Dr. Woods's words. Maybe Mama didn't have straps on her boots like Auntie did. Auntie went on living after her girl died even though a part of her heart would always embrace Nellie. I didn't have the energy to talk any more. I still felt guilty that I'd never told Mama I overheard Dennis planning the railroad escapade that cost Joey his life.

Dr. Woods most likely could see I was wearing down. "I think that'll do for today. I'd like you to consider the trip to Chicago and make plans. Also, think about the little girl you once were trying to understand an unfair, adult world." She took my hand.

I stood by her desk as she jotted down my next appointment. "If your trip plans overlap our schedule, just call."

We said our goodbyes, and I strode out of the building into the fresh autumn air. Colored leaves crunched under my feet, and birdsong echoed in the breeze as I headed for my car, a slight bounce in my steps.

•   •   •

Coincidentally, the call came that evening. Maureen's voice soft and raspy. "Betty, it's Dennis. He—he—"

My heart stopped. Then pounded. "Is he okay?"

"Yes, he will be, but the dumb ass overdosed on Unisom and booze. He spent the night in Mercy Hospital. How could he do that?" Maureen choked on her words.

"Jesus, Mary, and Joseph," a phrase I hadn't uttered in years. My thoughts raced. "What happened? Who found him?" Phil came beside me in the living room. He mouthed the words, 'what is it?'

I held up my hand, requesting his patience. Maureen coughed. "His AA sponsor, a guy named Al found him passed out on the living room floor. It's lucky he went over last night, otherwise—"

"You mean this happened last night and you're just now calling me?" Anger gushed through my veins. One more time kept in the dark.

"Don't start on me, Betty. It's been a hell of a day, going to the hospital, having John and friends stay with the kids and—"

"All right, sorry. Tell me more." I listened as Maureen explained that Dennis hadn't answered Al's calls; he'd been worried when Dennis missed two meetings in a row. So Al went to the apartment. The door was locked, so he got the super to open it. They took one look at Dennis on the floor and called the police. An ambulance rushed him to Mercy where they pumped his stomach and kept him overnight. Al had called Maureen, and she'd taken him back to his apartment around noon the next day.

"Why did he do it? What did he say?" I thought of Mama's same experience.

"He just said he didn't want to go on. No reason to live. No happiness in life. He's had girlfriends since Sue left him, but they end up leaving him too."

The sweat on my palm caused the receiver to slip. I realized I'd been clutching it for dear life. "Maureen, I need to get down there. I'm gonna talk to him whether he wants me to or not." I was heartbroken and terrified at the same time. "In fact, I was planning to come down and see Jenny. I was ready to talk to Phil about it, and my new doctor said it would be good for me."

Maureen agreed and said I could stay with Daddy or her; she'd make room in her crowded house.

"Hell, I forgot about Daddy. How did he take the news?"

Maureen sighed. "I visited him after I took Dennis home. He's cut down his hours these days, so he was home. He was upset about Dennis, of course, but really angry. He kept swearing, saying stuff like how could Dennis do something so damn stupid and what more can a father take, he already lost one boy and now another, and he rambled on."

"Maureen. I'm so sorry you're going through all this alone. I should be there. You must be exhausted. Does Auntie know?"

"No, I don't have the energy to call her. I just can't do anymore right now." I heard the sobs coming. I realized Maureen wasn't as tough as I'd unfairly expected.

"All right, listen. I'll plan to come down as soon as I can. You try to relax. I know that's dumb to say, but try not to worry. We'll be together soon." My comforting Maureen was a switch. She'd always been the strong one.

After we hung up, I collapsed in Phil's arms. He got the gist of the conversation and was his usual understanding self. "I'm so sorry, hon. You take the trip and together you and Maureen will get through this." Phil had only met Dennis one time and could only speculate about his struggles.

The boys had been glued to the TV, so they were unaware I was upset. Phil went in the family room. "Almost bedtime, guys."

"Awww, Dad." The usual chorus of moans and groans.

After our good nights, Phil and I planned my trip to Chicago by train on Saturday, day after next. I arranged for the boys' care so I could stay several days.

I was shaken by Dennis's actions and couldn't accept the reality of what he'd done. I admitted that sadly, I knew only too well, the feeling of not wanting to go on living. In my dark times with the Shadows, there was no light at the end.

Someone like Phil couldn't understand what the darkness feels like nor why anyone would want to end their life. I never could explain. The Hour of Lead.

CHAPTER 50

Maureen met me at the train station in Chicago on Saturday morning, and by noon, I sat at Maureen's kitchen table, holding my niece, Jenny, on my lap. What a lovely child, with her dark wavy hair and sapphire eyes like her father's. At seventeen months, she toddled about, chattering nonsensical words. "Can you say, Aunt Betty?" I rubbed my nose with hers.

"Abbaa," was her reply. I hugged her pudgy little body dressed in a pink shirt and lacy overalls.

Maureen busied herself putting baloney sandwiches on the table for the three boys. "Then you and I can eat in peace when they're done." They'd grown in the past year, especially Tommy, who at age twelve stood tall and sturdy.

John joined us at the table. "You gonna babysit this crew tonight, Betty?"

"Sure thing." I knew he was kidding. He'd put on a little weight over time, but looked fit and muscular. Several years ago he had enrolled in Bridgeport's police academy and was now an officer.

"I always loved a man in uniform," Maureen had said more than once.

After scarfing down their lunch, John and the boys left for baseball practice, and Jenny busied herself around the kitchen with every mother's go-to kitchen toys, Tupperware containers.

Maureen broiled tuna melts in the oven and served them with an orange jello salad. "I need wine, how 'bout you?"

"You bet." She poured us each a glass of Chablis.

"Andy's almost the age Joey was when—" I took a sip of wine.

"I know. Of the boys, he reminds me most of Joey." She spooned salad onto my plate, then hers.

"Has Dennis ever had therapy or seen anyone for his problems?" I said.

"Yeah, in rehab there were counselors and at AA there's Al. But a real psychiatrist like you've had, not that I know of." She sipped her wine. "I'm glad you got the right help, Betty. This last hospital stay really did the trick, right?"

"So far. It's a matter of maintaining now, and Myrna Woods is really good and so intelligent. I'm taking a new antidepressant that's helping."

Maureen exhaled. "Too bad Mama didn't have that kind of help, like the improved shock treatments."

I cringed at the term since everyone at the hospital called them ECT. "That's right. I hope to see Mama sometime if you can get away."

"I don't think so, Betty. I'm up to my neck with all this. I guess you could take a bus there."

Disappointed, I said, "I'll see how things go."

"No no. Not in that cupboard. Come on." Maureen swooped Jenny off the floor and into her high chair. "Here's a cracker."

Maureen winked at me. "It'll shush her up for two minutes."

"When did you say we could see Dennis?" I took a bite of sandwich.

"Tonight or tomorrow." She paused. "After John and the boys get home, I can put Jenny down for a nap, and then we can go see Daddy."

"Okay." My suitcase was still in Maureen's car, and I'd stay at Daddy's in my old bedroom. I didn't want to impose on my sister's family, which I thought would be awkward since there was no extra guest room. Daddy would be gone some of the time.

Maureen said we'd call Dennis later and arrange a time to stop in. I hadn't seen him for several years and was anxious for us to talk; have an honest conversation. I'd never been close to him growing up since he was six years older and viewed me as the annoying little sister.

Later, Maureen drove us to our old house, passing Uncle's store. Like much of the neighborhood, the store had undergone changes. I hardly recognized the new red brick façade in place of the worn white clapboard siding. "The yards change every time I come," I said, gazing out the window. "Fewer vacant lots, more trees."

"Yeah, guess it always looks the same to me since I'm here seeing Daddy a few times a month."

"There's still a tinge of the old perfume in the neighborhood." I yanked the window down a couple inches. "I want to go to the cemetery too. Sounds crazy, but I don't want Joey to feel forgotten."

"Sure, we'll go. I know what you mean, I try to visit on his birthday and in December. He'd be almost thirty-three now." Maureen parked in front of the house.

"Hard to fathom." I tried to imagine what Joey would look like. Twenty-one years since the Accident.

I followed Maureen to the front stoop, my suitcase in hand. Chipped yellow paint surrounded the windows, and several shingles hung loose from the roof. "I'll get John to come over and fix stuff before winter." Maureen knocked on the door, then opened it. "Anybody home?"

"Just us chickens." Daddy came to the door. "Here's the bluebird, come home at last." He gave me a bear hug.

Seeing him, I felt my throat tighten. I took in the intricate spider webbing on his cheeks and pouches drooping mournfully under faded eyes. He'd turn sixty in a couple months, but looked seventy. The stockyards took their toll.

"Sit down. Just made a fresh pot. Or how 'bout a beer?" Familiar tobacco aroma permeated the room.

"I'll put my suitcase away, and then I'll have coffee," I said.

"Coffee for me. Betty and I had wine with lunch." Maureen went to the kitchen to help serve.

We settled in the living room, chatting about the weather, Maureen's kids. I grinned at Daddy. "How do you like your first granddaughter? She's a beauty."

"Yeah, lucky she got the O'Leary looks. When are you gonna have a girl, Missy?"

I gave a short laugh. "No more for us, Daddy. Two boys is all I can cope with." It hit me what I'd just said. "I mean, you know, I don't—"

"It's all right, bluebird. Life's tough sometimes." He took a swig of Old Style from the can. "I'm gonna retire one of these days. Then I can move in with your sister."

Maureen feigned a gasp. "That'd be the death of me."

Daddy laughed. "Don't know what I'll do, maybe take up whittling like other old codgers."

"You can go to the library. Get a card, check out books. Sit there and read newspapers from all over the world." I sipped my coffee, strong and satisfying. "Mmm, good coffee, Daddy."

He shrugged. "Can't see me sittin' in a library. What would my mates at the corner think?"

We went on bantering, warily avoiding the subjects of Mama, Joey and Dennis.

An hour or so later, Maureen and I left for her house. I insisted on treating the family to dinner at David's on Halsted and 31st in Bridgeport. The place teemed with customers, but we didn't mind waiting while Tommy played "Mack the Knife" on the jukebox.

That evening, Maureen called Dennis to see about a visit. When she hung up, she said, "He claims he's really tired tonight and wants to wait till tomorrow. Maybe afternoon."

I was hoping for earlier, but what could I say. "Sure. I might go to Mass even if Daddy doesn't. I'll see."

I knew Maureen's family would attend Mass and Sunday School, so I was relieved to stay out of the way.

. . .

The next afternoon, a slight knot formed in my stomach as Maureen and I drove toward Dennis's apartment in Archer Heights. "Does he still look the same as—as I don't know when?"

"Of course, you'll know your own brother. He's probably thinner, but otherwise the same."

I straightened the collar on my lightweight jacket. Another fresh, sunny day, with reds and yellows splattered on trees. Puffy clouds shaped like bears and gourds hovered against a cobalt sky. We rode along I-55 southwest, then south on Pulaski Road past strip centers, and after more turns, Maureen slowed, parked in front of two brick apartment buildings. "It's the one with the green awning," she said as she opened her door.

The place looked decent enough, with a narrow yard and trees in front. I could feel my heart hammering as we entered the building. A grid of mailboxes covered one side of the vestibule, labeled in alphabetical order. "He's on the third floor," said Maureen. "No elevators."

We trudged up the stairs, stopping mid-way to take off our jackets. We each had on cardigan sweaters over cotton blouses. I wore corduroy slacks, Maureen, plaid flannel-lined jeans rolled above her ankle.

My forehead was damp by the time we reached Dennis's door on the third floor. Maureen held the foil-wrapped peanut butter cookies she'd brought. She knocked several times.

I heard shuffling, and the door opened. Dennis's light brown hair and blue eyes, the same as always. "There's the pipsqueak. Come on in." His voice thick. He guided me inside, his hand on my arm. We faced each other, awkward for a second, then hugged.

"Good to see you, Dennis." I choked out the words. A trace of roast meat wavered in the room.

"Cook us dinner? Smells good." Maureen put her jacket on an easy chair.

"Too late. Just devoured Swanson's special Swiss steak dinner." He took the wrapped cookies Maureen offered. "Looks like dessert. Thanks." He put them on the coffee table.

I looked around as we settled in the small living room. Dennis sat on a gold fabric couch, and I joined him at the other end. Maureen flopped into an overstuffed brown armchair.

Dennis wore a plaid flannel shirt and baggy jeans. The same hollow expression of Mama's showed on his face, yet he was handsome in a gaunt, Gary Cooper way.

"Hey, you look good, pipsqueak. Sorry to call you that. We're not kids anymore, Betty."

"It's all right, I don't mind." I smoothed my short page boy off my face.

"You got pictures of your kids? I've seen enough of Reeny's brats already."

"Very funny," Maureen said.

He looked at the boys' photos, and we made small talk for a while. Maureen rose. "Do you have any water?"

"May surprise you, but I do." Dennis picked up the cookies. "Betty, you want water or pop? I got Coke."

"Coke, thanks." He followed Maureen into the kitchen.

A plethora of unspoken words hung overhead. I was determined to muster the courage to tackle the forbidden subject of Dennis's troubles.

Chapter 51

Maureen and Dennis, drinks in hand, set them on the blond veneer coffee table, using folded napkins as coasters. I took a glass of Coke and sipped.

"You know—"

"Well—"

Speaking at once, Dennis and I chuckled. "Go ahead, Dennis," I said.

He took a drink of his Coke. "You know, we've been sitting here, all polite, and it's just bullshit. I know you wanna know what happened."

I started to protest, but hushed. Dennis continued. "My sponsor, Al, and others in AA say you should have honest conversations with your family and good friends. People important in your life. Reeny, you know about AA. Betty, don't know if you know much about it. But I want to come out with it. You just gotta be patient and listen."

"Of course, Den, we wanna help all we can," Maureen said.

"You probably know AA is a twelve-step program, and long story short, after rehab two - three years ago, I was supposed to join AA if I wanted my job back and shit like that. Sorry, Betty."

"Dennis, I've heard that before." I wanted him to keep talking.

"I met Al, who's been a lifesaver. I've skipped around and stumbled more than once, but now I'm doing step nine, which is making amends to those you harmed due to your drinking. Reeny, I know I've caused you a lot of grief and worry, and Betty too, even though I haven't seen you, I know you've heard about the shit I've done. So I want to say that I am sorry for causing you to worry and the hurt you've had 'cause of me."

"Den," Maureen sniffed, wiping her eyes. She sat beside us on the couch; together we gave Dennis an awkward hug.

I brushed at my eyes. "I'm sorry too, Dennis. You know we love you."

I was surprised at my words, and he seemed to be as well. "I know. I know," he whispered.

Suddenly, I saw that young boy at the railroad tracks who witnessed the death of his younger brother, forever blaming himself and never receiving the help he so desperately needed.

What had we done to this once-healthy, normal boy? I felt a surge of anger toward both Mama and Daddy for being ignorant to the ways of being human, to placing needless, false blame on a boy too young to be an adult.

"I'm thankful for Al," I said. "He's helped you a lot. But have you ever, ah, ever seen a doctor, a psychiatrist who might give you some medications to help, just for awhile?"

Dennis's mouth twitched. "Haven't seen a real head shrinker. They cost a lot. Don't know if my benefits would cover it. Besides, I can tell Al anything."

Then I poked the hornet's nest. "Dennis, have you talked about Joey? Not that I know everything, but I've learned from my doctor that when people cover up their pain, it comes out in other ways, like—like—"

"Drinking? Suicide attempts? Might as well say it." Dennis's heel tapped on the floor. His jaw clenched.

"Gee, I don't want to make you mad—you know from Maureen that I was in a mental hospital a couple months ago and—"

"Shit, Betty, I didn't know that." Dennis eyed Maureen. "You never told me—"

"Now, don't blame me. I didn't want to add to your problems. I thought you'd worry about Betty and—"

"See," I said. "There've been too many family secrets, people afraid to say Joey's name, but doctors have come a long way in knowing stuff like this. I'm just in the process of spilling my whole insides to my doctor, including Joey and Mama and being kicked out of my family—"

I stumbled on my words. We sat speechless for a few moments. Dennis reached over and held my arm. "Christ, Betty, I had no idea—no idea you still held onto all that." He paused. "Reeny, guess you came out the best of all of us."

She shrugged. "Who knows. My life isn't perfect, but yeah, Betty was always so shy, and I just, I dunno, got over stuff faster."

I took a sip of my drink. "You were the pretty one, had such confidence, outgoing and liked yourself. That's what my doc is trying to instill in me. To think of myself as a worthy, good person." I moved closer to Dennis on the sofa.

"But you had such a burden. Blaming yourself and Daddy too for the Accident. But there's still a part of me that thinks I could've saved Joey if I'd tattled to Mama after I overhead you planning to get the coal. So we can all blame ourselves, but in the end, it was an accident."

Maureen cleared her throat. "Yeah, I know Daddy blames himself and Mama blamed him and you, Dennis, I hate to say."

"Yeah, I know. One of these times I'm gonna go to Elgin and see her, even though she'll have a fit. I know she's out of it, but she's gonna hear what I have to say." He paused and jiggled his foot. "You know, I started having nightmares about that night at the tracks—Joey floating around above the coal car, then he's on the ground. But I didn't see—I thought he was right behind us—then that green scarf, I still see it on his jacket." Dennis took deep breaths.

I frowned at Maureen to keep quiet. It was good for Dennis to relive details, painful as they were. Dr. Woods told me in order to heal, you need to go through the pain, not around it.

"What else do you remember?" My voice soft.

"Ah, ah I heard shouting, Billy and the others, yelling, then a brakeman came running, more shouting, a couple bulls came and bent over Jo—Joey, I kinda went in another zone, then the sirens, oh God, the damn shrieking sirens." Dennis's breaths heaved. "Dennis, someone shouting my name, a man's voice, he's in shock. Yeah, I was in shock all right. Didn't sink in for days what'd happened. Then the guilt, oh Jesus, the guilt. Father John tried to tell me that God wanted Joey, that Joey was taken home to heaven and that bullsh— I think that was the moment I knew deep down there was no God. Like Ma, she quit the Church for good after that. I bet Pa did too, but still went to Mass for show."

"Do you still feel guilty, Den?" Maureen said.

"Not as much, but yeah, I think I always will. I should've kept a better eye on him."

"No, Dennis," I said, "it was Mama and Daddy's job to keep him safe. He never should've gone, but neither should any of you. It was the times. We were poor, needed coal. Other kids did the same thing." I was wearing down, exhausted.

Dennis sniffed, stifled a sob. My heart broke for him. I wished I could make his pain go away. "I know you don't want to, but I have to ask you about the night you—"

"Tried to end it all?"

"Betty, if he doesn't want to—"

"Reeny, I can stand up for myself. No, I don't wanna talk about it, but damn, I hate to admit it, but Betty's right. I need to face it. In a way I'm better already just for talking about our brother." Dennis drained his glass and held it out. "Get me more, will ya?"

Maureen scoffed and took the glass. "I should tell you to go to h—, get it yourself, but I'll wait on you this one time." She smirked and headed for the kitchen.

"Always could boss her around," Dennis said, intentionally loud enough for Maureen to hear.

Maureen returned with another glass of pop and handed it to him. "You're welcome."

"Thanks, kid." He took a gulp. "Okay, here's the story. I'd gone off the wagon a day or two before that night. Called in sick, but could tell the boss didn't believe me, I didn't give damn, stayed home. Got hammered. I just wanted to end it. End the pain of living. My girlfriend had left the week or month before, hell, I dunno. I wasn't sleeping, and when I did, the nightmares came."

We sat quietly for a minute. Dennis coughed, brushed his hair back. "I couldn't think straight, ah, no kidding. I'd switched from beer to whisky. I remember the pills in the bathroom, my sleeping pills, and gulping them down with booze. I couldn't see an end, like I'd never get rid of the pain." He leaned forward, covering his cheeks with his bear-size hands. "Next thing I knew I was in the hospital—I'll spare you the details. Al was there. I'd missed a meeting and he came here, banging on the door he says. Super and he came in, called the cops and you know the rest."

"Oh Den," Maureen sniffled, "it scared the hell out of us. Daddy was so upset."

"Can we have a contract?" I said. "We want to make sure it won't happen again. If you ever feel that way in the future, you must call one of us."

"Yeah, I actually signed something like that with Al. So I'll promise right here and now, I'll call if I wanna do that again."

"Thanks, and I know Maureen feels like I do, relieved that we won't live with that fear anymore."

"Whew," Dennis said. "I never thought I'd spill my guts like that. Gotta say, it's a load off."

"I really am relieved," I said. "And amazed at how much good all this has done."

"That's for sure." Maureen shifted in her chair. "You gonna be all right, Den?" She checked her watch.

"Yeah, you can take a powder now, Reeny. I got a meeting after a while."

We said our goodbyes with hugs and promises and headed out the door. I felt drained and knew I would visit Mama another time.

For the first time in my life, I felt a profound connection with my sister and brother. The three of us bound together by a decades-old tragedy, leaving a legacy of untold sorrow and guilt, all but destroying our family. Dennis and I were on our way to healing ourselves by keeping Joey in our hearts and speaking of him without hesitation. It may take a long time, but with each other by our side, I knew we'd carry on and not only survive, but flourish.

CHAPTER 52

1960

The months streamed by with no recurrence of the Shadows. I managed to live a comfortable rhythm of ebb and flow, gentle swings of serenity interrupted by bouts of unshakable gloom. I knew if my low times lasted more than a few days, I'd call Dr. Woods, but fortunately, I felt better after a day or two.

I continued easing off ECT, and by summer, I was down to once every six weeks. My only medication was Marplan, continuing to be effective. My eczema had disappeared, so my life was in good order.

Curious why ECT helped me recover, or at least manage depression, I worried about what the treatments actually did to the brain. One day I asked Dr. Woods. "I'm no scientist, so I'm sure it's beyond me, but what happens during treatment?"

She straightened her glasses. "Even scientists can't explain for sure how the seizures affect the brain. When ECT induces seizures, it seems to restart the electrical circuits and chemical balances in the brain that affect mood. The downside is that improvements like yours might need maintenance for months or perhaps years. We don't know, and it most likely depends on each patient." Dr. Woods crossed her ankles. "You may not need more ECT by next year, but major depression like yours will require regular check-ups."

I paused. "All sounds reasonable. I think the only thing still in my craw, as my aunt would say, is my mother. I want to try and reach her before she—she—"

"Dies," Dr. Woods finished. "It's all right to say it, Betty. You opened up with your brother, which helped both of you, and your sister as well. Do you have plans to visit your mother in the next few months?"

"I'd like to go in a week or two. Phil's taking the boys to Duluth for a few days to see his folks, so it's a good time for me to go." I felt slightly guilty about not visiting Phil's family, but he'd assured me I needed to visit Mama and my family.

"Just remember not to set your expectations too high for your mother. She may never be able to make peace or resolution with you for not giving you what you needed as a child. You must let it go at some point and live your life with parts missing, which is okay."

I left Dr. Woods's office feeling uplifted and encouraged about trying to make peace with my troubled mother.

$$\bullet \quad \bullet \quad \bullet$$

A week later, I leaned against the window of the train rolling south to Chicago, its steady zoosh sound and hypnotic clack of wheels over tracks soothing me as I shifted from wife and mother back to childhood. I loved the nostalgic rhythms and hushed whirr of the engine as my thoughts returned to my Back of the Yards, my early days of sunshine and reminiscence. *Gonna take a sentimental journey, gonna set my heart at ease.* I sang to myself, the words gently traveling through my mind as the train swayed back and forth. I thought of those halcyon days of innocence until Joey, when everything changed.

Men's voices behind me jarred my trance. "Nixon's sure to win. We gotta stay outta that Viet Nam business."

"I'm not so sure. Kennedy's leading in some—" the words faded off.

I'd heard Ida and Gus say that a Catholic would never be elected President, but time would tell.

I opened my copy of *Night* by Elie Wiesel, which had recently been published in the US. Phil bought the book for me, knowing it would open my eyes to the hard truth about the war. It was a short book, but I read it slowly, shocked at the author's horrific experiences. I was curious what Maureen's husband, John, had witnessed.

Before I knew it, the train screeched to a stop at the bustling Union Station. I tugged my suitcase from the overhead rack and wound my way through people of all ages and color, ending up in the vast depot and out the doors, trying to spot Maureen. I hung around the front for a few minutes and then caught sight of her coming toward me. "Hi, Betty." She gave me a hug. "I'm down the way, come on." Maureen looked the same, dressed in a white blouse and tan slacks.

We settled in her car, and she pulled out of the lot onto Canal Street. "How's Daddy?" I said.

"He's better. He got over the bronchitis, but he needs to retire." We continued driving toward Congress, then onto 90 going south. She told me about hers and Dennis's visit with Mama several weeks ago. "I think Dennis felt better in the long run, even though Mama didn't or couldn't have an honest conversation about Joey."

I adjusted my denim skirt over my knees. "I hope Dennis believes that Mama deep down doesn't blame him, but her illness just overcomes her and she can't think straight."

Maureen beeped the horn at a truck that nearly sideswiped us. "Dumb ass," she yelled. Nothing shy about her. "I think Dennis is finally letting himself off the hook for Joey. He was obeying Daddy's orders, and he was just a kid himself."

"Hard to think it's been over twenty years since that happened. Imagine, in one or two seconds, our whole lives changed, and years later we're still paying for it. Not you so much."

"Yeah, I was lucky, the grief didn't hit me like you. Of course, I was sad for a long time, and my life isn't perfect, you know." She had said that before.

I spotted familiar churches and buildings as we bypassed Greektown, then Little Italy. "Can I ask how your life isn't perfect?"

Maureen sighed. "Betty, no one's life is. You know, I wanted a large family, but it wears you out. And John—he has a temper sometimes. When he drinks, especially."

I grimaced. "I know he likes his beer, but I didn't know it was a problem. I'm sorry that someone else in the family has—" I let the thought trail off.

"He claims he's not like Dennis. He doesn't need AA, that he can control it. And most of the time, things are fine."

I didn't want to sound like a doctor, so I said nothing, but I was worried about John. However, admittedly, I felt some comfort that Maureen's life wasn't perfect. "You know, he might have seen unspeakable things in the war—a lot of soldiers have shell shock and they—"

"I know." Maureen sounded impatient. "He won't talk about it. I heard from his uncle that John's unit liberated one of the camps, Dachau, and how horrible it was. But John has it locked up, he has nightmares sometimes, and has mumbled some German words. Of course, I don't understand them."

We neared the turnoff onto I-55 and then Ashland. I rolled my window down halfway. "Hey, my hair's blowing all over." Maureen's right hand flew to her head.

I laughed. "I need to inhale the old childhood sniff of the yards. I miss it."

"You are nuts for sure, no offense. Guess I'm numb to it."

"Ah, the aroma of animals and manure, nothing like it." It was true. Offensive to many, the distinctive odor evoked in me a nostalgia and gentle yearning.

We pulled up in front of my old house, always the same, but different. A note from Daddy was on the kitchen table saying he would be back later.

"He's at the corner, I'm sure," said Maureen. She took the empty coffee pot from the stove. "Want some?"

"Sure. I'll put my suitcase away."

After unpacking a few items and freshening up, a whiff of coffee lingered in the air as I returned to the kitchen. Maureen had straightened up the counters and rinsed some plates and cups.

"Daddy never keeps the place clean." Maureen wiped the counter with a damp cloth. "I stop in every couple weeks and tidy up."

We sat at the table, visiting and drinking coffee out of plain green mugs. We decided to have dinner at Maureen's, and then tomorrow she would take me to see Mama.

Maureen filled our cups. "Remember I said last week that the doctor reported that Mama was showing signs of hardening of the arteries or becoming senile?"

I hadn't thought of it since. How could the doctor tell? "Mama's conversations rarely made much sense."

"I just want to warn you that she might sound even more nutty than ever. Last time I saw her, she thought she was back on the farm where she grew up. I think she thought I was her mother, 'cause she called me 'Ma' a couple times." Maureen paused. "Daddy said she has good and bad days, and he saw her once when she was normal as apple pie, and he wished he could've brought her home."

"Let's hope she's having a good day tomorrow. I really want to talk about things that were taboo, like Joey's death and shipping me off."

Maureen made a clucking sound. "Betty, it wasn't like that. You were too young for her to cope, ah, take care of."

"Yeah, so I heard all my life. I just want to say things to her, and then I'll let the situation rest."

That had been my plan for months. Tomorrow would be my day of reckoning.

CHAPTER 53

A warm, dandelion summer day awaited me as I woke up the next morning. I convinced myself it was a good omen for my trip to Elgin. Daddy stood over the toaster when I traipsed into the kitchen wearing my cotton duster.

"Top o' the mornin' to ye, lil' bluebird." His Irish brogue heavy.

"Someone's in a good mood." I poured myself a cup of coffee and sat at the table.

"Aye, indeed. Toast? Cereal? Don't do eggs." He buttered his toast and slathered a healthy portion of strawberry jam on top.

"I'll get toast," I said. Daddy looked gaunt from his recent illness, but some color had replaced his skin's grayish tinge from a few months ago. I dropped a slice of bread in the toaster; when it was done, I joined Daddy and buttered and spread jam on the crisp brown bread.

We conversed about Maureen's family and other general topics like his job. He'd complained for years about the decline of the meatpacking industry leading to layoffs. "I'll be retiring at the right time, before they close down and kick me out." He took a bite of toast, chewed slowly. "I wanted to say that I'm—ah sorry about your troubles, um, your—"

"It's all right, Daddy. I know Maureen told you about the hospital. The important thing is that I'm, um, not exactly back to normal, but much better." I sipped my coffee. "It's a shame Mama didn't get the treatment I got, but it wasn't available then."

Daddy shrugged, cleared his throat. "Yeah, damn shame. Nora, your ma, just fell apart after Joey—hell, we all did. Hit her the worst. Her cousin out East had the same thing, guess it runs in the family."

"There is a biological risk involved, my doctor said. But at least things are better now with me and Dennis too. You know he saw Mama—"

"Yeah, I know." Daddy finished his coffee. "Don't get your hopes up, bluebird. Maybe she'll be all right, but you never know from day to day."

"I know, but I'll hope for the best." I checked the round clock on the wall. "Maureen will be here soon, and I'm not ready. Gotta run."

"Harrumph. Just trying to get out of clean-up," Daddy smirked.

•   •   •

Within two hours, Maureen and I strode up the familiar sidewalk leading to the entrance of Elgin State Hospital's main building. The sky was blue as Mrs. Kowalski's cornflowers, and the sun warmed my body and spirit.

"I'll leave you and Mama alone after a few minutes." Maureen straightened the collar of her madras blouse as we approached the stairs after signing in.

I agreed, noticing the sunshine had not filtered its way into the shadowy hallways. A young blond nurse's aide sat at the main desk at the unit station. Her smile surprised me. "How can I help you?"

After Maureen gave her Mama's name, the girl directed us to the lunchroom. "They're just finishing up now, so you should find her there."

A whisper of pot roast wafted in the hall as we approached the dining area. Pots and pans clanged out of sight, and chairs scraped on the floor as patients and aides rose and made their way toward the exit.

"There she is." Maureen guided me past mostly skeletal people lost inside loose-fitting housedresses or trousers. Mama sat alone at a round table, her head back, drinking the last of her water. She set the glass down and looked up. "There you are. They said you were coming." She scooched backward in her chair.

I put my arms around her shoulder, catching a familiar tang of Pond's cold cream. "Hi, Mama. So good to see you." Her bony hands grasped the table edge as she eased herself up. She gaped at me, faded hazel eyes framed with spidery etched lines.

"Betty, you came." She gave a faint smile. "And with your sassy sister of course."

"Now, Mama, you be nice." Maureen kissed her on the cheek. "Should we go to your room or the lounge?"

Mama shrugged. "My room's so cramped. Guess the so-called lounge."

Turning to me, Maureen said, "The former activity room. Someone decided the lounge sounds better, less like a nursery school." She laughed. "Time to finger paint, Mama."

"Don't get fresh, Missy. I'm still your mama." She clicked her tongue. "Still uppity, your sister is."

We chuckled as we headed down another hallway to the lounge where Mama sauntered toward the large windows overlooking a courtyard and landscaped lawn. She had a pass for outdoor visits, but we'd decided it was too warm to sit outside.

I joined Mama on a small worn couch and Maureen settled on an upholstered chair. "Where did you come from?" Mama frowned at me.

"I took the train from Wisconsin yesterday. I wanted to see you again."

"Oh. That's good." Mama twisted her fingers on her lap. "That food here is pig slop, you know. Trying to poison us."

"I'm sorry," I said. I caught Maureen's eye.

"You got married, didn't you?" Mama peered at me, adjusting her floral cotton skirt over knees that looked like broken matchsticks.

"Betty is married with two boys, Mama." Maureen rose. "I'm going to the ladies room. I'll be back soon."

Mama looked around. "It's through that door and down the—"

"I know, Mama. I'll be back." She left us alone on the couch.

Nervous, I took Mama's hand. "I've been wanting to talk to you about some things. Things that are hard to bring up."

She raised her barely-visible eyebrows. "What?" She withdrew her hand.

"About our family, about what happened years ago." Mama sat stoic. I continued, "I'm sure you've told your doctors about—about Joey." Still no reaction.

"Mama, I want you to talk about Joey. About Dennis. Have you put that to rest? Do you still think about it?"

She shifted toward me, her lower lip quivering. "Lord, Betty, you always were exhausting, even as a baby. I'm sorry. Sorry that you were—when the banks crashed, people were poorer than ever. We had to cut corners. We had three children, enough mouths to feed." She studied her feet.

I knew what was coming. "It's all right, Mama. I know I wasn't planned, was a surprise. I overheard things. I can imagine how hard it was. You know, I had problems with my first baby, trying to cope."

Mama sneered. "You had it easy. Had enough money. Back then, you cried all the time, and I was ready to—"

"Run off?"

Her eyebrows shot up. "Either that or, ah, do myself in."

"Mama, I've learned from my own doctors that mental illness affects people, rich and poor, old and young. I know it's in the family—"

"Betty, I've had enough of this. I can't—" Both eyes twitched.

"Mama, I'm not leaving until you talk about Joey and Dennis. And that you admit and realize Joey's death was a tragic accident. You can blame anything. Blame the Depression. Blame the railroad. Blame God." I couldn't help the tears springing to my eyes.

Mama's lips pursed, becoming nearly invisible. "What good is it to stir up the pot again? It's best left buried in the past where it belongs. Would it help you to know Joey was my favorite? But you all knew." She furiously rubbed her hands together. "Lordy, the times I wished it had been Dennis or one of the rest of you who'd been taken from me." She glared at me. "There, do you still want more? I will never forgive Dennis or your drunk of a father. So tell that to your fancy doctors."

Stunned, I shot up from the couch, anger coursing through my veins. "All right, Mama. I won't bother you anymore. You're a damaged old woman, so broken you can't be fixed. You hurt me when I was a kid, sending me away. But I'm strong now. My so-called fancy doctor warned me this could happen."

Mama sat, head bowed. My hands trembled as I straightened my purse strap. "So I'll concentrate on being with Maureen and Dennis and Daddy. We love each other and I'll put you to rest like Dennis has. I'll leave you to rot away in this place. There's no hope for you."

I started to march out when I nearly collided with Maureen. "What's going on?" Her eyes looked frightened.

"I expected too much from our mother. I admit defeat. I give up and would like to leave now." I had never spoken to Mama like that. A strange combination of guilt, liberation, and triumph swept over me.

"Mama? What did you do?" Maureen sat beside her.

"Ha, now you're all ganging up on me. You're the last one, Missy. You gonna desert me too?"

"I don't know, Mama. I'll let Betty tell me what happened. So it's goodbye for now."

"Come on, Betty." She took my arm.

I glimpsed at Mama. Were her eyes shining with tears? My anger faded to confusion as I realized in this instant, her mind was in the here and now, no signs of senility or dementia. I still didn't know if she'd meant her unforgivable words, or if they were a product of her illness.

Maureen tugged my arm. "Let's go."

"Oh crap. I don't know what to do." We faced each other. Two women at a nearby card table gawked at us. Were they eavesdropping?

Mama started muttering softly. I slowly drew near her and bent down. "What are you saying, Mama?"

"In the gloaming, oh my darling, think not bitterly of me, though I passed away in silence, left you lonely, set you free," she barely whispered the melody of the old sorrowful song.

"Mama." I took her fragile hands in mine. "Where are you?"

Maureen drew near. Something faraway seemed to capture Mama's gaze. Then she squeezed my hands and let go. "Don't you see, Betty? I left you to set you free. Free of me. Yes, I didn't want you at first. But you grew to be so shy, unsure. After that happened to Joey, I knew, I knew, just like the song." She sniffled and sang, choking on the words, "It was best to leave you thus, dear, Best for you and best for me." She motioned for Maureen to join us on the couch.

She bowed her head, then, "When the lights are soft and low, Will you think of me and love me, As you did once long ago."

By this time, tears streamed down all of our cheeks. "Oh, God, I'm sorry, Mama. I don't know what I'm doing or saying."

Maureen sniffed. "I don't either, believe it or not."

Mama tugged a linen hankie from the front pocket of her white blouse. "I'm tired. So terribly, terribly tired. I just want to sleep. Maybe never wake up."

"Let's go to your room," Maureen said. "You can take a good nap." She helped Mama stand and the three of us, our mother in between, slowly made our way to Mama's room and sanctuary.

When I slipped into her pocket-sized room, I smelled rosewater and broken dreams. Mama sat on her twin bed atop her green hobnail bedspread. She bent down to untie her shoe laces. "Here, let me do that, Mama," Maureen said.

"All right, good night, sleep tight." Mama leaned back, her head on the pillow. "I don't wanna get under the covers, just bring that throw blanket." She indicated a lightweight covering on a wooden armchair.

"Bye, Mama," I said, bending to kiss her parchment paper cheek. "I love you."

Maureen gave her a kiss as well. "We all love you, Mama."

"A-huh," she murmured, and closed her eyes.

We crept out of the room and silently moved down the well-worn corridors until we reached the main entrance and left the building. Would I ever come back?

CHAPTER 54

On the ride home, Maureen and I didn't speak for several minutes. I felt a modicum of satisfaction, but I still needed time to reflect on the twists and turns of Mama's conversation. Maureen sped up when we reached I-20 heading southwest. "Was this worth the trip down here?"

I thought a moment. "Yeah, not exactly what I hoped for, but I'm sure it's the best she can do. We were really mad at each other at one point."

"I could tell," Maureen said. "Maybe that was a good sign. She has feelings."

"Maybe." I leaned forward and fiddled with the vent. The sun blazed through the windows, warming my arms and neck. "I still think she's broken beyond repair. It's been what? Twenty-two years, and she's not much better. But she finally talked about Joey and Dennis. And me too, saying I wasn't planned and all. But yet she thought she needed to abandon me, to set me free so I could—could thrive."

Maureen met my eyes. "I'm sorry you went through that."

"It's all right. I could go on saying 'poor me' till I'm blue in the face. But I think I've finally come around to being okay with the way things were."

I thought about Dennis. "You know that AA prayer they say about accepting what you cannot change, and the wisdom to know the difference. That says it all. Some of my depression was caused by events out of my control, but I couldn't let go until recently."

"You've done so well, Betty. Another part of that prayer is the courage to change what you can. It took guts to confront Mama and Dennis like you did."

"Thanks, I am feeling better now. I'm ready to go home and see Phil and the boys. I'll call Dennis tonight to say hello."

"Let's hope his new lady friend works out." Maureen adjusted the rear-view mirror.

"Think he'll tell me about her?"

"Highly doubtful," Maureen said. "He's afraid to jinx it."

We drove several miles without speaking. I realized how strongly we're entwined with our mothers, the first human connection we have. Our only universe until others enter. Was that tie broken between me and Mama before Joey's death? Did I need to become my mother in order to set us both free?

I felt lighter in mind and spirit, determined to become a better wife and mother, a fresh start. I felt fortunate to have a strong family, one that would always be on my side. I'd continue to see Dr. Woods, who, along with Phil, encouraged me to enroll in a class or two this fall. Literature, poetry, perhaps even psychology.

·   ·   ·

The next evening I was home, nestled on the family room couch with Phil. The boys watched *The Andy Griffith Show* while I told Phil my plans to take a class.

"I'd like to take a psychology class, then winter quarter another lit course, maybe poetry." I curled my legs on the soft fabric of the sofa.

"Sounds good, hon. You'd take intro to psych, and then if you're interested, go on to applied or abnormal."

"Yeah, that's me. Abnormal. But I am interested in the field because of my own problems and Mama's too." I had told Phil earlier about my visit with her.

"Let's go in the living room so we can talk in peace," he said. "You don't mind if we leave, boys?"

David looked at him and rolled his eyes. At age nine, he'd not only grown taller, but acquired a self-assurance I'd lacked.

We flopped on the loveseat away from Andy and Opie's twangy voices. "It was so worthwhile, even forcing Mama into facing things she didn't want to. But the main thing is I finally accepted who she is. Whether it was her fault blaming Dennis and sending me away or the family sickness, I'll never know. And it's all right now."

"I'm proud of you, honey." Phil put his arm around my shoulders and drew me close. "You worked hard going through treatment, and we're lucky you found Dr. Woods."

I was lucky all right. Lucky to find the doc, but most of all, lucky to have found Phil. Every sappy song and poem described him. "I know. Last time the doc said that I'm getting stronger and will have the tools to cope with the hard times. She also told me that people often think they're supposed to be happy all the time, but life is meant to be seasons of joy, sorrow, and so on."

"Yes, like Longfellow says, *Into each life some rain must fall—*"

"*Some days must be dark and dreary*," we both chimed in.

"Aren't we a couple of sentimental lovebirds?" Phil nuzzled my neck.

"Something else I want to do. I've never told the boys much about Joey. I'm going to do that tomorrow."

Phil nodded in agreement. "Just remember, Betty." He sang softly, "*I'll spend the rest of my days Near you.*"

•   •   •

Later after the boys were sleeping, I sat on my bed and opened a drawer on my end table. I reached in the back corner and drew out a navy velvet-covered box. I slowly opened the lid and gently lifted up a tiny red car.

"All will be well, Joey."

EPILOGUE

August 1980

Sitting on a wooden bench, I breathe in the cool green aroma of leaves and lakes. I watch the waves lap the shores of the "shining big-sea water," their song lulling me into peaceful recollections of waterfalls, a lighthouse, and Phil on bended knee in the sand. We celebrated my fiftieth birthday yesterday with family gathered at a scenic resort nestled in the pines of northern Minnesota. The years have been kind, embracing new lives, parting with others.

Auntie was ninety when she joined Uncle ten years ago. I'll always miss her unending compassion for me, her needlepoint wisdom.

It will be four years this fall since Phil's father, Gus, died. Ida at eighty-two is in good health, still doling out unsolicited advice on plants and recipes.

Dennis married years ago and has two step children; Maureen welcomed another son, Mike, in 1961, Jenny's fourth brother.

Daddy died shortly after the stockyards closed in 1971. A bittersweet farewell to him and Back of the Yards. After the funeral, we gave him a resounding send off at the corner where the road surely rose up to meet him.

Odd how I can still evoke the smell of the yards. I guess it's true, the scent is always with you, but for me, it's like Auntie's wooly afghan enveloping me.

Two months ago, Mama was reunited with her beloved Joey who rests between her and Daddy, forever protected. She lasted longer than we thought, but sadly she died before anyone in the family could be with her. I think of her and Joey, now in the gloaming singing together.

In 1961 I enrolled at Milton College and received a BA degree in English and taught the literature and poetry I love to high school students. Two years ago, I began my master's program in psychology and hope to fulfill my dream of becoming a family therapist.

Our family moved to Madison in 1965, where Phil accepted a position at the University of Wisconsin. The boys attended college there, graduated, and moved out of state. David at twenty-nine, settled in Denver, married, and gave us a granddaughter last summer. Her name is Elizabeth Carole, a lovely reminder of Jenny as a baby. Steve, twenty-six, recently married, and lives near Tampa.

I turn at the sound of a familiar voice. Jenny sits beside me, her dark hair shining in the sun. Her first job as a nurse starts next week. She wonders at the velvet box I hold on my lap. I open it, and she leans near, eyes the contents.

A tiny red car rests there; she knows it belonged to the uncle she never met. I lift the other object from the box. "A nurse found this under Mama's mattress in the hospital after she died."

Jenny holds out her hand, and I place the long-ago amethyst rosary in her palm.

It will be hers some day.

NOTE FROM THE AUTHOR

Word-of-mouth is crucial for any author to succeed. If you enjoyed *Back of the Yard*, please leave a review online—anywhere you are able. Even if it's just a sentence or two. It would make all the difference and would be very much appreciated.

Thanks!
Meg Lelvis

For fans of **Meg Lelvis**, please check out our recommended title for your next great read!

Bailey's Law by Meg Lelvis

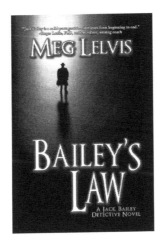

"An intelligent, immersive police procedural that will leave you pining for another Jack Bailey novel." *–BEST THRILLERS*

Made in the USA
Middletown, DE
06 December 2023